**The kiss she'd shared  her world.**

Since Willow had never ~~been~~ ~~kissed~~ before, she didn't know if it was always like this. So intense. So powerful.

And when she'd felt his body swell with desire, her womanly parts had come alive. She'd wanted him, in a gut-wrenching, visceral way.

Apparently he hadn't felt the same.

The sense of loss that had come over her when Ruben had turned away had been shattering. Used to hiding her inner pain, she'd gathered her shredded dignity around her like a cloak, glad she'd been able to look calm and relatively normal when he'd finally turned back to her.

When they'd first stepped into her world, she'd let the peace of the woods surround her. As usual, the sounds and scents of the forest were a calming, balm upon her troubled soul.

But her sense of tranquillity was only fleeting as she forced herself to remember why they were there. Into this beauty, a killer had gone.

## Books by Karen Whiddon

### Harlequin Nocturne

### Silhouette Nocturne

### Harlequin Romantic Suspense

### Silhouette Romantic Suspense

*The Pack
**The Cordasic Legacy

## KAREN WHIDDON

started weaving fanciful tales for her younger brothers at the age of eleven. Amidst the Catskill Mountains of New York, then the Rocky Mountains of Colorado, she fueled her imagination with the natural beauty that surrounded her. Karen now lives in north Texas, where she shares her life with her very own hero of a husband and three doting dogs. Also an entrepreneur, she divides her time between the business she started and writing. You can email Karen at KWhiddon1@aol.com or write to her at P.O. Box 820807, Fort Worth, TX 76182. Fans of her writing can also check out her website, www.karenwhiddon.com.

# THE WOLF PRINCE

## KAREN WHIDDON

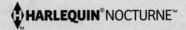

Recycling programs
for this product may
not exist in your area.

ISBN-13: 978-0-373-88567-1

THE WOLF PRINCE

Copyright © 2013 by Karen Whiddon

**HARLEQUIN®**

**Printed in U.S.A.**                    www.Harlequin.com

Dear Reader,

In *The Wolf Prince*, I once again revisit the imaginary kingdom of Teslinko. And in addition to the shifters you've come to know and love in my Pack series, you'll meet in this story yet another kind of mythical being—a fairy princess named Willow. Writing about these two mythical people who join forces and learn that love is indeed possible was a real treat for me.

Add into the mix beautiful scenery, a loyal German shepherd dog named York, various relatives on both sides of the veil, a murder that must be avenged and a dark force that means danger and death, and you've got a fast-paced book that is dear to my heart and soul.

I hope you enjoy reading about Prince Ruben and his Fae princess as much as I enjoyed writing about them!

Best wishes,

Karen Whiddon

As always, to my husband and my daughter. My family.
You are and always will be everything to me.

# Chapter 1

As dusk settled over the land like a tattered cloak, Prince Ruben of Teslinko stood alone in the crumbling, condemned tower of his ancestral home and wondered if madness had finally come to claim him.

If not yet madness, then complete blackness of soul. Worse, he could see no way out. He was trapped, as surely as a wild animal caught in a snare.

At the thought, his inner wolf snarled. The beast had been furious as of late, clamoring for him to shape-shift, to change. Stubbornly deliberate, Ruben had remained human for two entire days now. Normal for most Shifters. As for him, forty-eight hours felt like a death sentence.

If only death could come so easily.

Again, the black thoughts. Nothing would help him. Nothing save changing, letting his beast take over once more. Each time, he remained wolf longer and longer, having to battle the

wolf inside to shift back to human. And then once he had…
he wanted to die.

He'd lost control. More than that. No matter how he tried,
he couldn't seem to regain that part of himself he'd given
over to the wolf. The human part, necessary to survive in
the kingdom of his parents, the world of his people. Something had broken inside him and he didn't know how to fix
it. Being human felt like how an addict must feel without the
drug. Craving it, shaking, unable to sleep, or eat, or function.

He was damaged, ruined, borderline insane. And he—or
rather his wolf—didn't care. Always, the idea of changing, of
remaining wolf, beckoned like a glittery bauble forever out
of reach. The struggle to keep from giving in grew more and
more difficult, compounded by the fact that he really did not
care. He'd *rather* be wolf than human. And though he knew
this was considered wrong, it was the way he felt.

Worse, he could only think of one reason *why* he should try
to repair his damaged psyche, because he sure as hell would
rather stay wolf than man. But as his father's sole heir, the
fate of his bloodline rested squarely on him. Unless his hidden
madness overwhelmed him, Prince Ruben would rule Teslinko one day. Therefore, he couldn't give in to his deepest,
darkest desire and vanish into the vast forests surrounding
his father's lands. Forever to walk on four legs instead of two.

Even the thought made his insides quiver with longing.

Damn it.

Rather than pace the confined space, stepping carefully to
avoid the crumbling stones and gaping holes, Ruben gripped
the stone window ledge so hard his knuckles turned white.
Breathing rapidly, he watched as vehicle after vehicle snaked
up the winding, ancient road toward the royal castle. Not to
the old part where he now hid, but the sleek, renovated, mod-
ern building where his family resided.

No one but Ruben ever visited the decrepit ruins. He preferred it this way, relishing his solitude over the hundred irritating daily tasks a royal prince must perform.

He counted this night among those onerous duties.

His parents, King Leo and Queen Ionna of Teslinko, were having a huge ball. Tonight, and again one week from tonight, and once more a fortnight from tonight, and so on. As long as it took, they had said, making no secret as to their reason. Now that his sisters, including Alisa had been married, all eyes had turned to Ruben, the youngest child and, as the only male, the royal heir. His parents had decided Ruben needed to settle down and produce an heir of his own. This event would be the first of the many it took to find him a suitable wife.

Which was the absolute last thing he wanted.

Ruben could have told his parents they were wasting their time. But as much as he loved them, he was well aware of their shortcomings. They heard only what they wanted to hear, steadfastly refusing to believe their only son could do any wrong.

He certainly hadn't told them of the dark cloud that had settled over him. They weren't aware of the possibility of his encroaching madness, nor that he'd reached a decision never to marry. How could he, when he could be a danger to anyone who got too close to him?

So he'd suffer through who-knew-how-many balls, dances or parties, all the while hoping for a miracle that would likely never come. Pity he didn't believe in either magic or divine intervention.

These days Ruben didn't believe in much of anything. Least of all, in his ability to lead his people.

Below his vantage point, a door closed and a woman's bright laughter trilled through the air, drawing his attention. They came alone and in groups, every young, marriageable woman in Teslinko and beyond. Dressed to impress, they chattered and giggled and plotted. Though he despised the label, he knew he was known far and wide as the catch of the season. Therefore he could, in theory, have his pick of gorgeous, desirable and well-connected women. Sadly, he wasn't interested, not in the least. He had too many issues to burden anyone else with them.

Of course, unaware of this, his parents plunged full-steam ahead in their plans of finding him a mate. Shifter or human, they'd told him they'd be happy as long as he was happy. They had no idea that happiness for him was an unattainable goal.

A party only made him feel worse rather than better. And what a gala this would be. For this event, the royal decorator had spared no expense. A hundred thousand tiny lights illuminated the trees, the drive and the entrance.

Glumly, he continued to stare down at the festive scene below as more and more guests arrived. How many were there? From what he'd seen so far, he'd guess at least two or three hundred single women, all fixated on the same goal. Him.

Inside, his wolf stirred, intrigued by the variety of new scents and sounds. The beast wanted to be set free to investigate. As always, the notion tempted him.

No. He shook his head, mentally pushing his wolf back into a cage and locking the door. Once finished, his chest ached with the familiar and now forbidden longing. Better if he could simply shape-shift into wolf and never change back to human. At least this impending madness didn't seem to bother his lupine self.

And there it was. Again. Temptation. If he valued what was left of his mind, he knew he could not give in.

Watching as expensive car after expensive car rolled up the drive and disgorged its contents, he sighed. He'd better go change and prepare to do his time. If he was lucky, he could snag a couple of glasses of strong Scotch to help him survive the ordeal.

* * *

Trudging through the forest, the watered silk of her best formal dress bunched up in her fist, Willow of the SouthWard Brights tried to think happy thoughts. Because she couldn't take a chance on getting dirty, she ignored the siren call of the wild animals watching her from their various hiding places around the thick forest.

All she'd have to do was crook her little finger and whistle, and they'd come. When they were with her, carnivores ignored their natural prey, and the most skittish of beasts calmed under her gentle hand.

It was a gift and one she had kept hidden, by necessity. The one time she'd tried to tell her mother, she'd been treated with scorn and derision. After that, she'd supposed everyone else would view her gift the same way, so she had kept it secret. Not only from the rest of her family, but from everyone in the kingdom. In a place where the level of magical ability meant power, Willow's was a secret best kept inside.

Just like the tear in the veil.

She'd discovered the portal by accident a year ago while on one of her solitary strolls through the forest. Just because she didn't cast spells or use magic like her mother and sister, didn't mean she couldn't sense it. And the lure of the shimmering veil had drawn her as surely as a bear to honey.

With it, she could cross between her world and that of the humans. She'd taken advantage of this numerous times in the months since, yet another secret she held close to her breast.

She quite enjoyed her anonymity in the human world. There, no one knew she was a princess. No one thought she looked different or looked down on her because she was lacking in magic.

A loner by nature, Willow had few friends among her kind. With a rueful smile, she stepped over a fallen log. Make that *no* friends. At least, not among her people—the Bright.

Forcing herself to focus on the present, she felt the siren thrum of the magic as she approached the veil. Her heartbeat quickened and the scents of the forest became sharper, more intense. Damp earth and plant, and the slightly acrid, barely detectable scent of its animal inhabitants.

As she neared the shimmering space, she felt an unfamiliar tickle of anticipation.

The royal family of Teslinko was having a ball. Tonight, in fact. According to the chatter she'd picked up hanging around near their castle, they'd been preparing for the huge event for weeks. Rumor had it that the king and queen were determined to find their son, Prince Ruben, a bride.

Willow cared about none of that. As the youngest—and least desirable—daughter of a powerful queen, she had her own worries about that area. According to her older—and much more beautiful—sister, Tatiana, Willow would remain unwed the rest of her natural-born, magic-less life.

Which, though occasionally sounding lonely, was all right with Willow.

Growing closer to the veil, she felt the pull of its magic. She took a deep breath, then another, allowing herself to feel the power of the ancient earth gathering under her feet and the rush of air swirling around this, an opening between worlds.

Ahead, in a clearing between two tall ash trees, the space flickered, odd shapes sparkling through a fog, as though one might be able to see them if one turned quickly enough. The magic was strong here, visible even to the untrained eye. Briefly she wondered how it was that a hapless human hadn't managed to wander straight into it and wind up among the land of the Bright—her home.

Maybe, because the power felt so odd, humans instinctively avoided this area.

Shaking her head at the absurdity of it all, Willow stepped into the shimmering veil and gave herself over to the magic.

* * *

Bored, drifting from one cluster of simpering women to another, trying not to gag on the choke of their strong perfume, Ruben glanced at his watch for the twentieth time and wondered how long he needed to stay. At least until the meal had been served, he estimated grimly. Naturally, the dinner service was a drawn out process that could take as long as two and a half hours. So for now, he was stuck.

His mother, Queen Ionna, had already taken him by the arm and dragged him around the crowded room, introducing him to what seemed like every unmarried woman under the age of forty. He'd taken care to be pleasant, nothing more, well aware of his mother's displeasure when he didn't choose one female to single out for his attentions.

He suspected several of the women were disappointed as well, though most took care not to show this. There were so many of them, women of every shape and size. Young and old, virgin and widow, his skin crawled as each eyed him as eagerly as if he were a prize stud up for auction to the highest bidder.

Which in a way, he supposed he was. His sister Alisa had often complained about this very thing. Aware of her tendency toward the dramatic, he'd never taken her complaints seriously. Now that she'd been married off and his parents' focus had turned to him, he'd begun to see her point.

Restless, his wolf tested the edge of his control. Gritting his teeth, Ruben forced the beast back into his mental cage, a task growing more and more difficult.

At the thought, a wild longing swept him, freezing him in his tracks. To run free. Wild. As he pushed the desire away, he swore he could feel his wolf's savage amusement.

Not good. So not good.

The evening was early yet, the music soft and the food and drink plentiful. He eyed the guests lingering over their cocktails, standing in clusters and conversing about financial markets, the latest fashions or the employment crisis in other nations. All topics which held zero interest for him.

He'd already downed two strong Scotch-and-waters and now sipped his third. Mildly intoxicated, he was well aware that he had to slow down if he wanted to keep the wolf at bay and the darkness inside him from leaking out. Wouldn't do, he thought cynically, if the guests were to realize the heir to the throne grappled with bouts of insanity. The humans would be horrified and the Shifters…they'd be appalled. He could imagine the varied reactions. He wouldn't be regarded as such a catch then.

Again, he nearly smiled, his wolf pacing restlessly, full of nervous energy. The idea almost sounded…good to him. Proof positive how unbalanced he'd become.

In the crowded ballroom, Shifters and humans mingled, the majority of the humans unaware that there were those among them who could change into a wolf at will. His boredom growing, Ruben began picturing their reactions if he were to calmly stroll out to the middle of the empty dance floor, strip off his tuxedo and drop to all fours to initiate the change that would turn his human form into that of a huge, nearly Feral, wolf.

Panic from the humans. His wolf snarled, enjoying the mental image. From his own kind, the Shifters, he expected he'd see a mixture of shock, anger and disgust.

His parents would be mortified. After the first moment of horror, the damage control would begin in earnest.

The thought made him smile again, a record as of late. Again, the idea felt tantalizing. As if he could close his eyes, let his tattered willpower fall away, and allow events to happen as they would. His wolf would take over. Everything would be out of Ruben's hands.

So simple… He swayed, tempted. Snapping his eyes open,

he took another slug of the strong liquor, letting it burn its way down his throat.

And therein lay the twisted path to madness.

Giving himself an inner shake, putting a choke hold on the furious wolf inside, he again began to make another circuit of the room, trying to regulate his breathing, his thoughts, his steps. As he looked up, he noted his mother's sharp gaze fixed on him.

Inhaling the mixed odors of perfume and human sweat, he shuddered, longing for the clean, crisp scent of the pines, the damp muskiness of the earth. The lure of the forest beyond the castle, where he spent so much of his time, pulled at him, though he knew part of that was tied up in his wolf's desire to break free.

While he strolled about, gritting his teeth and hiding his indifference, inside his wolf snarled and paced and raged. Ignoring the capricious beast took effort, but he managed. He wanted nothing more than to disappear into the ruins at the edge of the forest, but he fixed what he hoped was a pleasant expression on his face and attempted to socialize.

His mother's earlier decree replayed in his head. *Find a wife. You are heir to the throne. It's long past time you settled down. Marry. Have children.*

His absolute worst nightmare. No, he paused, twirling the ice inside his almost empty glass. His *second* worst nightmare.

And the women. Every one of them made no attempt to hide their hope that he'd chose them. They smiled and simpered and tried to seduce him, but he barely gave any even a cursory glance. Despite their varying beauty, none of them interested him. He knew many of them, had run into them at one event or another over the years. Some he'd grown up with, played childhood games alongside, and even stolen his first kiss from while hidden in a high-walled garden and thrilling at the forbidden taste. He sighed with annoyance. Such memories were a thing of the past.

Of late, he'd lived the life of a monk, abstaining from all feminine companionship. Another attempt to keep the darkness that haunted him secret.

Glancing at his watch, he prayed this night would be over.

And then, as fate played some sort of ironic trick on him, he saw her from across the room. Unfamiliar, tiny, exquisite, the dusky rose of her skin faintly shimmering with life. Desire stabbed him, sharp and strong and so gut-wrenchingly powerful even his wolf was stunned into silence.

Unlike the others, who resembled overdressed peacocks, she wore a simple long sheath in a muted yellow, devoid of ornamentation or jangle. Head high, smooth shoulders back, she carried herself with the unconscious bearing of royalty. Though he could tell from her lack of aura that she was not Pack, he found himself wondering if she was even human. Something about her…

Damn and double damn. He swayed, wondering if he'd had more to drink than he'd thought.

For the first time in a long time, his wolf approved. Though he'd not yet taken measure of her scent, the beast wanted to mate with her.

Letting his wolf guide him, he began moving toward her, determined to claim her as his.

When their gazes met, every jangling noise inside Willow went still. Who was he? *What* was he? Whatever he was, he wasn't human. The darkness emanating from him drew her. She wondered if this was because of her secret Shadow heritage or if, as always, the part of her that was Bright felt a compulsion to bring light to the faintest bit of darkness.

Of course, since she had no magic, she never could. But that didn't stop the longing.

As he began to move toward her, certain and sure and clearly determined to reach her, she panicked. Glancing left, then right, she quickly calculated an escape route and tried to leap toward it. She didn't know if she was afraid because she'd crashed his party, or because he was so damn beautiful. She went with her gut reaction to flee. However, she'd completely forgotten about her long skirt and high heels, and as a result, she stumbled and nearly fell.

Miraculously, she caught herself. Casting a quick glance over her shoulder—he was drawing impossibly closer—she slipped in between two groups of women and hurried away. Keeping to the most crowded part of the room, she weaved her way toward a balcony she noticed on the other side.

Finally there, she opened the French style door and slipped out into the cool darkness, lit by the brightness of the full moon. Safe, at least for now.

As she gripped the iron railing, she wasn't surprised to note her hands were trembling.

Inhaling the sharp, fresh air, she wondered when she'd become such a coward. Behind her the door opened with a click. Even though she'd remained in the shadows, she knew he'd found her, even before he spoke.

"I'm not dangerous, you know." The husky-as-sin voice sounded exactly that. Dangerous as hell.

Slowly she raised her head. Years of experience at her parents' court enabled her to put a pleasantly surprised expression on her face. "I think if you feel the need to even say such a thing, then you must be very unsafe indeed."

When his smile came, the sight of it made her pulse race. She futilely tried to get her now scattered bearings, when he spoke again.

"Walk with me." He held out his arm, his words a command rather than a request.

She swallowed hard and tried to think. *This* she hadn't

planned for. She gazed up at him, a dark figure of a man with powerful shoulders and broad chest, and her mouth went dry. Blindly she reached out and took his hand. The roughness of it gave her an unwanted sense of protection. She glanced down at their entwined hands and realized his fingers were beautiful—long and strong and oddly graceful, like those of an artist.

"Who are you?" she asked, finding her voice.

"Ruben," he answered simply, his dark gaze locked on hers. Despite herself, she shivered.

"Don't be afraid," he murmured.

At that, she straightened her shoulders. She might be many things, but coward was not one of them. "I'm not," she said, wondering why the words felt like a lie.

He gave her hand a gentle tug. Moving with him out onto the terrace, when they reached the balcony that in daylight would look out over the lush and green forest, she let go of him, taking a small step sideways to keep their bodies from touching. He didn't react to this, gripping the smooth marble rail and staring straight ahead, almost as if he'd forgotten she was there.

Together they stood, side by side, gazing out over the darkness toward the mountains, the silence growing between them. The faint swell of music from inside provided background noise. She fought the urge to fidget or to speak, simply to hear the sound of her own voice.

Evidently, despite the way he'd sought her out, he had nothing to say to her. Just like she was back at home, the ugly younger sister. Though she knew she ought to be used to it by now, it still hurt.

Turning to face him, she lifted her chin and flashed a carefully casual smile. "I have to go," she said, no trace of regret in her voice.

Tall and straight, he swung his head to gaze down at her. "Please, not yet. Stay with me a little longer. Please."

Though his husky voice simmered with enough sensuality to make her feel dizzy, she suspected he might be toying with her. Though for what reason, she couldn't tell.

"Why?"

"A simple enough question." He sighed, running a hand through his dark hair. "Though my answer is more complicated. I'm the prince."

"The prince?" she repeated, shocked.

"Yes. This—" he waved one hand "—This is all for me. My parents' idea of a good time. They're putting me through ball after endless ball, all to find me a wife."

At the word, he gave an exaggerated shudder, making her laugh despite herself. "I take it you don't like the idea?"

"That would be a major understatement. I don't want to marry." Casually, he placed his hand on her shoulder. Despite the heavy material of the dress, she felt the heat of his beautiful fingers and had to fight not to lean into him. To be able to choose one's own fate…now that was a luxury she wished she had.

"Me, either." She sighed, unwillingly reminded of the unknown prince her parents had promised her to.

"You never told me your name," he said.

Since she now realized the man, this prince, rather, needed a friend rather than a date, she relaxed. "Willow."

His disheveled dark hair gleamed in the lights from inside. "That's an unusual name."

More at ease now, she grinned up at him. "I'm an unusual person."

As he continued to gaze at her without responding, she felt her face heat. "I'm sorry," she said. "I'm not really good at flirting." The words came out in a rush.

He shrugged. "Who is? I'd rather run in the woods."

At his words, she couldn't help but silently agree. How could this be possible? He'd unknowingly echoed her earlier thoughts. "You run in the woods? Me, too, though I roam more than run. I love the forest."

He grinned, devastating her, and then he laughed, the deep, rich masculine sound curling around her like a shawl.

"Come with me." Again, he held out his hand.

This time, instead of blindly accepting, she shook her head. "First, tell me where we're going."

Gravely, he regarded her, the flickering interior lights casting shadows on his craggy features. "To dance, of course."

And just like that, he made her want him. So intensely her entire being ached with it.

"Let's go," she said, surprised her voice didn't crack.

As they entered through the French doors, the band had begun to play a waltz, as if on cue. Because her mother had seen to it that Willow had received the same dance lessons as her sister, she knew all the steps.

He swept her into his arms and she had to remind herself how to breathe.

In that instant, she felt sharply the loss of every magical power she'd never had. Because dancing with Ruben was all that and more. He was tall and fit, his broad shoulders tapering to a narrow waist. By the laws of physics, he should have been clumsy, a stumbling bear of a man. Instead, he moved with the grace of a born athlete. Women watched them enviously. And the men…the men eyed her, wondering no doubt why such a beautiful man wasted time on such a skinny and frumpy girl.

"They all want you," he rumbled in her ear, making her start. At his playful words, she couldn't help but laugh.

"I know," she murmured back, enjoying the joke. "How could they not want the one who can get the prince to dance?"

He peered down at her, mischief making his eyes sparkle.

"You're right about that, you know. I haven't danced at a single one of these things since I was twelve."

"Why not?" The instant she asked the question, she knew the answer. A man who'd rather be running in the wild forest would eschew dances and banquets and all the other social nonsense that came with being royalty. She should know. She was exactly the same way, though no doubt for dissimilar reasons.

Still, this was different, somehow. Her beautiful skirt floated around her ankles and she felt as if she were gliding on air.

They'd barely begun—this time a fox-trot—when someone screamed, a shrill sound of absolute panic. As Willow, along with everyone else, turned to look, the rear of the ballroom exploded.

## Chapter 2

The blast knocked them to the ground. Instinctively, Ruben tried to direct his fall to protect the unique woman who'd allowed him to spend the evening with her.

*Willow.* Hellhounds, he hoped she was all right. Ears ringing, he called her name, even as he hauled her to her feet amid the debris raining down on them.

She sagged against him, causing his heart to skip a beat. So tiny, her bones. He cupped her soot-covered chin in his hand and lifted her face to his. Her amazing caramel-colored eyes were open, if dazed. *Alive.* Relatively unhurt, as far as he could tell.

Relief flooding him, he slipped his arm around her impossibly small waist, helping her to steady herself.

"Are you okay?"

She opened her mouth to speak, and then licked her cracked lips instead, drawing his gaze. "I think so," she finally croaked, sounding uncertain. Tentatively, she moved, testing her joints, and finally shook her head. "At least, I don't hurt anywhere."

She wasn't bleeding, so for now he had no choice but to take her words for truth. As he turned away, there was another explosion, this one smaller and farther away.

Damn. His guests…his family…his home.

Releasing her, he turned to survey the damage, praying there were no fatalities. Several people were still down. Smoke rapidly began to fill the room, which meant there was a fire nearby. Flash. Another mini-explosion. Hell, he didn't see his parents anywhere. The sounds—moans and wails and crying, fire crackling, something— What? Dripping? Smoke, more smoke. The tainted air grew rapidly difficult to breathe. How many were injured? How many were…dead? Hounds. He hoped none.

Need. To. Move. Now.

He took a deep breath. "I've got to help get everyone out. Are you well enough to assist me?"

Blinking, she nodded. The effort seemed to make her dizzy, as she swayed on her feet. Ruben cursed under his breath. He couldn't leave her, but he wasn't sure if dragging her around with him was the best idea, either.

At this point, he didn't really have a choice. She wasn't seriously hurt, so she either had to help or take herself to safety.

A prince's first responsibility was toward his people. His family. His home. Damn and double damn.

"Come on." Taking her arm, he led her through the thickening smoke toward the closest group of people, with the intent of leaving her with them. Most had scrambled back to their feet; those could make their way out, to safety.

Near them, several lay still on the floor, unmoving.

Ruben's stomach lurched as he dropped to his knees next to an older man he recognized from court. So many people hadn't yet risen. He didn't dare think that they might not be alive. This man—George something or other—blinked and lifted his head, gray hair tinted red with blood. Hurt, but alive. Ruben helped him to his feet, pointing him and the others who were able to move toward the door.

The next several minutes—hours?—passed in a blur. Though he'd had to resort to crawling under the smoke, Ruben managed to get from group to group, with Willow surprisingly right alongside him. She'd refused to leave for safety with the others.

As they led more and more people toward the door, her strength appeared to improve rapidly, for which he was thankful. Together they tended to the wounded, helping people who'd been stunned by the blast to their feet, assisting others in moving their wounded outside, where it was safer area.

Gasping for air, three times they had led groups of people toward the door, coughing and hacking all the way. They couldn't stay much longer. The smoke had grown so thick everyone was getting disoriented.

Was everyone out? He still had not seen his parents, which chilled his blood. He knew his father and if King Leo had been able to move, he would have worked tirelessly to save his people. Ruben prayed the older man worked in another part of the castle, or even better, outside doctoring the wounded. He couldn't stop long enough to search for him.

With time of the essence, Ruben grabbed several of the palace guards to help him drag the wounded outside, away from danger. This helped speed things up. Soon, the smoke-filled room emptied and, gasping for air, Ruben finally staggered outside and collapsed on the grass.

While he tried to suck in enough air to his burning lungs, Ruben pushed away the hated and eerie feeling of déjà vu. This had happened before, when his sister Alisa and her now husband Braden were here. Bombs had gone off inside the palace. Then, many had supposed the attacks were targeted at Dr. Streib, Alisa's husband who'd initially traveled to Teslinko to do research on her.

But over time, they'd learned differently. The bombings hadn't been directed at the American doctor. Rather, the royal family had been targeted by a group of extremists, those who claimed they felt more connected to their wolf selves and believed remaining human for longer than a week or two was an abomination to their true natures. Only Alisa had known how much Ruben was like them, though he didn't share their propensity for violence. Their methods, which involved violence such as bombings, were deadly. They believed such things would draw attention to their cause.

Their cause, as he knew better than most, was futile. Shifters could not stay wolf without losing their mind. Until recently, the Society of the Protectors had been dispatched to bring in Feral Shifters for rehabilitation. Those who had refused, or were deemed too mad, had been eliminated. Fortunately, that barbaric practice had been outlawed.

Still, everyone knew about the limitations placed on changing. Everyone except these extremists. Considering what had happened to him when he had tried to stay wolf more than human, he couldn't help but wonder what sort of madness drove them.

Their bombs killed and maimed, accomplishing nothing but death and destruction, but still they persevered. The royal family of Teslinko had taken precautions to prevent this from ever happening again, but evidently those hadn't been enough.

More death. More destruction. Senseless.

Shoving his thoughts to the back of his mind, Ruben summoned his last reserves of strength and began checking on his people. Now that they were out of the ballroom and safe, minor injuries could be attended to. Water was found and distributed and Ruben accepted a bottle gratefully, draining it in several gulps. He wished it did more to soothe his raw throat, but this would have to heal with time.

As he made his way through the throngs of people, Willow remained silently at his side, patching up the wounded, providing a slender shoulder when needed. Though she was covered in soot, her beautiful gown ruined, she worked tirelessly, selflessly, earning his gratitude and his admiration.

Finally, he thought everyone had been helped. As far as he could tell, they might have saved them all. With no casualties—at least that he knew of. All of the ones who'd been knocked out were all right.

He had yet to find his parents. Wearily, he pushed himself up off the grass. Willow looked at him quizzically, her exhaustion evident by the dark circles under her eyes. They had to be safe, he thought, seeing numerous members of the King's personal guard milling about. If something had happened to either the king or queen, no matter how minor, there would have been an outcry and someone would have been sent to fetch him.

Finally, he found one of their assistants who, wide-eyed from shock, stuttered as he assured Ruben that the royal couple was fine. Apparently they'd been in another part of the palace when the explosion had occurred. They were now ministering to the servants and the most gravely injured.

Another part of the palace. Hearing this had brought a slight smile to his face, the first since the explosion. Even after all these years spent together, his parents were still deeply in love and were known to sneak off in the middle of a gala to grab some together time. He—along with all his sisters—used to find that mortifying. Lately, he'd viewed their amorous behavior more tolerantly, even finding it amusing.

This time he breathed a sigh of relief, believing this proclivity to sneak away to spend private time with each other might have saved their lives.

Relieved, he returned to his place on the grass by Willow and watched as a team of firefighters from the village worked frantically, attempting to put out the flames. Still, part of the ballroom continued to burn, the flames flickering, roaring hungrily and sending billows of thick smoke into the night sky.

Finally, the fire was extinguished. One last dousing of water had been sprayed. The remains of the ballroom were coated in watery soot and the sour odor of smoke still curdled the air.

Shoulders rounded with exhaustion, the firefighters silently put away their equipment and prepared to return to the village.

As he pushed again to his feet, Ruben realized he was exhausted. Even his wolf had slunk back deep inside him. He glanced at Willow to find she also stood at his side, clearly equally done in, yet uncomplaining.

When he turned to face her, she stumbled, nearly going to her knees. Easily he caught her, relishing the feel of her against him before setting her on her feet.

"I think we're done." Hand at her elbow, where soot made the material a dirty grayish black, he steadied her and smoothed her smoky, ash-covered hair back from her face. "Thank you so much for your help. We did a lot of good tonight. There was no loss of life."

Appearing distracted, she nodded, biting her lip, almost as though she was on the verge of tears. Swaying, she glanced at all the people huddled together in various groups. Then, lifting her hand in a gesture that seemed a halfhearted wave, she staggered away. She weaved slightly and headed down a winding, cobbled path that led only toward an old stone bench which sat alone in a secluded arbor.

This bench had once been one of his sister Alisa's favorite places. She'd gone there when she'd needed solitude in order to think. No one had used it since Alisa had gotten married and gone to America with her new husband. Following Willow, he wondered how she'd known how to find it.

With only the full moon shining in the cloudless night sky providing light, she rounded the final bend in the path. Then, smoothing her ruined skirt, she took a seat on the bench. As he came up on her, she gave him a tired smile. "Sorry. I couldn't bear the smell of the smoke any longer."

He nodded his understanding. With a sigh, she patted the space beside her for him to drop down next to her.

He did and they sat, shoulders touching, silently contemplating the night. Again he marveled at the way she'd helped for hours, uncomplaining or expecting any kind of preferential treatment normally given to a beautiful woman in a ball gown. A stranger, she hadn't run from the chaos but rather dove right in to help people she clearly didn't know.

In short, if he'd thought her amazing before, this was doubly so now. His feelings had expanded to a sort of exhausted wonder. How could she be both so lovely and so…good? Chest tight, he gazed at her, finding her soot-stained face extraordinarily beautiful.

"What time is it?" she asked him, her voice still raspy from the smoke.

He glanced at his watch, unsurprised to find that it would soon be morning, despite the huge moon hanging in the western night sky. "Four a.m. Can you believe the sun will be rising in a few hours?" he mused. "What a night. And I still have to make a statement to the authorities."

At his words, she inhaled sharply, sitting up straight. "Four?"

Wide-eyed, she pushed to her feet, her movements still unsteady. She glanced at him before looking out at the still-dark forest beyond the castle. "I'm sorry, but I've got to go," she told him. Was that the faintest note of panic he heard in her voice?

He rose with her, eyeing her curiously. She'd been calm before, in the face of disaster. And now, panicked at the idea of being late, she seemed like a different woman.

"I'll vouch for you," he told her. "Sit back down. I'm sure whoever is waiting for you will understand."

"I doubt it." Glancing wildly around her, as if she expected someone to jump out of the shadows and grab her, she gathered her shredded composure about her like a cloak. Dipping her chin formally, she mustered up a shaky smile. "It was very nice to meet you, Prince Ruben. I'm sorry that your party didn't turn out as well as you'd hoped."

And then, as he tried to process her remark, she leaped away like a wild animal, without a backward glance, and took off running into the dark woods.

Mind muddled with exhaustion, Ruben considered her retreat blankly. What the…? By the time he took a step to follow her, she'd vanished from sight, disappearing into the forest.

But why? The way she'd gone led to nothing but wilderness. The nearest town was in the opposite direction.

From the castle, someone shouted his name. The authorities must have arrived and they needed him to make a statement. Duty called. Reluctantly, he turned and headed back along the way he'd come.

The local police—along with the media—had indeed arrived. Amid the red and blue lights and the flash of cameras, a cluster of reporters had gathered to await the official statement.

Waving at them, Ruben again went looking for his father. Usually the king handled press conferences, though Ruben would do so if needed.

The Captain of the Royal Guard, a large, dark skinned Pack member named Drake, informed him that the king would indeed deal with the press. He'd asked Ruben to tie up any loose ends before he did so.

Though it was nearly morning and he was weary to his bones, Ruben took care of business. While he conferred with palace guards and picked his way through the rubble that had once been the enormous foyer and receiving room of the palace, Willow's image hovered in the back of his mind. Not the beautiful woman in the beautiful ball gown, but the grimy, soot-covered one who'd so selflessly helped him. Who was she? Where had she come from? And why had she run away?

Had she been frightened, or had her fleeing been something else entirely? He froze as an awful thought occurred to him. Had she known something about the bomb or who had planted it? Had she seen something or was she much more intimately involved? Did she know something about the extremists?

As much as he tried, he couldn't immediately dismiss the idea. He'd thought he was familiar with every noblewoman around, not only in Teslinko but in the neighboring countries. But he had no idea who she really was, what nationality, or even who her people were.

When he'd first found her, she'd been hiding, keeping to herself, speaking to no one. She'd been practically skulking about. Had what he'd put down to shyness been in actuality an attempt to remain unnoticed?

One thing he knew for certain. When all this was over, he had to find her again.

Finally finished, he straightened his shoulders. Since the press conference would be starting in a few minutes, he turned to go in search of his parents again. As he did, he glanced down. There, among the soot and the rubble, near his feet, something shimmered. He bent, his muscles sore, and picked it up.

A woman's earring, a dangling pearl, now sullied by ash

and soot. An image flashed into his mind of the earring swinging gently as Willow turned her head. The earring was hers. She must have lost it in the craziness after the explosion.

Jaw set, he slipped the jewelry into his pocket. He'd seek Willow out, ostensibly to return her earring. While he was there, he'd ask her to explain exactly why she'd run and what she'd seen.

Kicking off her heels and lifting her sodden, ruined skirt in one hand, Willow took off. She ran, full-out, panic fueling her, grateful for the sudden spurt of energy that enabled her to go. She relished the feel of her legs pounding the earth and the wind whipping her hair, pushing away her weariness. When she reached the veil, she didn't hesitate, leaping toward the shimmering space as though the hounds of hell followed her.

For all she knew, one of them did.

When she'd discovered the veil, she'd quickly learned not to stay overnight. If she did, too much time passed on the other side. Once she'd come home after spending eighteen hours among the humans, only to learn over a week had passed at home.

She couldn't chance that happening again. Especially not now, when her parents had warned her that the two princes from EastWard would be arriving by the next day. One of these men—Prince Chad—was to be her betrothed. The other, Prince Eric, would wed her older sister, Tatiana.

There would be a ball—the irony of this didn't escape her—and she would be expected to make an appearance. As a matter of fact, she'd planned to wear the dress she'd worn tonight, which was now hopelessly ruined.

Once she'd landed—this time, miraculously on her feet— she hurried home. As soon as the glistening gold of the castle came into view, she felt some of her panic subside. Judging from the way the moon still hung low in the horizon, time had remained the same, or close enough that her lateness wouldn't matter.

Out of breath with her heart pounding from her exertion, she skidded to a stop and smoothed down her hair. There was nothing she could do about her ruined and filthy dress. At least everyone should still be asleep in their beds.

Hurrying up the glittering steps and grasping the huge handle of the castle door, she pulled the heavy door open and slipped inside.

All quiet, exactly as it should be. So far, so good.

Then, as she turned the corner that would lead toward the stairs, she heard it. Coming from down the hall, emanating from the direction of one of the receiving rooms, the sound of harp music and muted laughter.

Oh, dark. Her heart in her throat, she froze, listening. Was this a party that had continued into the predawn hours? What else could it be? Had the EastWard group already arrived? Her stomach clenched. She hoped not. If she'd missed some kind of welcoming reception, her mother would be furious with her.

Another laugh, deep and masculine, drifted down the hall. Immediately following, her sister Tatiana's signature giggle. If this wasn't the EastWard group, then her older sister had been entertaining another gentleman caller for the entire night.

*Blech.* Though Willow wouldn't put it past Tatiana. One last fling before settling down to a boring married life would be the way her older sister would look at it.

Hoping she was wrong, Willow gave the room a wide berth and hurried to her room to shower and change out of her ruined dress into her pajamas. Hopefully she could manage to catch a few hours of sleep before anyone came looking for her.

The next morning, full sunlight lit her room when she finally opened her eyes. The clock on the nightstand next to her bed read eleven thirty-five. Nearly noon.

Though her first instinct was to panic and jump out of bed so she could rush through her normal morning preparations, after a moment of thought, she reconsidered. Stretching, she allowed herself to wallow in the unexpected luxury of sleeping in. Since no one had bothered her or, more specifically, come to chew her out, she'd have to assume that the EastWard group hadn't yet arrived.

As she snuggled under the covers, her door swung open. Tatiana rushed into the room, slamming the door behind her. She wore one of her most glittery dresses, the shifting colors of white, gold, silver and blue giving Willow an instant headache.

"Good, you're here," Tatiana gushed, her golden hair all done up in ribbons and curls. Then, as she took in the sight of Willow snuggling under the covers, she frowned. "Why are you still in bed?"

Briefly Willow entertained the thought of telling her sister that frowning made a deep furrow appear right in the middle of her perfectly shaped eyebrows, but decided against it. "Thanks for knocking," she said. "What do you want? I was sleeping."

"This late?" Tatiana snorted. "Right. You forget, I know you. You're hiding, aren't you?"

Cautiously, Willow peered up at her sister. The waist of Tati's sparkling dress had been cinched so tightly, it was a wonder the older girl could breathe. Her full breasts threatened to spill out if she moved the wrong way. The glittering material barely covered them, though the way it had been arranged put them on blatant display.

Of course. Tatiana was getting ready to meet her fiancé. She wanted to look her best.

"Why would I need to hide?" Cautiously, Willow sat up.

Narrow-eyed, Tatiana studied her. Her painted lips finally spread into a malicious grin. "You honestly don't know?"

"Know what?"

"I'll bet you didn't show up at the welcome reception last night, did you?"

"Didn't you notice?" Willow volleyed back. What kind of sister doesn't discern whether or not her younger sibling was in attendance? She knew the answer to that one. Unless they were in direct competition with her for attention, a completely self-absorbed person like Tatiana rarely noticed any other woman in the room. And, since Willow clearly was no competition, Tatiana rarely knew—or cared about—her whereabouts.

Shaking her head so that her waves of bright, golden hair swung about her in a glorious cloud, Tatiana moved forward and perched on the chair at the side of Willow's bed.

"The princes are here," she said dreamily, though her bright violet eyes remained as sharp as ever. "Prince Eric is nearly as beautiful as me. And Prince Chad…"

Tatiana laughed, the sound so high-pitched and false Willow had to fight the urge to put her hands over her ears.

Tatiana's perfect red lips widened into a mocking smile. "He's perfect for you."

Since Tatiana showed no signs of leaving and hadn't yet arrived at the reason for her visit, Willow played along. "In what way? Is he also short and dark?"

"No. Quite the opposite. As a matter of fact, in his own way he's very…appealing." Tatiana gave a nervous laugh that was totally unlike her normal high-pitched giggle. This, along with the fact that her sister rarely even visited her room, made Willow instantly suspicious.

Slowly, she sat up, keeping as much of herself covered as she could for protection. She wouldn't put it past her older sister to get in a few jabs about Willow's lack of serious cleavage. About to ask for a second time what Tatiana wanted, Willow closed her mouth as Tatiana continued speaking.

"There's a big breakfast this morning." The words came out in a breathless rush, again not like her. "Since you missed the welcome reception last night, they've arranged for you to meet your intended in a few minutes over coffee and pastries. I was sent to fetch you."

"A few minutes?" It took every ounce of restraint not to jump from her bed. Not only would she be rushed, but she'd be late for her worst nightmare. A big breakfast with a male stranger whom she was supposed to marry.

"I'll stall them for you," Tatiana offered.

Since her sister never did anything without expecting payment, Willow tilted her head. "Why would you do that?"

Tatiana abruptly fell silent, her huge violet eyes filling with tears. This made Willow instantly suspicious, as she knew her sister only cried to manipulate someone.

"I'm sorry I've been so awful to you lately," Tatiana said. And there it was, or at least the beginnings of it. Exploitation. Though what Willow could possibly have that Tatiana would want, was beyond her.

Instead of acknowledging the apology, Willow simply crossed her arms and waited, knowing eventually Tatiana would get to the point.

But even she was shocked when her older sister suddenly burst into tears. And not fake tears either, but gut-busting, mascara-ruining *real* tears.

# Chapter 3

After her initial surprise wore off, Willow got out of bed and hugged Tatiana awkwardly. Years ago, Tatiana had trained her that any attempt at touching her would not only be rebuffed, but ridiculed. Apparently, that rule had been suspended, at least temporarily.

Still silent, Willow patted her sister's shoulder and let her cry.

"I don't want to marry Prince Eric," Tatiana finally sobbed, raising her mascara-stained face to Willow's.

Doubly shocked, Willow stared. Tatiana's ruined appearance, combined with her words, proved she actually meant it.

Aware she needed to tread carefully, Willow ventured a comment. "I thought he was the golden one, the prize among all princes."

"And the way our two kingdoms can join forces against the Shadows," Tatiana recited, as if by rote. "I know, I know."

"You said he was beautiful." In the past, appearances had been all that had mattered to her gorgeous older sister.

"He is, he is," Tatiana moaned. "Like I said, he's almost as beautiful as me."

What would have been extreme vanity in others was a simple statement of fact. Tatiana was the most beautiful among the Bright. And all knew it.

Again, Willow waited, knowing it would be better if she didn't speak just yet.

"But…" Tatiana began.

And here it came. The big *but*. For the life of her, Willow couldn't figure out what it might be. Prince Eric was wealthy, powerful and the heir to the EastWard throne. Once married to him, Tatiana would be in line to become Queen of the EastWard and, if their parents' dream came true and the South-Ward and EastWard people united, Queen of all the Brights.

A power that had never before existed.

If Willow knew her big sister—and she did—it would have to be something *awful* to make her want to give up that much power.

"That's the problem," Tatiana sniffed. "He's too beautiful. Everyone will be looking at him. No one will even notice me."

Willow shook her head. "That's not possible. And think of the adorable children you'd have."

"Children born of two good-looking parents are usually ugly. And I'd rather…" When Tatiana didn't finish but instead dissolved into another bout of sobbing, Willow continued to pat her back and wait her out.

Meanwhile, she tried to figure out why Tatiana was acting this way. Was she drunk? Had she gone without her much vaunted beauty rest for the entire night and this breakdown was because of simple exhaustion?

Or—and darker thoughts began to arise—was Prince Eric

some kind of sadist? Had he—horrified, Willow swallowed hard—had he *hurt* Tatiana? Abused her in some way?

Finally, as Tatiana continued weeping, Willow prodded. "But?"

"I think I could fall in love with Prince Chad."

"Huh?" Willow blinked. "Eric's younger brother? The one our parents promised me to?"

Tatiana's perfect, creamy skin blushed bright red. "Yes. And I'm quite certain he could love me, too, if he were given a chance."

Skeptical, Willow crossed her arms. "And you determined this in, what, a few hours last night?"

Tatiana shook her head so vigorously her hair whipped Willow in the face. "Don't say it like that." Her sorrowful expression hardened. "You've always treated me like I was stupid. I'm not. When I see what I want, I know it. It's as simple as that."

Willow's head had begun to ache. Rubbing her eyes, she tried to make sense of her sister's words. "And you're telling me this because you want me to do…what?"

Tatiana snapped her head up, her tears drying instantly. "Switch with me. Seduce Prince Eric. Make him want you."

Willow couldn't believe what she was hearing. "Switch with you? Listen to yourself. As if someone as perfect, as golden, as *Bright* as you've described would want someone like me over you." Not to mention the outcry such a public rejection would cause. The gossip! The rumors! Tatiana would never live them down.

Which meant there had to be a catch. And because she was who she was—tigers didn't change their stripes—Tatiana wouldn't mention this catch until it was way too late for all involved.

In her childhood and teenage years, Willow had been down

that road more times than she could count. She wouldn't make this mistake again.

Her self-depreciating comment had pleased Tatiana. Grinning with a false modesty, she dipped her head in acknowledgment. "True, but Prince Chad has told me one something about his older brother that isn't well known. Eric's magic is weak, like yours. Again, I have to think of my future children."

Since Willow's magic was more than weak, it was nonexistent, she crossed her arms. "Prince Chad told you this why?"

"Were you not listening? I talked to them both last night. That's how I know I can't marry Eric. One, he's too good-looking and two, he has inferior magic. Chad's magic is as powerful as mine, plus he's less beautiful than his older brother. He is much more to my liking."

Stunned speechless, Willow considered her thoughts. Was this a simple case of Tatiana wanting whatever Willow had? No, she decided. Not possible. Especially since everyone knew Tatiana's intended husband was every bit as beautiful as her.

"But the eldest son's wife will be queen," Willow said, trying another tactic.

"Of the EastWard Brights." Tatiana shook her head. "You can have that."

"You'd give up the throne?" This definitely meant Tatiana was up to something. Unfortunately, whatever it was wouldn't be good for Willow.

"Only *that* throne," Tatiana finally conceded. "I'd still be able to rule SouthWard once Mama and Daddy step down."

"Which won't be for a long time," Willow put in.

Tatiana's smile held a hint of darkness. "Oh, you never know. It might be sooner than you think."

Did she plan to help things along? Willow shook her head. She didn't really want to know. However, she'd need a mate with a lot of magical power if she planned to try and stage a coup. Which would explain her sudden desire for the younger, less handsome brother.

They were still eyeing each other when the door opened and Queen Millicent swept inside, peering at them with disapproval. "The breakfast will be in one hour and neither of you are ready? I expect this sort of behavior from Willow, but from you, Tatiana? Honestly."

The queen had barely finished speaking when she caught sight of her first-born child's red nose and face streaked with black. Instantly she rounded furiously on Willow.

"What have you done to your sister?" she hissed, gathering Tatiana close while her gaze shot daggers at her youngest daughter. "Today of all days she must look her absolute best and you've made her cry."

Willow didn't bother to try and form a response. She knew from experience that her mother wouldn't believe her anyway.

Without waiting for an answer, the queen turned and shepherded Tatiana from the room. At the doorway, she paused, glaring back over her shoulder at Willow. "I'm going to take your sister and see if I can repair the damage you've done. As for you, get ready for the breakfast. All I ask is that you try to look decent."

Willow nodded.

"Thank you." Giving Tatiana's hunched shoulders a hard squeeze, Millicent delivered the final shot. "After all, every dog will have its day. Don't blow yours."

"Wait, Mother." Squirming out of the queen's hold, Tatiana dashed over to Willow's side. "Let me help her get ready. A little makeup will fix this." She waved her perfectly manicured hand at her own face. "You know it'll just take me a few minutes."

"Fine." Unable to refuse her eldest daughter anything,

Queen Millicent nodded. "Just make sure you both are on time." And with that, she left.

Tatiana sighed. "You don't know what a burden it is being the eldest."

It took every ounce of self-control Willow possessed to keep from rolling her eyes. "Try being the ugly duckling of the family."

"No thanks." The fact that Tatiana didn't even bother trying to refute Willow's words should have stung, but she supposed she was used to it.

"You have to make the best out of what you have." Stalking over to the closet, Tatiana went through the day dresses. Finally, she pulled out one made of light blue watered silk, the sparkles interwoven into the fabric, which made them much less noticeable. The dress was dull by Bright standards, but Willow loved it. She hadn't yet had an occasion to wear it.

"Whatever you do, don't wear this one," Tatiana ordered, tossing the gown on the floor as though it were garbage. "Wear something fun!"

She pulled out a hideous chiffon concoction of orange, hot pink and yellow, held it up and nodded. "This is perfect." Tossing it at Willow, who miraculously caught it, she grinned. "See you in an hour." Then she, too, swept from the room, slamming the door behind her.

The overpowering scent of heavy perfume lingered in the air.

Willow shook her head and tossed the frothy dress on her bed. She went to open the window and let in fresh air. Inhaling the smell of fresh pine, she gazed longingly at her beloved woods, missing the gentle creatures that lived there. They knew nothing of subterfuge and lies. They didn't care that she didn't look anything at all like a Bright was supposed to look. How she wished she could simply slip out of the castle unnoticed and escape to the forest.

Attempting to escape her life, that's what she was doing. She'd done so many times already, running to the forest and lately, to the human world.

As she had when she'd danced with Prince Ruben.

The thought nearly made her smile. But, true to the way her luck seemed to go, even her one magical night was shattered by a bomb explosion. In the ensuing chaos, she'd tried to help as much as possible, escaping back to the veil at the last possible minute.

Home again. And now this. A meet-and-greet breakfast dressed in uncomfortable formal clothes. Already, the ball last night and the human prince who'd treated her as if she was beautiful felt like a dream, a fantasy.

With a heavy heart, Willow went to shower. When it came time to select something to wear, she chose the more discreetly elegant watered silk rather than the rainbow-colored chiffon. She could only imagine how Tatiana would roll her eyes when she saw that.

Willow sighed, bracing herself for the ordeal ahead. Even though she wanted no part of her sister's secret plans, she knew she was about to walk smack-dab into the middle of them.

The next morning dawned with a leaden sky and the promise of rain whispering in the wind. The acrid scent of smoke and soot hung over everything, a constant reminder of the explosion and fire.

Heart heavy, Ruben accompanied his father, King Leo, in an inspection of the damage caused by the bomb. He'd gotten barely an hour of sleep, and most of that had been standing up when he took a quick, hot shower to cleanse the ash from his exhausted body.

The events of the previous night felt like a dream—meeting Willow, dancing and spending time with her. A promising dream that had been interrupted by a nightmare. He couldn't believe the extremists were back. But who else would have done such a thing? Until he was given reason to think otherwise, he had to believe the extremists were behind the bombing. They always felt violence was the best way to prove a point.

Ruben didn't understand this line of thought. Last time they'd set off bombs and had tried to harm his sister. The only thing they'd achieved had been jail sentences and widespread scorn and censure.

None of that had fazed them, he guessed. Because they'd regrouped and tried their foolish terroristic actions again. To what end? Ruben couldn't see what they had hoped to gain by blowing up the palace. Did they even have a plan? Somehow he doubted it.

He suspected they were all crazy. What they wanted was impossible. They wanted Shape-shifters to be able to stay wolf longer than human. Even if such a thing were physically possible—which it was not—Ruben knew better than most how that could mess with one's mind.

Pushing aside his thoughts, he walked with his father through the still smoldering rubble.

"We're lucky no one was killed." Grim faced, in the watery light King Leo looked older than his years. As he watched his normally jovial father shoulder the responsibility for the destruction, Ruben suppressed fury. The strong emotion stirred his wolf to instant alertness. The beast was spoiling for a fight.

He felt his father's wolf respond in kind, which was unusual. Normally, both his parents' beasts were sedate animals, content with their lot. Unless… Of course.

"How long has it been since you changed?" Ruben asked the king. Standing right next to each other, both their wolves could sense the other's restlessness. As usual, at least lately,

Ruben had difficulty keeping his under control. He watched as his father instantly subdued his own beast.

Ruefully, Leo smiled. "Quite a while, actually. I've been so busy. And now…" He spread his hands, visibly struggling with slipping control. "I don't know when I'll ever find the time."

"You must," Ruben began, stopping as he watched his father engage in a battle with his beast that felt both odd and eerily familiar. He'd encountered so many of these same battles himself recently.

The king's inner wolf fought him, struggling to break out, to force a change. Since Ruben had never seen this happen with anyone beside himself, he watched helplessly.

"Sorry." His father grimaced. "I've been fighting my wolf for a while now. I really need to make time to change."

Ruben felt a combination of emotions. Sadness, fury and anticipation. He realized the latter was fueled by his own wolf. The animals were in sync about one thing—the urgent need to change.

A quick glance at his father made him realize the older man was having similar thoughts. "How about we go right after we finish with this?"

Ruben nodded. Sometimes it was easier—and safer—to give in.

Together they finished their inspection of the damaged area. Through it all, the sense of finality that the king wore like a cloak fascinated Ruben. He couldn't help but compare his father's issue to his own. Did King Leo share his son's problems with his inner wolf, the constant battle to remain human, to maintain control, often with a high mental and physical cost? If so, Ruben wondered if that meant he wasn't as abnormal and as isolated as he'd feared.

The potential felt enormous. Just the idea that he might not be alone in this felt like a huge weight had been lifted from his chest. He took his father's arm, trying to frame the words properly so that he didn't give too much away. "How long have you—"

Someone shouted for the king, cutting Ruben off before he could finish asking his question. As they hurried over, he figured maybe it was for the best. He could probably learn more by keeping his mouth shut and observing. He definitely didn't want his father guessing that something serious might be wrong with his only son and heir.

As she quickly made up her bed, Willow saw something stuck between the pillow and the edge of the wall. Leaning in, she picked it up and froze. An earring. One of the dangly pearl earrings she'd worn last night. Her heart thudded hard in her chest. The ancient and valuable set had belonged to her mother and, as most of the queen's jewelry did, contained magic only she could access. Willow had borrowed them without permission, intending to return them quickly, before her mother noticed. With everything that had happened, she'd completely forgotten about them.

One earring. Her hand shook as she cradled it in her palm. One perfect, slightly sooty, pearl earring with unknown magical powers. Oh, shades. The queen would certainly notice if the set wasn't returned intact. She had to find the other.

Frantic, she looked. A search of her bedding revealed nothing. Ditto under the bed and on the surrounding floor. *Think, Willow. Think.* Since she'd obviously showered last night with the jewelry on—how could she have been so oblivious?—she checked the bathroom and the shower. Nothing.

Shadefire and double shadefire. Heart sinking, she tried to think. One of her mother's perfect pearl earrings was missing. How long until her mother noticed? The way Willow's luck seemed to be running, the queen would decide to wear them today. She'd fly into a rage when she couldn't find them.

And Willow knew where her mother would look first. Not to Tatiana. No, Willow would have a lot of explaining to do.

After the breakfast, she had to find the other. If it wasn't here… Her pulse skipped a beat. She must have left it in Teslinko, at the prince's palace, most likely somewhere in the ashy ruins of the ballroom. After the breakfast, she'd return there. That is, if she could sneak away without anyone noticing, and try to find it.

Plan made, she hurried to get ready for the breakfast, well aware her mother wouldn't appreciate it if she was late after her conspicuous absence at the welcome reception the night before.

And she'd have to do her best to steer clear of whatever scheme her sister was concocting. She had enough trouble already. No sense in borrowing any more.


"Something is going on with my sister," Tatiana murmured to Prince Chad. She liked him, she really did. They'd been seated next to each other at the breakfast table, Chad on her left and her betrothed, Prince Eric, on her right.

Chad's faded violet gaze sharpened. "How so?"

Since Willow hadn't shown up yet, and he had no idea what kind of bride their combined parents had saddled him with, she hid her smile and shook her head, sending her glorious hair swaying. "I'm not certain. I'll watch her and see if I can get her to tell me."

He nodded, already looking bored with the subject. As he held her left hand under the table, he'd begun drawing circles in the middle of her palm with his thumb. She shivered, unable to believe how erotic such a small touch could be.

That, plus the fact that he dared take such liberties right under the watchful eye of his brother made it doubly thrilling.

They were two of a kind, she and Prince Chad. If Willow

wouldn't play along, Tatiana would try some other scheme to switch bridegrooms.

"What are you two talking about?" Eric turned and leaned closer, his perfect white teeth flashing in a face that carried exactly the right amount of tan. Studying him, from his patrician features and bright violet eyes, to his hair the exact same shade of gold as hers, Tatiana knew on the surface that no one would understand why she didn't want him. He was perfect, every girl's dream of a prince. Like Prince Charming in the old stories.

In looks, he was exactly like her. Her mirror image.

Tatiana never fooled herself or tried to hide from her flaws. She was, she knew, vain and shallow and often bad tempered. The most important person in her life was, and would always be, herself. She didn't care about others' feelings or charity work or any kind of endeavor that might involve selfless giving. She adored luxuries, adulation and being cosseted, not necessarily in that order.

She sensed Prince Eric was the exact same way. Like her inside as well as out. She'd known instinctively an instant after meeting him. Left alone together for too long, they'd either kill each other or—and this was more likely—their relationship would eventually dissolve into icy indifference. After that, the affairs and love children and scandals and misery would swiftly follow. The stain on her reputation would be more than she could bear.

There were quick scandals—such as what would happen if she switched fiancés—and those that were soul-sucking, psyche-damaging and lasted for an eternity. Marriage to Eric would cause the latter.

Therefore, Tatiana would not marry him, regardless of what her parents had promised his. The way she figured, she had one way out, as unlikely as it might seem. Her plan was comprised of two parts. First, she had to get Prince Eric to fall in love with her younger sister.

And second, she had to make Price Chad fall in love with her.

The second part was easy. No man had ever been able to resist her once she started batting her long lashes his way. Judging from his hand-holding activity, Prince Chad would prove to be no exception.

Yet another challenge that wasn't. Oddly disappointing, that.

Tatiana found she genuinely liked the younger prince, at least on first impression. Though also fair skinned with golden hair and about the same height, he lacked a certain symmetry of features, and was a rugged-looking man rather than a beautiful one. Personality-wise, she could already tell he was as different from his older brother as she was from her younger sister.

Plus, she suspected he worshipped her already, which in her opinion would make their union a match made in heaven. One absolute in her life was that she needed to be the wor-shippee rather than the worshipper.

"Would you fetch me some more coffee, my dear?" With a smarmy smile, Prince Eric tapped her on the shoulder like she was his personal maid.

Stiffening, Tatiana fought the urge to tell him to get it himself. Instead, she smiled sweetly. "We have servants for that. All you need to do is hold up your hand and signal one of the waitstaff. See, there are several standing over by the silver coffee urn."

Instead of being mollified, he pouted. "I'd rather you get it. Such a personal gesture carries so much meaning, don't you think?"

Right, she thought. So much meaning. In a sad little way, he was right, because if she scurried to do his bidding, she'd be setting a precedent for the rest of their lives together. That is, if she was unlucky enough to actually marry him. She simply had to finagle her way out of this.

Clenching her jaw, she kept her pretty smile in place. No, she wouldn't be jumping up to fetch and carry for him. Not now, not ever.

Pretending to misunderstand, she tilted her head. "Of course. I'll do it." And she lifted her hand, signaling a servant over. "Prince Eric needs more coffee."

Immediately, the waiter brought over a new, piping-hot cup and set it down in front of the prince.

"There you go," Tatiana said brightly, pretending not to notice Eric's frown as he gaped at her, apparently stunned into silence that she hadn't jumped when he had snapped his fingers. "Next time, you'll know what to do so you can get it yourself."

And with that small insult, she turned back to her left, keeping her sweet and slightly dopey smile in place. She'd learned early on that her beauty tended to intimidate men. Yet if she acted less intelligent, that one flaw appeared to negate the other, at least as far as they were concerned.

While Eric stewed silently, Chad leaned closer, smiling a small, secretive smile. "Well done," he murmured. "Most women are so busy fawning all over him. I wager he has no idea how to react to one who doesn't."

Pleased, Tatiana took a sip of her own coffee, now lukewarm. She wished she could say more, but she had to be careful not to overplay her hand.

Speaking of which, Prince Chad squeezed hers under the table, apparently intent on continuing his sensual thumb massage.

Enough. Aware of the dangers of acquiescing too early, she moved both her hands to the top of the table, folding one over the other and pretending to inspect her flawless manicure.

He gave a snort of laughter, which she ignored.

Casually she glanced at her watch. Where the hell was Willow? Their mother had been quite clear in letting her know that she was to attend this breakfast on time. First she'd missed the welcome reception and now this? Already she was over thirty minutes late.

A quick glance at Queen Millicent showed her mother had definitely noticed and was greatly displeased. Though she kept her face expressionless, well aware of the consequences brought on by a frown, the queen's eyes snapped with annoyance.

About to push to her feet and fetch her sister, Tatiana breathed a sigh of relief as the door opened and Willow strolled inside. Tatiana noticed her sister had not taken her advice and had chosen to wear the blue silk dress.

Both men turned to look. Inside, Tatiana prayed Prince Eric would somehow find Willow attractive, if only because of the sharp contrast between her coloring and everyone else's.

Apparently, the weight of everyone's stares made Willow falter. She nearly stumbled, regaining her balance only at the last moment and flashing the group a weak smile. "Good morning, everyone," she murmured.

Even though this dress wasn't as flashy as what most considered fashionable and Tatiana herself wouldn't be caught dead in it, reluctantly she approved. She had long ago noticed that Willow looked better when she wore less glitz and glam. She had no idea why that would be so—in her opinion, the more glitter the better—but it was true.

And the sky-blue color of the gown made Willow's dusky complexion glow. She had, Tatiana noticed, even taken the time to twist her long, dark hair into a chignon. If she was feeling charitable, Tatiana might even say her sister looked… pretty. In an odd, shadowy sort of way.

To Tatiana's right, Prince Eric puffed out his chest, believing here would be another easy conquest. To her left, Prince Chad went very, very still. As Willow approached with her father, King Puck, in order for him to make the introduction, Tatiana noticed the younger EastWard prince's set jaw. He narrowed his eyes at the woman he'd been promised to marry. If anything, he looked furious.

Good, she thought with satisfaction. Evidently he hadn't been told of the youngest princess's physical shortcomings. And there was no way he could know Willow had no magic, either. Which was fine with Tatiana, since she planned to tell him herself. Once he believed himself to be doomed to marry such an ugly, non-magical woman, Prince Chad would be that much riper for the picking. He'd crumple under the massive assault she had planned.

She watched from under her lashes as his nostrils flared, obviously trying to maintain a bland expression.

She'd seen men do that before, though usually they'd been looking at her, overcome by her loveliness and trying not to show it.

All her life, Tatiana had been the beautiful one. Sought-after, cosseted, beloved eldest daughter. The world was more than her oyster—it was her pearl. And her baby sister, Willow, had proved to be the perfect foil, reflecting back Tatiana's beauty and amplifying it by comparison.

For that, Tatiana was grateful, though she'd never expressed her gratitude to Willow. How could she, when to do so would mortally offend the younger woman?

Both of the EastWard princes watched Willow walk toward them, appearing riveted. Tatiana knew that had to be a ruse. They didn't fool her. After all, who know better than her what men wanted?

## Chapter 4

*Here we go,* Willow told herself as she propelled herself forward, aiming for the single empty chair at the table. She tried to move gracefully, even though exhaustion from the night before made her legs feel hollow and wobbly. Eyeing her sister as she approached, she wondered why Tatiana looked so smug, like a cat that had wandered across a mouse farm.

Of course the moment she took her attention from what she was supposed to be doing, Willow stumbled. She flailed her arms in a passable imitation of a windmill, nearly tearing her dress in her painful attempt to keep from falling flat on her face.

Despite the exhausted weakness of her traitorous body, she miraculously managed to keep standing.

Both princes immediately leaped to their feet to offer their assistance. Face flaming, she waved them away, not missing the wry look her father gave her.

At least her family was used to her complete lack of social skills. While this was her first fall, she was frequently guilty of other faux pas, like saying the wrong thing at the worst possible time. No doubt these two visiting princes had heard stories about her. Even as they once again took their seats, their backs stiff and unyielding, she felt their silence as a form of judgment. She didn't even try to look at her mother, already aware of the furious condemnation she'd find there.

Instead she glanced again at her sister. Tatiana only tilted her head and narrowed her eyes. Normally, she would have made cruel jokes and laughed meanly. Instead, she sat solemnly, her golden beauty glowing, a sympathetic look on her beautiful face. False, but sympathetic nonetheless.

Weird. Really, really weird.

As she resumed her progress toward her seat, remembering what her sister had said, Willow tried to check out their visitors surreptitiously. Tatiana sat between the two princes, their three fair heads the exact same glorious gold, their eyes varying shades of violet, though close enough that they might have been related.

They were perfect examples of the Bright. As shimmering, as golden, as Willow was not. In fact, all of them were as unlike her as it was possible to be. Yet this time, she refused to let them make her feel…less. Because she knew she wasn't. Prince Ruben had shown her this. If only for one night. She'd felt beautiful, perfect, *shining*. As she never had before. She wanted to keep that feeling close to her for as long as she could.

The only empty chair for her sat next to the man on Tatiana's left, which meant he must be the younger son, the one her parents intended her to wed.

Her father stood and pulled out the chair as she approached, glaring at her as though he dared her not to do anything else to humiliate herself and by proxy, them. Only when she was safely seated did he speak.

"Prince Chad, may I present my youngest daughter, the Princess Willow."

Chad stood, his expression shuttered. He didn't meet her gaze while he bowed over her fingers. Since this was a formal breakfast, protocol dictated that he kiss her hand, something Willow had always hated. Some kisses were too much, slimy and wet. Others were dry, reminding her of snakes and bats. She'd endured them all time and time again, ever since she'd been a small girl. Always, there was no escaping this archaic ritual, so she suffered through it with a bland smile. When Prince Chad met her smile with an ironic one of his own, she realized he must hate the old-fashioned greeting as much as she did.

His mouth moved over her hand, the barest whisper.

Finally, he released her, dipping his cleft chin in a mock bow. The small glimmer of hilarity she saw in his violet gaze warmed her. Surprising. She thought she might actually *like* this man, despite his too-good-to-be-true handsomeness.

The other—Prince Eric, no doubt—leaned across in front of Tatiana, his corded arm scraping her considerable bosom, causing Tatiana to draw her breath in a sharp hiss. If he noticed, he paid her no heed, fixing his bright violet eyes on Willow and flashing a dazzling smile that would have been painfully beautiful if it weren't so practiced.

"I'm Prince Eric," he intoned, his rich baritone both deliberately seductive and impossibly arrogant. Tatiana's intended. Willow nodded in acknowledgment.

As her sister had mentioned, Eric was beautiful, in the same way as Tatiana. They were both flawless, golden and oh-so-Bright. Together, they would make a breathtaking couple. And their children would be perfect visions of Brightness. She tried to ignore the envy that coiled in her stomach.

Instead, she opened her mouth to pay them the compliment, remarking on their great beauty and how that would affect their potential offspring. She then realized Tatiana might not appreciate it, especially after what she'd said earlier.

"Pleased to meet you," Willow said lamely instead.

Was that actually amusement that flashed in her sister's bright violet eyes?

Though she'd already taken her seat, Chad began to fuss with her chair, ostensibly to help her get settled comfortably. She glanced sideways at him and felt…nothing. Which actually was a relief. He was no Prince Ruben, that was for sure.

The thought startled her. Merely thinking of the human prince made her entire body feel warm. Until she remembered the earring—oh, her mother's pearl earring—and her stomach turned.

Her mother's precious, no-doubt-magical, pearl earrings. Precious, not only because of the pearl, but because of the magical power contained within, although only their true owner knew how to use them properly.

She glanced at the queen. Luckily, though she'd decked herself out in a dazzling array of jewels for this breakfast, evidently her mother hadn't yet realized they were missing. Willow crossed her fingers, hoping her luck held out long enough for her to travel through the veil and retrieve the lost one. Whether or not the baubles were magical, they belonged to Millicent and thus, were valuable beyond compare.

She had to find it. Or there would be hell to pay. Her mother would make sure of that. Therefore, failure wasn't an option.

When she looked up again, she realized Prince Chad was watching her, as though trying to discern her thoughts. She pasted on her best social smile and pretended to be interested in the table arrangement.

As the servants stepped forward with an array of delicacies, her stomach growled, making her realize she was actually starving. Left to her own devices, she'd have preferred to break her fast with a hot bowl of oatmeal and fresh berries, but instead she allowed her plate to be filled with scrambled eggs, grits and sourdough toast. Though the meal looked heavy, the scent of freshly cooked food made her mouth water.

Glad to have something to do with her hands, she dug in, halfheartedly listening to the conversation swirling around her while she chewed and tried to develop a plan.

"Bright to Willow." Prince Chad gave her a gentle nudge, nearly causing her to spew her orange juice. She gasped instead, choked and unfortunately began coughing, her eyes filling with tears as she grabbed her napkin to cover her mouth.

"Are you all right?" he asked, sounding concerned, even though a bit of ironic humor lurked in his gaze.

"Swallowed wrong," she gasped out, waving him away. When she finally looked up, helpless, wishing she could make a quick exit from the room, everyone at the table was ogling her as though she'd grown two heads.

Some things never changed. Except they had, last night at the ball in Teslinko. That night, everything had been ideal.

She gave them a sickly smile, grabbed her napkin and wiped at the tears streaming down her cheeks. When she did, she saw her mascara had run and that she'd ruined her makeup. Another addition to a morning already gone bad.

Briefly, she considered excusing herself and either going to repair it or—and she liked this one better—excusing herself and never coming back. Only the steely look in her mother's eyes warned her that she'd better not try either.

"Pssst, Willow." Leaning around the back of Prince Chad, Tatiana rapped her on the shoulder.

Resigned, Willow leaned back. Now her sister would make sure her humiliation was complete. "Yes?"

"Lean closer," Tatiana ordered, making Willow wonder what she was up to. Tatiana had many cruel tricks in her repertoire; she'd been perfecting them since the two were children together.

Still, Willow'd learned either to do as Tatiana asked or risk making a scene. Another scene. She leaned closer, crossing her fingers that her sister wouldn't be too harsh this time.

"Hold still." With gentle hands, Tatiana cleaned her face. Stunned, Willow couldn't move. When her sister made a second pass, using some kind of compact makeup to repair the damage, Willow couldn't help but wonder if she'd just had her face painted bright green or something.

"What are you doing?" she finally asked, careful not to touch Prince Chad's rigid back. Unsure of the protocol, the prince was doing his best to eat and pretend the two women weren't having a conversation directly behind him. Grudgingly, she found she admired that, too.

Meanwhile, at the head of the table Prince Eric carried on a one-sided conversation with her parents. Either he was trying to help distract them, he was oblivious, or just didn't care. Willow was betting on the latter.

A rueful look from Tatiana showed she thought the same thing. Finally, she finished fixing Willow's face. "There you go, sis. Good as new."

Since Tatiana had never called her *sis* in her life, Willow wasn't sure how to react. "Thanks," she finally muttered, trying not to watch as Tatiana flashed a warm smile before turning away to pick at her own, mostly uneaten breakfast.

Uneasy, Willow tried to do the same. The food on her plate had grown cold, but she was still hungry, so she doggedly ate it anyway.

Everyone else resumed their breakfast, as well.

While they ate, Prince Eric continued to talk, often with his mouth full, a lapse in manners that normally would have horrified her mother. But no, a quick glance at the queen showed her mother pretended to hang on Eric's every word.

But by the time he got around to bragging about his talents with horsemanship, Queen Millicent's patience had obviously frayed. Mouth a thin line, she sipped at her coffee and glowered at the young man.

Finally, her father, experienced at deflecting this sort of thing, deliberately shifted the conversation to include Tatiana and Willow. As King Puck went on about their prowess on horseback, Willow felt her eyes glaze over.

Chad, too, barely stifled a yawn.

After listening to this for a few minutes, Eric magnanimously decided they must all go riding after the meal.

Gazing at Chad, Tatiana smiled and breathlessly agreed.

Willow clenched her jaw and continued eating. Riding. On horses. Where she'd be expected to pretend to be gracious and magical and…Bright. Everything she was not. This would be another possibility for an epic disaster.

Though Willow didn't demure, she had no intention of accompanying them. This was her perfect opportunity. While they were out riding, she'd have time to get to the veil and cross over to Teslinko. With any luck, she could find the missing magical earring and be back before anyone even noticed she'd been gone.

After all the plates had been cleared, everyone dispersed to get dressed in their riding gear. They had agreed to meet at the barn in half an hour. Rather than give an excuse and waste valuable time, Willow planned to simply not show up.

She had to hurry. Dutifully heading to her room, she rushed down the hallway with her heart pounding. She prayed no one—particularly Tatiana—would follow her. She needed a few minutes to change—into jeans rather than breeches— and then make her escape into the woods.

This one time, at least, she hoped her prayer was answered.

She took a deep breath. The meeting with the EastWard princes had rattled her more than she'd expected. Though

Prince Chad seemed charming enough, something about him unsettled her. She suspected it was the possibility that they were a bit alike. Used to living unnoticed in the huge shadow cast by their perfect older sibling, like her, he was able to do many things unnoticed. Slipping underneath the family's radar was a trick she'd perfected ever since she could walk. Chad most likely did the same. She had the feeling he saw way too much. For once Tatiana had been intuitive rather than self-absorbed.

A knock on her door startled her. Heart pounding, she opened it. Chad.

"I didn't want to go riding, either," he said, flashing an easy smile. "How about we go for a walk and get to know each other?"

Stars. Her plans not so secret anymore, she said the first thing that came to mind, which happened to be the truth. "I can't. I've lost one of my mother's earrings and I've got to find it. Once I do, I'll come looking for you, all right?"

To her relief, he dipped his head in a nod and left her alone. She closed her door and locked it, willing her rapid heart rate to slow.

After changing into jeans and boots, feeling much calmer, she went to her window and, grasping the trellis that she'd had installed a few years ago as an escape route, climbed down the outside wall. She looked both to the left and the right and seeing no one, she hurried away and slipped into the woods. Her woods.

The moment the shadowy forest enveloped her, all the tension left her. The scent of damp earth and leaves, pine and oak filled her senses. The dappled sunlight felt welcoming and warm. Here, she felt at home as she did nowhere else. She rolled her shoulders, breathing deeply, her footsteps quiet on the cushion of leaves.

Nearby she sensed several of the numerous forest creatures she'd befriended, but she didn't call them to her as she usually did. Time was of the essence today. She had to get to Teslinko, find the missing magical earring and return to SouthWard before anyone noticed she was missing.

With this in mind, she hurried toward the veil. Once she thought she had heard footsteps behind her, but when she had slipped behind a tree to listen and watch, there was no one.

Because it never hurt to be careful, she picked up her pace. Dead leaves crackled underfoot as she hurried toward the portal.

Jogging, then sprinting, she found herself breathless by the time the shimmering power of the veil made itself known. She felt it long before she finally saw it, but once she did, she leaped forward, leaving her home the same way she'd returned, as though a demon from hell was on her heels.

Only this time, one actually was.


Prince Chad of EastWard couldn't decide whether to be amused or angry that the SouthWard royalty had thought to marry him off to their youngest daughter. Obviously, Willow wasn't of pure royal blood, not looking like that.

Again, he grimaced. Not that Willow was ugly. Quite the opposite, in fact. She was just…different. Both her parents had the standard Bright appearance—blond hair, violet eyes and pale skin. Like all the SouthWard and EastWard people. The Bright. Boring, but the epitome of both feminine and masculine beauty, as far as he was concerned.

No, Willow looked more like the Shadows. The people of the north and west—the Shadows—were completely different in their appearance. They were the polar opposite of the Bright. With her dark hair and dusky skin, Willow easily must have come from either NorthWard or WestWard. She was the quite obvious by-blow of some Shadow lover.

Which meant the rumors were true. For years, it had been

whispered that Queen Millicent had strayed with one of the Shadow princes. Willow obviously was the result of that union. Evidently King Puck hadn't wanted to risk humiliation and had accepted her as his own.

Furious, Chad clenched his jaw. As second son, he was always given second best. Once again, as eldest, Eric would get the most beautiful daughter. The bastard one, who was rumored to have weak magic as well, would be foisted off on Chad.

Like that would ever happen. Though he grudgingly admitted Willow had her own exotic beauty, he could never marry a woman who looked like that. There were his future offspring to consider. His children. Mating with her would risk tainting his bloodline.

Acknowledging this, he realized something else. She intrigued him. Something about her innocent sensuality appealed to his bloodthirsty nature.

While he couldn't marry her, he still wanted her. He'd freely admit that Willow of the SouthWard fascinated him, unlike her sister who—like his brother, Eric—had absolutely no secrets. Willow moved with an unconsciously sensual grace, and the slight tilt of her almond eyes was alluring. Her lush mouth gave her an earthy sexual appeal.

Though he knew she wasn't aware of it, Willow had passion simmering underneath her complacent, dusky beauty. Chad thought he might just be the one to awaken that in her, even if he had to use honeyed lies and false caresses.

He wouldn't marry her, but he *would* have her. Of that he was determined. His brother Prince Eric might be showy, but Chad always got what he wanted, no matter how underhanded the methods he had to use to obtain it.

Always.

His initial fury subsided. This entire situation had actually surprised him, not an easy feat these days. When the marriage between Eric and the spectacularly lovely Tatiana had been arranged, the SouthWard royal couple had wanted to throw their youngest daughter into the bargain. Chad had thought it a bit odd, but what the hell. Eric was expected to marry and produce an heir. It would be to Chad's advantage to do the same, just in case something happened to his elder brother. And you never know, he thought wickedly. Something just might.

An earring, eh? Even better, a *magical* earring belonging to Queen Millicent. Who knew what impressive powers the piece of jewelry might contain? Willow might have lost it, but if he could find it before her...

Whistling under his breath, he'd rounded the back corner of the palace just in time to see the Princess Willow climbing down a trellis and taking off into the woods. Alone, acting as if she had feared being caught.

Chad hadn't even stopped to think. Intrigued, he'd followed her, intent on learning her destination without her discovering his pursuit. No doubt she went in search of the earring.

Adrenaline fueled him as he rushed through the forest, taking care not to let his quarry catch a glimpse of him. Amazed that he'd discovered a new way to get his heart pumping without drawing blood and causing pain, he grinned.

He pushed the thought away, continued his pursuit, going from tree to tree, using the underbrush as cover. She was easy to track as she took no care to hide her presence, clearly believing no one would ever attempt to follow her.

Even as she hurried through the forest, there was something sensual about her. As if this was where she belonged, he thought with a startling flash of clarity.

The idea nearly made him stumble. More than any of the other Brights, he'd studied many of the types of beings in the human realm. There were the Shape-shifters that called themselves Pack, and then Vampires, Mer-people, Warlocks, Wizards, Witches, Tearlachs and those that were a various combination of these.

Many had their own powers, but none of them had the inherent magical abilities that his people, the Bright, and the others of his kind, the Shadows, had. Each form of magic was different. The Brights controlled the elements of air and of fire, while the Shadows had earth and water.

Except for Willow, who was rumored to have no magic at all.

When she had stopped, he had ducked behind a tree. He felt the shift in the air, raising the fine hair on his arms, and frowned. What the…? The feel of magic crawled along his skin. Magic. What was she doing? Peering out at her, he realized the magic wasn't emanating from her slight figure. Then where?

Now he concentrated. Using his inherent magical ability, he sensed the gate long before he realized what it was, slipping out from behind a tree just long enough to see Willow hurl herself into the shimmering space and vanish.

His heartbeat kicked into overdrive. A portal. Shades of fire, could things get any more interesting? He thought not. Now to see what lay on the other side.

Striding forward, he stepped into the veil and let the magic take him where it may.

# Chapter 5

After watching his father hold the press conference, Ruben had given his statement to the police. When he'd finished, King Leo was waiting for him.

Together, they'd walked the perimeter of the ruined ballroom, inspecting the damage and dictating their report to the attending scribe. Now that the damage to the castle had been noted and repairs scheduled, Ruben knew he should rest. Beyond exhaustion, he wondered how he had kept from doing a face-plant into the rubble.

As he turned to ask his father's leave so he might grab a few hours of sleep, the wolf inside him protested. Lunging at an invisible barrier, the animal wanted out. As did his father's beast.

Clearly equally exhausted, King Leo gave him a rueful grin. "Your wolf is restless. Mine is responding in kind. Since they won't let us sleep, are you up for a quick change and run?"

Fighting to hold back his inner beast, Ruben nodded. "When?"

"How about now?"

As his father clapped his hand on his shoulder, Ruben finished corralling his wolf into temporary submission. He grinned up at the older man. "That's one of the reasons I love you, Dad. The ability to make quick decisions."

This compliment made the king laugh. "Quick and good, I hope," he said.

"Do you mind if I bring York?" Ruben asked. "He'd love a good run. He's been cooped up since the ball last night." His German shepherd dog had been brought up with the Pack and often accompanied him on trips into the woods. When Ruben changed, the dog eagerly ran at his wolf self's side.

"Sure." King Leo loved the large dog almost as much as Ruben did.

Rather than go all the way back into the castle and locate the kennel master who was looking after York, Ruben dialed him up on his cell phone. A moment later, he whistled and the huge dog came flying around the corner toward them.

"Settle, boy." Ruben calmed him with a few words and a light touch. King Leo stroked York's silky head also.

"Let's go." Ruben waved the dog ahead of them. Tongue lolling, York gladly led the way.

King Leo chuckled. "Too bad that's a dog, not a wolf. If anyone ever sees us all together, there will be talk in the village about the giant shepherd who runs with a pack of wolves."

Ruben chuckled, knowing his father's words were true. "Are you ready?"

"I am," the king answered. Side by side, they strolled out of the castle, both in relatively good humor despite their weariness.

Walking down the path past the bench where Ruben had

rested with Willow, Ruben again wondered where she'd gone. To all outward appearances, she'd disappeared into the same forest they were going to in order to shape-shift into wolves. Maybe as wolf, he could find a clue.

He didn't want anything to interfere with this moment so he pushed the thought from his mind and bumped his father with his shoulder. His father bumped him back.

Both wearing identical faint smiles, they continued, companionably silent, along a well-trod path that wove through the dense woods in a seemingly random pattern. Centuries ago their ancestors had cleared this path and built the small stone temple at the end of it. All for the sole purpose of enabling the royal family to have a private—and beautiful—place to shape-shift from human form to wolf.

When they rounded the last turn and the ancient temple was no longer hidden, King Leo shook his head and let out a long breath. "I need this, my boy!"

Then, as Ruben was about to agree, the older man took off running. "Last one to change is a rotten rabbit!"

After a moment of shock—they both had been up all night, after all—Ruben leaped forward. Taking up the challenge, he tore after his father. They reached the old building roughly at the same time, though the king won by mere inches.

"Not bad for a man my age," he huffed.

Ruben had to agree.

Still chuckling and slightly out of breath, they stepped inside, shedding their clothes as they went.

King Leo was the first to change. Ruben had barely gotten undressed when the air around his father began to shimmer, heralding the beginnings of the change. With his own wolf raging to be free, Ruben dropped to the ground and counted to three. Then he let the change rip through him as his wolf rejoiced to be free.

A moment later, two wolves stood in the spot where before there'd been two men. King Leo was a huge graying beast, while Ruben's pelt was close to the same sable color of his human hair.

Muzzle to muzzle, they inhaled each other's scent. Then, with a glad bark, Ruben took off, aware of his father racing at his side.

Later, much later, with the hunt completed and their wolves sated happy, and pleasantly worn out, they headed back toward the changing temple, luxuriating in their heightened wolf senses. As a human, Ruben relied primarily on sight. As a wolf, he used his nose. He missed that super sense of smell when he existed as man. He felt its absence with a sort of sharp sorrow.

It was good to have this experience with his father. These days they didn't get to spend enough time together.

As they neared the path that would take them back to the old temple, Ruben felt a disturbance in the air. A shift, a slight breeze, a shiver up his spine. Nothing tangible, at least not by scent or by sight. A quick glance at his father revealed the older wolf felt it, too.

Instantly, they went low to the ground, seeking cover under vegetation. His sharp lupine hearing picked up a sound and he went still. Footsteps. Human. Uttering a low growl in the back of his throat, he glanced at his father. The other wolf dropped to his belly, well hidden. Ruben did the same.

He smelled her before he saw her. The scent, tantalizingly familiar. And the instant the woman's dark head came into view, he knew why.

*Willow.*

His father growled, making Ruben realize he'd moved forward. A foolish and futile move. She wouldn't know him now, not as wolf. And where had she come from? He'd swear she'd simply appeared from thin air. Whatever she was, she wasn't Pack, wasn't Shifter. But she wasn't human, either. Her scent was off.

She'd appeared in the middle of the royal ancestral woods. Nothing that way but forest and mountains. Where on earth had she come from? Maybe, he found himself thinking cynically, she hadn't come from anywhere on this earth.

The instant the thought occurred to him, he shook his head. Fanciful and ridiculous, even for a man who shape-shifted from human to wolf.

Then again, there *was* something different about her. Once more he wondered if she had somehow been involved in the explosion. But if so, why was she alone? She would have needed help to pull off a blast on the scale of the one that had taken down part of the castle.

Still hidden, the wolves let her pass. And remained hidden, as they were about to rise when their keen ears had picked up more footsteps. This time, Ruben did not recognize the scent. He only knew it, too, was not human.

And when the unfamiliar man wearing odd clothing appeared a few moments later, they let him pass, as well.

Though this time, Ruben wanted to trail him. A quick glance at his father showed he concurred. They set off together, easily able to stay out of sight.

Willow arrived at the castle right before the noon meal, which was perfect. If everyone was occupied with either preparing a meal or eating, that gave her a better chance of slipping in and out of the place unnoticed.

Though she'd been there when the bomb had gone off, how the destruction looked in broad daylight still shocked her. The section of the castle where, only hours before, there'd been music and dancing had been reduced to rubble. And, she saw as she drew closer, she realized the royal family of Teslinko had placed guards over the entire area.

Not good, especially since that's where she suspected she'd lost the earring.

So much for moving around unnoticed. Now what?

Though initially she'd planned to skirt around the damaged area and enter through the kitchen, trying to pass herself off as kitchen staff, there was no way to get near the castle without getting past the guards. And, since she didn't have a legitimate reason to enter, she knew she wouldn't get far.

She glanced down at her jeans and faded T-shirt; she didn't look like royalty. Even though, on the other side of the veil, she actually was.

Backtracking, she slid into the shadows before anyone noticed her. Heart pounding like a trapped bird, she weighed her options. There was one other place she could try. When she and Prince Ruben had stood on the balcony off the main ballroom, she'd noticed another couple balconies farther down the castle wall. Several of them were near large trees. It was a long shot, but at the moment, her only option.

Going around the perimeter didn't take as long as she'd expected. Still keeping to the cover of the forest, she passed up the first two balconies as too close to the wrecked part of the castle and far too visible. And, while the second and third had some tree cover, neither was close enough to any limbs.

Finally, on the fourth balcony, she thought she had a winner. Three large trees formed a triangle and two of them had branches that extended out nearly to the balcony's edge. Even better, one of the trees looked easily climbable.

Glad of her jeans, she went around to the opposite side of the large tree so she'd be hidden in case a guard happened to look this way. Shimmying up the trunk was more difficult than she'd expected, but she made good progress and reached the lower part of the balcony without any trouble.

Glancing one more time toward the guards, she realized she couldn't even see them. Perfect. She climbed up another foot or two, then took a deep breath, grasped the largest of the four branches and swung herself out over the balcony. And then she let go.

Landing was awkward and loud and only slightly painful. She stayed crouched on the floor while she assessed the damage to her body. Not bad. Only her ankle hurt and it wasn't that bad. She doubted it was even strained.

Waiting another moment to see if she'd been noticed, she pushed herself to her feet and went to try the door. To her surprise, it wasn't locked. All of her intuitive alarms began chiming. This was too easy.

She thought about abandoning her attempt and leaving it for another day. Then she pictured her mother's reaction if she noticed the missing earring and decided to go for it. In the end she didn't really have a choice.

So she pushed open the door and boldly stepped inside.

Like some sort of supernatural caravan, Ruben and his father followed the man who followed Willow. Of course the two high Royals of Teslinko remained in wolf form. They hadn't taken the time to change back to human. Yet.

From the shelter of a grove of aspens, the stranger stopped to watch as Willow shimmied up the tree. They all saw her drop onto a balcony, try the door and go inside.

Apparently satisfied, the other man turned and went back the way he'd come. Clearly unaware that he'd been followed, he made no attempt to hide his passing.

Ruben glanced at his father. Since as wolves they couldn't speak, he whined once, jerking his head in the direction of the stone temple.

King Leo shook his shaggy gray pelt and made for their castle instead. Ruben understood and followed. It would take too long for them to return to the stone temple in the woods and change back to human.

Their captain of the guards was Pack. He kept several changes of clothing stashed in the guard house just in case. They'd change there. That way, they could get inside and catch Willow before she had a chance to plant another bomb.

And, Ruben thought grimly as he loped alongside his father toward the guard house, he'd send some soldiers to find that man in the woods. Just in case.

Again, Ruben realized he'd underestimated his wolf. Once allowed to take form, the beast resisted the necessary change back to human. Heart pounding, Ruben battled his inner animal, praying his father was sufficiently distracted and didn't notice the savage fight.

Ruben won and forced the change back to human. Each time, it grew more and more difficult. He could easily foresee a day when the wolf would win and he'd remain in his lupine form forever. On that day, he knew he'd slide over the last slippery slope to madness.

What worried him was how badly he wanted to.

A few minutes later, human and fully clothed, King Leo and Ruben alerted the guards. Men were dispatched to the woods to search for the stranger, and the palace was quietly put on high alert. Willow would be caught and interrogated. Ruben hoped she wouldn't resist. Despite everything, he didn't want her hurt.

Yet.

Of course he'd already decided to question her himself. Though their association had been brief, he'd foolishly believed they'd connected on some visceral level. More proof that his mind was slowly unraveling, he supposed. Now, he wanted her to look him in the eye and explain.

Fuming, Tatiana put on her riding boots, trying to keep from scowling as she didn't want to cause wrinkles. First her sister—whom she'd planned to pair with Prince Eric—had managed to disappear unnoticed, but now Prince Chad had begged off, claiming he had a headache. As if. And when she'd questioned him, he'd had the audacity to say he felt it better if she and her fiancé spend time alone. He'd grinned mockingly as he'd spoken, taunting her.

This not only infuriated her, but aroused her, as well. Tatiana had never met a man who wouldn't let her have her way.

A challenge was exactly what she needed. But first... She stood, adjusting her ponytail. She had to deal with the buffoon she was supposed to marry.

Sparkles of Fairy dust. This was going to be a long afternoon.

Prince Eric waited, standing beside his mount. She noted he'd chosen the largest, flashiest horse in the royal stable, a cantankerous gelding appropriately nicknamed Trouble. She wondered if the stable hands had bothered to tell their visitor that he was indeed asking for...well, trouble. The only one Trouble would allow to remain on his back was King Puck. And that was only when the giant beast felt like it.

At the moment, he stood docilely, mouthing his bit while Prince Eric eyed her and preened. Since she knew he was waiting for her to compliment him and say how handsome he looked next to the magnificent steed, she kept her mouth shut and pretended not to notice. After all, he hadn't bothered to comment on her appearance—and she knew she looked absolutely, freakin' gorgeous—so why should she bother with his?

Her own horse, a beautiful gray mare her father had given her for her twenty-first birthday, had been saddled with her favorite saddle. Trying to appear lighthearted, she swung her leg up and over, settling on her horse with the abundant grace she'd been born with.

"Are you ready?" she chirped brightly. Just once she wished she didn't have to put on the act of beautiful, gracious princess. She'd have hoped, with the man she was supposed to marry, at least she'd get a chance to be herself.

Not that this oaf would notice. She suspected Prince Eric was such a narcissist that he only noticed others if they made him look bad. Which of course, she would never do.

Or would she? Even thinking such a thing made her shiver with delight. She was twenty-four years old. Maybe the time had come to make some changes in her life.

Tatiana had always been the good child, doing what was expected of her. When she'd been little, her mama, Queen Millicent, quite enjoyed treating her like a doll, dressing her up and changing her elaborate outfits sometimes as much as three times a day. She knew she was spoiled and if she often felt suffocated, well, it made her dear mama so happy. How could she even think of disappointing the one who'd given her life?

Despite the fact that Tatiana had grown increasingly bored and unhappy, she'd always taken care to please her parents. She'd found other avenues to vent her frustration and unfortunately her poor younger sister had taken the brunt of things.

But Willow never seemed to mind. At least on the surface. Tatiana suspected that she also kept her true feelings locked away inside.

They might be sisters, she reflected grimly, but neither truly knew the other. Maybe that too would have to change.

Prince Eric cleared his throat, bringing her attention back to him.

"Daydreaming?" he asked, his bored tone indicating he didn't really care what she answered.

So she didn't. Instead, she urged her horse forward, ignoring the man trying to mount the skittish gelding. As he swung his muscular leg over the animal's back and Trouble bucked, she held her breath, hoping she'd get to watch Eric get thrown.

To her surprise, he got the horse under control easily, with-

out too much fuss. Once Eric was certain Trouble would respond to the touch of his heels, he rode up alongside her. "This
is a fine animal," he told her, grinning triumphantly. "I'll
never understand why you'd geld a horse that looks like this."

Instead of answering, she considered him. He looked
human, for the first time since she'd met him. Albeit, a spectacularly beautiful human. Certainly, his smile transformed
his handsomeness into another realm entirely; the kind of
male beauty about which songs are written.

Though used to such beauty—she possessed numerous
mirrors—Tatiana couldn't help but stare.

Seeing this, he laughed out loud.

"What's so funny?" she asked him, cross.

"You don't really want to marry me, do you?" he asked.

Insight and beauty? Would wonders never cease? Now it
was her turn to laugh. "Is it that obvious?"

"Only when I look at you." His smile faded.

"Then don't," she popped off, making him laugh again.
Oddly enough, she actually liked him now, when he was making absolutely no effort to impress her.

"How about this?" he offered. "Why don't we quit wor-
rying about impressing each other and just hang out like
friends? We're pretty evenly matched, at least in the looks
department. Why don't we try and get along?"

She thought about that for a moment. "I'm not sure I know
how," she finally admitted, bracing herself for his derision
and scorn.

Instead, he merely cocked a brow at her. "It's an acquired
skill," he said, his tone dry. "I promise you, it took me a while
to learn it, as well."

Urging his horse sideways until their knees were nearly
touching, he held out his hand. "Friends?"

Though she wasn't sure this wasn't some sort of trick—

after all, in her experience men like him were always exactly like they seemed—she took his hand and shook it.

"Friends." Then, yanking her hand free, she urged her horse away and into a run. Trouble's ears went back and she suspected he'd buck at any moment. "Catch me if you can."

At first, the darkness of the room Willow had entered threw her off. Then, as her eyes gradually adjusted, she looked around her with great interest. The only part of this mammoth palace she'd seen had been the ballroom area downstairs.

She'd entered a bedroom. A masculine one, judging from the abundant leather and metal used to decorate the room. She took a step forward, the animal skin so plush and deep that she left footprints. Resting her hand on one of the leather chairs, she shuddered, unable to keep from wondering if the animal had suffered and hoping not.

A certain scent lingered in the air. She sniffed, a memory tickling at the edges of her mind. She knew this scent and if she had all the time in the world… It was tantalizingly familiar, though she couldn't quite place it. But she liked the smell. It made her smile.

Now to find her mother's precious pearl earring. Once she'd located that, she could beat a fast retreat, hopefully unnoticed. Especially by the handsome Prince Ruben. Moving confidently, she started toward the door.

A sound from the hallway made her freeze. Someone shouted. Another man answered. Footfalls, coming close. Heart pounding, she glanced around the room, searching for a place to hide. There. Quickly and quietly, she crossed the room to a set of double doors that could only be a closet.

More footsteps out in the hall. Several people, running. Guards, most likely. Someone must have seen her breaking in. Trying not to panic, she gave the closet door a tug. Nothing. Another tug, this time with more force. To her relief, the door opened. She stepped inside, closing the door behind her. It made a small sound as the handle clicked into place.

As she stood in the middle of someone's clothes, she tried to breathe quietly when her body wanted her to inhale in great gasps. She willed herself calm and began to take in the scent surrounding her. This was the same masculine cologne she'd noticed earlier. All at once, she realized whose closet this was. If she closed her eyes, she could see his face and once again smell this particular scent of candlewood and spice.

Prince Ruben. Bad enough she'd broken into his room. But now she was hiding in his closet. And he was the last person she wanted to see right now.

Liar. Even as she formed the thought, she knew it wasn't entirely true.

Listening hard, she heard nothing else from outside the hallway. Still, she waited, her heart beating slow and steady.

She would succeed. She would not be caught. If her mother learned she'd taken her jewelry without permission… Even thinking about the possibility made her shudder. Avoiding her mother's ire was worth any risk.

After a few seconds had passed without any more sounds, she cautiously opened the door a crack. And waited again.

Finally, satisfied that the danger of discovery had passed, she pushed the door open and stepped into the room.

The instant she did, the lights came on.

## Chapter 6

"Care to explain yourself?" Prince Ruben, muscular arms crossed, blocked the doorway into the hall. Another man, who looked so much like him that he had to be his father, the king, stood in front of the balcony, cutting off that way of escape.

Caught. Swallowing hard, she hoped her voice didn't betray her fear. "I came to get—"

He cut her off. "Who are you working with?" The ice in his voice felt like frost hitting her heart.

"I don't understand," she began. "I'm not working with anyone."

"You cannot expect me to believe you caused the explosion alone."

Stunned, she narrowed her eyes. "Explosion?" Fear forgotten, she drew herself up straight. Now her wintry tone matched his. "You honestly think I had something to do with that?"

"Are you saying you didn't?"

"Of course I am. I helped you with the wounded, remember? How could you possibly think that I could..."

Words failed her. To her shock, she found herself blinking back tears, one of her flaws that she hated with a passion. She always cried when she was angry. Indignity warred with exhaustion as she pushed herself away from him. "That's it. I'm out of here."

"Sit down," he ordered. "You're not going anywhere."

She nearly laughed in his face. Instead, hands clenched into fists, she raised her head and looked him in the eye. "I'd rather not sit, if you don't mind."

Almost nose to nose, his gaze shot daggers back at her. The older man still hadn't spoken. Willow glanced at him, surprised to see his mouth twitch in the beginnings of a smile. This was amusing him? Really?

"Look." Moving back half a step, she took a deep breath, including them both in her apology. "I'm sorry I broke into your palace, but I swear I had absolutely nothing to do with the bomb. I came here looking for my earring."

Something flickered in his gaze. "Your earring," he repeated back.

Noting his complete lack of surprise, she took heart and continued. "Yes. It's made from pearls. I was wearing it at the ball last night. Maybe you saw it? Dangly and very old. It's a family heirloom and therefore quite valuable. You've found it, haven't you?"

Instead of answering, he uncrossed his arms. She couldn't help but notice how the fabric on his shirt pulled against his muscles as he moved. She also noticed the way he had his hands clenched into fists. Just like her. Taking another deep breath, she forced herself to relax and try again. "That earring doesn't even belong to me. It's my mother's. I have to return it to her."

"I'm sure she'll understand," he drawled. "Especially when

she finds out her daughter is being held until we have some answers."

"Held?" Her stomach churned. This wasn't good. They had visitors back at home. Now was the worst possible time for her to disappear. "You can't keep me here. I've done nothing wrong."

"Prove it." His amber eyes dared her. "I'm perfectly willing to hear a plausible explanation. That is, if you have one."

"I've told you the truth."

"No, I suspect you haven't. Why would you break in and try to search my home for your missing jewelry? Why not simply ask to see me and request my help?"

Put that way, he made her sound like an incompetent bungler and a thief. But that still didn't make her a mad bomber.

The man over by the window cleared his throat, drawing her gaze. "Who are you, my dear?" he asked, his voice as warm as Prince Ruben's was not.

For one startled instant, she almost gave her true name and title. As in *Princess Willow of the SouthWard Brights*. But her people didn't exist in this world. "My name is Willow," she said instead.

Prince Ruben snorted. "Is it really?" he asked rudely. "Or did you make that up, too?"

Shades help her, she saw red. "Too? I'm telling you the truth. Look, I know I made a mistake. I shouldn't have broken in here. But—"

"Then why did you?" Again he interrupted her, his voice low and furious. "It couldn't have been because you didn't want to see me again, now could it?"

At that, King Leo chuckled. "Enough. Both of you. Ruben, bring your lady friend and let's go downstairs to my office. We have much to talk about."

Though his rigid jaw belied his anger, Ruben nodded.

"After you," he told Willow. "And don't try to make a run for it. You still have a lot of explaining to do."

She shook her head, docilely following the king. At least he didn't appear to think she was capable of bombing their palace. Truth be told, she didn't understand why Prince Ruben did. Had her disappearing the night of the ball angered him that much?

If so, then he was more like her sister and mother than she'd care to admit. And since she normally avoided toxic people as much as possible, she'd been right to take off without a word of goodbye. Though she still felt marginally guilty, for some reason.

"I've already explained," she grumbled as they marched single file down the long hallway to the circular marble stairs. She wondered what they'd do if she took off running—she was pretty sure she could outrun the older man.

But probably not Ruben. And if she tried such a foolish stunt, she would be in an even worse place than she'd been from the beginning. Without the earring *and* with Prince Ruben considering her his enemy. Which apparently he already did.

Oddly enough, that rankled nearly as much as the knowledge of the punishment her mother would dole out if Willow didn't return the jewelry.

She actually *liked* Prince Ruben. Or she had, until today when he'd shown his true colors. He'd given her the most magical night of her life, at least until the bomb had gone off. She just couldn't understand how he could even consider her as a suspect. How could he possibly think she could have been behind such as thing?

Finally they reached the bottom of the staircase. King Leo went right, heading down yet another long hallway. Willow glanced longingly left, toward the set of double doors that no doubt led to the outside and freedom.

The exact moment she did, Prince Ruben came up along-side her and took her arm. "This way," he murmured, steering her firmly after his father.

Shadefire be damned if she didn't feel a shiver of longing at his casual touch. How much more of a fool could she be?

Finally, after a few twists and turns, they reached a set of double mahogany doors. These were open, revealing a lux-urious office that was…well, fit for a king. King Leo took a seat behind a massive L-shaped desk, made of dark wood that was so highly polished, she could see her own reflection. The king picked up his phone and spoke a few words quietly.

Ruben closed the door behind him. The steely glare he gave her dared her to try to leave.

She took one of the armchairs in front of the desk, expecting the prince to do the same. Instead, he perched on the side, angling both the chair and his body in such a way that would block her if she tried to make a run for the door.

As if she would. The fear no longer governed her. Instead, the slow burn of anger that had begun low in her belly, fueled her, making her feel flushed. To accuse her of this? Her! Though this human prince had no idea who she truly was, that shouldn't matter. She'd actually thought they'd connected last night.

Finally, the king placed the phone in the receiver and looked expectantly at her. "Go ahead," he said, his eyes sparkling with warm humor. "Obviously you have something you want to say."

"Look, I understand that you don't know me," she began, including both father and son in one sweeping gesture. "But I can assure you I had nothing to do with that bombing."

King Leo nodded, encouraging her to continue.

"I have no reason," she said, spreading her hands. "I wanted to attend your ball, so I did. I came simply to have a good time. Nothing more."

"Do you have any friends?" The prince's eyes sharpened. "Is there someone who can actually vouch for your character?"

Shades of moon. Vouch for her character?

"No," she said, struggling to hide her annoyance. "I have met a few people, but made no actual friends. I have no one who can vouch for me."

"That won't be necessary," King Leo interjected, cutting off his son before he got a chance to speak. "We already know you had nothing to do with the bombing."

"We do?" Standing, Prince Ruben sounded as shocked as she felt. Once again, he crossed his arms. "Please, enlighten me."

King Leo picked up a sheaf of paper from his desk. He slid it over toward the prince. "My advisors phoned a moment ago. We've received a video from the extremists. In it, they claim responsibility for the bomb."

A muscle worked in Ruben's firm jaw as he read the paper. "How do we know she is not a member of that group?"

Willow couldn't help it—she snorted out loud at that. Most assuredly not ladylike, but this prince wasn't acting even remotely like a gentleman, either.

"I promise you, I'm not," she said, mentally daring him to contradict her.

As he glared back, she swore she saw a flicker of desire in his dark gaze. Mingled with his anger, so potent she almost responded in kind.

Of course, she wasn't a fool. And, she had to admit to herself, there was a strong possibility she'd simply imagined it.

Trying to stare her down, Ruben barely restrained himself from baring his teeth and growling. Something about her made his inner wolf wild. Just like it had the first moment he'd seen her, his beast fought to break free. Until recently,

Ruben would have sworn he was gaining ground on his inner battles. Not so much as of late. He used every ounce of self-control he had to keep the animal contained.

His wolf liked her scent. His beast wanted her, with a savage, single-minded intent.

Worse, his father knew. His father's wolf couldn't help but pick up on the restless frustration emanating from within Ruben.

Watching her with narrowed eyes, Ruben tried to figure out how such a small slip of a girl could have so much power over the other part him. At least his human side had emotions carefully under control.

"Where did you come from?" he asked abruptly.

Instead of answering, she simply gazed at him, her beautiful caramel-colored eyes huge and full of tantalizing secrets.

"Go ahead and answer, dear," the king urged. "He won't rest until he knows. For that matter, I'm a bit curious myself. I have my suspicions you see, and I just need you to confirm them."

Ruben could see her struggling to find the right words.

"Don't lie," he warned.

Anger flashed in her gaze. "I wasn't about to." Giving him one final contemptuous once-over, she turned and looked at his father. "I came from the forest. There's a…passageway there. It links my home and yours."

Her answer visibly startled the older man. "Are you one of the Shadows?"

She tilted her head. "No. Despite my appearance, I'm Bright. How do you know of us?"

"Because I've used that portal, when I was a young lad. I've met your king and queen once. Of course, that was a very long time ago."

Now her brave facade faltered. "Millicent is my mother."

"But your eyes…"

"Are the wrong color, I know." She sighed. "It's rumored my real father was a Shadow."

King Leo nodded, his expression contemplative. "This puts a completely different spin on things, Princess."

*Princess?* The entire exchange made absolutely no sense. Ruben nearly interrupted, but he wanted to see where his father was going with this nonsense. Willow was no princess. He would have heard about her long before now. Royalty and beauty were always talked about.

"And you attended the ball the other night?" the king asked.

"Yes." She shot Ruben a sideways glance, spearing him with heat. "For me, it was last night, but time passes different in our worlds. I danced with your son."

King Leo smiled. "I trust you enjoyed yourself?"

"Very much so." Though her voice vibrated with sincerity, she wouldn't look away from the king. Ruben inwardly demanded she meet his gaze, to no avail. "At least until the explosion. After the bomb went off, I assisted Ruben here in helping the wounded."

He nodded. "Very commendable, wouldn't you say, son?"

Ruben jerked his head in a curt nod.

"I only came back to find my earring," Willow continued softly, the rich texture of her voice washing over him and sending another sharp pang of desire straight into his core. "I wore a set of matching pearl earrings and went home missing one."

"Are they very valuable?" King Leo asked.

"Only to me. And my mother." She swallowed, drawing Ruben's attention to her slender throat. "Since the pearls belong to my mother, as I've said, I've got to get it back. She has a temper and she'll be very upset if I don't recover the missing piece. She, ah, doesn't know I borrowed them."

No surprise there. Of course she'd taken them without

permission. Just like she'd broken into the castle. Evidently Willow wasn't a fan of playing by the rules.

"Ruben, have you located her earring?" his father asked him sternly.

For the briefest moment, Ruben considered saying no. But because he didn't want to add lies to her deception, he nodded. "I found it last night. I have it upstairs in my room."

"Send someone to fetch it for the princess," King Leo ordered.

"The princess?" Fed up, Ruben looked from one to the other. "Are you saying you believe this nonsense? She's as much a princess as I'm a—"

"Enough," King Leo commanded. His implacable expression showed he meant it. "I'll explain later. Ring for one of the chambermaids to bring her earring to us."

Jaw aching from clenching it so tightly, Ruben reached for the desk phone and did as he'd been told.

When he finished, he hung up and forced himself to look at Willow, steeling himself against the unwanted sensuality of her dusky beauty. "Soon you'll have your precious bauble," he said, his tone like frost.

She stood resolute, completely not intimidated. His wolf approved of her courage, which unsettled him even more.

"I really appreciate that," she said without expression, refusing to take her eyes from his. As they locked gazes, his wolf thrilled at the challenge, daring her to back down. When she dropped her eyes first, he felt a sudden jolt of victory, of conquest, which he quickly doused.

"Once you have it back in your possession," the king put in, "I'll send an armed escort to accompany you into the woods. You will be free to go."

Now Ruben shot his father a sharp glance. "Just like that?"

"Just like that. As I've said, I'll explain later."

"What of the man who was following her?" Ruben crossed his arms. "Her accomplice. He came through this portal also."

This appeared to surprise her. "What man? I came here alone."

"You had a tail," the king said, his voice gentle. "He was tall, with bright gold hair and those strange purple eyes of your kind. He carried himself as if he were nobility."

She frowned. "Are you certain you weren't mistaken?"

King Leo shook his head.

"Who was he?" Ruben asked. "And why was he taking care not to let you see him?"

"Judging from your description, I'd say that was one of my people." Her firm tone indicated she wasn't willing to discuss this any further. "I'll see what I can find out when I return home."

Ruben opened his mouth to question her, but the king shook his head in warning. Apparently this was enough of an answer to satisfy him.

King Leo gave Willow a warm smile. "When you get back home, say hello to your parents for me, will you?"

She smiled back, the same warm expression with which she'd favored Ruben the night before. This inexplicably made his wolf dig in his claws. While they waited for the maid to return, Willow and King Leo engaged in small talk, completely ignoring Ruben, which was fine with him.

For his part, he found being in the room with her a peculiar sort of torture. Watching her, he had to fight the urge to touch her, to stroke her creamy skin and pull her close enough to capture her scent.

He glanced at his watch and gritted his teeth. What was taking the maid so long? She could have been to his room and back twice now.

Patience, he told himself. Just because time seemed to be moving at an excruciatingly slow place for him, didn't mean it actually was. His father and Willow certainly didn't seem to notice.

The instant the thought crossed his mind, King Leo looked up and frowned. "Shouldn't she be here by now?"

"I'll go and look for her," Ruben said. As he opened the door to do exactly that, someone screamed.

Chad hadn't meant to kill the maid, though he bowed to the capricious whims of fate. Following Willow and watching while she entered the castle by stealth, he initially had decided to hang around outside. But as he'd settled in to wait, two of the guards had stepped away to have a smoke, leaving a side door unprotected and ajar. It was a simple matter for Chad to slip inside. If they'd been his guards, he would have not only fired them, but imprisoned them for their careless foolishness.

Once in, he found the castle lay out was remarkably similar to his own family palace in EastWard. Since Willow had entered upstairs on the back side, he figured she'd probably come in to someone's bedroom. Now he simply had to learn if she'd traveled here for a dalliance of some sort or had another, more nefarious purpose.

A thrill shot through him at the thought. Who could have guessed that the dark little princess could be so fascinating? He'd never considered the possibility that she was more like him than anyone suspected.

Heart beating loudly in his chest, he made it up the marble staircase undetected, shoulders back, head up. He'd learned long ago in situations like this that the secret lay in walking with purpose, as though he belonged there. This proved true now, as well. He passed two maids and a butler without breaking stride, and none of them thought to even question his presence. No doubt they believed him one of the noble guests. Nobility was its own disguise, often as good as a mask.

As he turned a corner, he heard voices heading toward him. Normally, this wouldn't have been cause for concern, but he recognized one of them as belonging to Willow.

Bloody shades!

Glancing around quickly, he grasped the closest door and pushed it open, stepping inside.

Just in time. As he pulled the door closed, leaving a small crack so he could look out, they rounded the corner. First, an older man who walked with regal self-confidence as befitting a nobleman. Next came Willow, her pretty face looking disgruntled and even a bit panicked. Last, a younger man who bore enough resemblance to the first that he had to be his son.

The king and prince of this palace? How had the princess gotten mixed up with them?

This situation grew more and more intriguing.

He watched through the crack in the door as they marched off down the hallway, heading toward the stairs. Though Chad knew following them would be risky, he couldn't resist. Heart pounding, he waited a moment after they'd disappeared from sight, then strode off after them. This time he saw no one, so he wasn't stopped or questioned.

When the two men and Willow went inside what appeared to be a huge office at the end of the hall, Chad stopped in a small and empty waiting room, glad the attendant or secretary, if any, was not at his or her desk. This entire thing had been ridiculously easy. Almost too much so. Now, he simply listened to hear what Willow and her companions had to say. Because they left the door open, their words carried easily.

At first, Chad was entertained to learn the humans—at least that's what they had to be, though they gave off an aura of otherness—thought Princess Willow might be behind a bombing that had apparently happened the night before. His amusement grew as he realized Willow had taken all these risks to locate her mother's missing earring.

Which meant the bauble must be powerful indeed.

Now most definitely, he thought, inching closer to the wall nearest the hall, he had to get this earring before she got a chance to return it to her mother.

Listening as the man—or prince—named Ruben dispatched a servant to his bedroom to fetch the jewelry; Chad realized what he had to do. He hurried off, taking the marble stairs two at a time as he headed toward the bedroom area. He arrived just in time to see a maid going into one of the rooms, and leaving the door ajar behind her.

Perfect. Without a second thought, he hurried in after her.

She'd just retrieved the earring from a dish on top of the massive oak dresser when she noticed him. At first, she showed no fear—nothing but mild annoyance flashed across her plain face.

"I'm afraid you have the wrong room, sir." Her low voice, properly deferential, had a pleasing accent from a place he didn't recognize.

"No, I don't." He held out his hand. "Give me that." The earring positively glowed with power, though this human couldn't see it.

As he'd expected, she shook her head. "I'm afraid I can't. Prince Ruben has asked me to bring this to him. Now, if you'll excuse me…"

Did she really think he'd step aside and let her travel merrily on her way? This time, he wouldn't ask, he'd simply take.

He grabbed her arm. "Let me have it."

Rather than do as she was told, to his disbelief she fought him. "No."

Furious and savagely aroused, adrenaline pumping, he backhanded her, using his magic to silence her pitiful attempt to scream. When she pushed herself up, he hit her again. She stumbled backward and fell, losing her grip on the earring. It went tumbling to the thick carpet near his feet.

As he bent to grab it, amazingly, she managed to right herself and went for it, forcing him to backhand her a third time. This time, he put a bit more force into the blow. She went down for the count, her head making a sickening thump as her temple caught the side of the massive dresser.

She didn't move again.

A woman appeared in the doorway and, seeing the maid and her blood, began screaming. Her eyes met his as he retrieved the earring and dropped it into his pocket. The hum of its magical power felt reassuring, somehow.

Then he turned and went out through the balcony, using the same method Willow had used earlier to enter.

He didn't know if the maid was dead, nor did he care. Even though the older woman had seen his face, since Willow herself didn't even know he'd followed her, he wasn't of this realm. Once he slipped through the veil back into the land of the Bright, he'd be home free.

Making it to the forest unnoticed, he headed for the portal, intent on getting back to his own world long before Willow. Then he could examine the bauble at his leisure and learn what magical properties it contained.

## Chapter 7

The bloodcurdling scream reverberated through the castle, repeated again and again, reaching a horrifying crescendo that finally culminated in silence. Utter and terrifying silence.

King Leo was up and running before the first scream had finished. "That sounds like your mother," he shouted over his shoulder at Ruben, his expression revealing his terror. "Come on."

Needing no second urging, Ruben took off after him, his pulse pounding. To his shock, Willow followed, completely ignoring her one chance to escape.

"To your queen," King Leo shouted. "Aid your queen."

Numerous guards poured out of the side hallways, ready to join them, expressions grim, weapons drawn and ready. Rushing up the stairs two at a time, the small army barreled down the hallway toward the bedroom wing. Running, King Leo led the way. Ruben and Willow were close on his heels.

At the long, empty expanse of hall, they all stopped.

"There." Ruben pointed toward his own room. It was the only one with the door ajar.

"Step back," Drake, Captain of the Royal Guard ordered, stepping in front of the king and neatly shouldering him aside. A small force of his elite guards surrounded him, bodyguard style.

King Leo pushed past them, swearing loudly. "I don't need protection. This is my wife. Your queen!"

Ruben went with him. Barely inside the doorway, Queen Ionna lay in a crumpled heap. A few feet past her, also not moving, was one of the chambermaids, with blood seeping out from under her head, staining the carpet.

With a loud cry, the king dropped to the floor beside his wife. "Ionna," he cried, feeling at the base of her long throat for a pulse. At least there was no blood.

Chest tight, heart aching, Ruben crouched down as his father frantically tried to revive his mother.

"I don't know what's wrong with her," King Leo cried. "She has no wounds that I can see."

Ruben leaned forward, wanting to help. As far as he could tell, his mother was still alive. Her chest rose and fell with shallow breaths. Dropping to her knees beside him, Willow elbowed him aside.

"Let me," she said, her voice calm and certain. "I think I can help."

"Are you a healer?" Raw hope filled the king's voice.

After the briefest hesitation, Willow shook her head. "Only with animals, but I think I can help." She placed her hands on the queen's forehead and took a deep breath. "She has only fainted. Give her a moment to come around."

King Leo gave his wife a tiny shake. "Ionna," he said again.

To everyone's immense relief, this time the queen stirred at the sound of her name. A second later, she opened her eyes.

"What happened?" she mumbled, struggling to sit up. Then she caught a glimpse of the maid. Grimacing, her eyes widened. "Oh. Shadefire."

She looked at Ruben and swallowed hard. "I was walking by and noticed your door was open. As I approached and saw the maid, I also saw a man standing over her."

"Can you describe him?" Ruben asked, pushing away the hard knot of anger that had his inner wolf baring his teeth and snarling.

"Yes." Swallowing hard, she said, "Tall, blond, handsome. He had the strangest color eyes. They were purple. He looked right at me and then took something off your dresser before he ran away, out the window." She winced, looking queasy but resolute as she turned her gaze to Willow, indicating the maid. "Please, even if you are not truly a healer, help her if you can."

With a small nod, Willow rose and went to the other woman, kneeling down and feeling for a pulse. After a moment she bowed her head, her mouth moving silently.

When she finally looked up, her eyes were full of pain and regret. "I'm sorry. She's gone."

"How did she die?" the queen asked softly.

"Someone hit her." Pointing at the woman's face, she sighed. "Numerous times. It appears she hit her head there." She indicated the corner of the dresser. "See the blood? That final blow is what killed her."

King Leo cursed, a particularly virulent word that he normally wouldn't have used in mixed company. "First a bomb, now a murder."

"This had to have been the man we saw following Willow," Ruben said. "No one else has eyes that color."

He looked at Willow. "So I'll ask you again. Are you with the extremists?"

She lifted her chin. "And I'll tell you again. I am not. I

didn't know I was being followed, but all of my people have violet or purple eyes."

"Except you," Ruben said, not entirely certain he believed her.

"Except me," Willow agreed. "And that's a story for another day."

"So it wasn't the extremists," King Leo said, giving Ruben a sharp look that meant he wasn't to protest. "Which makes sense, as they've never done things on an individual scale before. They go for as much damage as they can get with a single blow. Which means this killing…"

"Doesn't make sense," Queen Ionna finished, her expression worried.

"I agree." The king began to pace. "And the more havoc they wreak, the less close we are to understanding the reason why."

Ruben realized what the open box on his dresser meant and Ruben frowned, barely keeping his fury leashed. Inside, his wolf fought to come to the surface, all teeth and claws and rage. Darkness warring with light—shredding the edges of his sanity.

As though she somehow sensed this, Willow held out her hand and let him help her to her feet. The instant his fingers wrapped around hers, he felt a calming sense, like she'd poured a healing balm over an open and festering wound.

"Whoever killed her took your mother's earring," he told her, unclenching his teeth in an effort to speak normally. "Apparently, they believed it to be valuable enough to kill for. I'm very sorry."

"I am too," she said, her caramel-colored eyes shiny with unshed tears. "While that piece of jewelry definitely is priceless, it's certainly not worth a life."

As she moved slightly closer, her scent reached him, lilac and vanilla and some other muskier spice. The heady combination made him want to pull her even closer, to burrow his face in her hair and inhale her. He found himself wondering if she would taste as good as she smelled.

This time, his wolf shook himself, as though shaking off water. This action brought Ruben out of the foolish—and dangerous—line of thought.

"Murder and theft? Who could have done such things?" Queen Ionna asked, her husky tone vibrating with a combination of shock and anger.

Rushing to his wife's side, King Leo met Ruben's gaze before facing his captain of the guard. "Drake, I want you to find out how the killer escaped."

"If he did," Ruben put in. "For all we know, he might still be in the castle."

Though he didn't say the rest of it, he could see from Willow's expression that she was thinking it, too. The killer might have been the same man who'd been following her. And he might have planted the bomb at the dance the night before.

If so, had the royal family of Teslinko actually been the target? Or had the intruder been after Willow all along?

Though Willow had no idea who had tracked her across her home forest and through the veil, from the description Prince Ruben and his father gave, she knew the man who'd been following her had to be one of the Bright. The humans had another name for her people, the Sidhe. This name comprised both people of the Bright and of the Shadows, though in human lore they were the Seelie and the Unseelie, or the bright and the dark.

From the stories she'd grown up with, she wouldn't put it past one of the Shadows to have followed her here and killed a human maid to gain a little bit of Bright magic. However both Ruben and his father had said the man was fair-haired with a pale complexion.

Which meant her tracker had to be Bright. Unless…she frowned, wondering why she hadn't thought of this before, unless there was a man among the Shadows who was exactly like her—the opposite of his own people.

Though the idea seemed intriguing, she immediately discounted it. She had no doubt she would have heard about such a man. Despite their animosity, she figured gossip traveled quite easily among the two Sidhe courts. Just as everyone among the Shadows was most likely well aware of her existence, if such an aberration existed among their people, she and all the Brights would know. Unless savages were better at keeping secrets, which she doubted.

Therefore, the man had to be a Bright. But her people did not kill. Such evil violence was strictly for those among the Shadows, or so she'd been raised to believe. For most of her life, she'd sensed undercurrents below the perfect, Bright surface. Was such darkness one of them?

Her thoughts must have shown on her face. When she blinked and looked up, she caught Prince Ruben studying her, his amber eyes intense.

"May I have a word with you in private?" he asked, taking her elbow in a firm grip so she'd know declining was not an option.

Even now his touch made her want to lean into him and rub against him like an affection-starved cat. Strange and oh-so-foolish.

To distract herself, she glanced at the king, still with his arm around his visibly shaken wife. Neither even looked at her, though the tense set of the king's broad shoulders revealed his anger. The queen would be all right, despite her earlier faint, and there was nothing Willow could do for the poor maid.

Taking a deep breath, she looked back at Ruben and nodded. She wished she had enough willpower to pull away from his touch. Either that, or lean into it.

Foolish, foolish, Willow, she chided herself.

They stepped into the hallway, still teeming with guards and other curious guests and servants. Ruben took no notice of them, steering her down the hall, into a quiet and relatively private corner.

As he stood gazing down at her, her heart rate sped up, so fast she wondered if he could see her pulse jumping at the base of her throat.

"I owe you an apology," he said, his expression inscrutable. "When I saw you breaking in to my bedroom, I—"

"I didn't know it was your bedroom," she felt compelled to point out, hating the breathlessness that crept into her voice no matter how hard she tried to keep it out. "But I owe you an apology, as well. I should never have tried to get my earring back the way I did. I should have just asked you about it."

At her words, his gaze darkened. "Why didn't you?"

She told herself she imagined the dangerous note in his voice. "Good question."

Lifting one shoulder in a shrug, she tried to sound casual. There was no way in shadows that she could tell him the truth.

She hadn't wanted to see him again. She'd been completely and utterly flabbergasted at the way he made her feel. Still was, in fact.

Instead, she thought it would be better to stick to business. "However, I can promise you if I'd had enough time to locate my earring, I would have been gone without troubling anyone. Most certainly your maid wouldn't have been killed." Her voice wobbled on the last.

"It's not your fault," he murmured, and then he did the one thing she both craved and wished to avoid. He pulled her close, tucking her into his hard and muscular side.

A jolt of desire shot through her. Shades, she wanted more.

Much, much more. Her body—and no doubt her face—burned
at the idea.

Luckily, he appeared too engrossed in his train of thought
to notice. "I'm going to hunt down this man and make him
pay for what he's done."

She was used to seeing the supernatural, and something
around him caught her eye. What the…? Eyeing him, she told
herself she must have imagined the wild beast shimmering
around his body. A wolf. An aura of a wolf. How was such
a thing even possible? She blinked and it was gone. Or had
it ever been? No. She couldn't have actually seen anything.
She must have been thinking of the creatures she knew in
the forest.

Forcing herself back on track, she took a deep breath. "I'll
help you all I can." Even as she spoke the vow, she knew she
would do whatever it took. Because if he was from her people, then she suspected the killer was no longer in this realm.

Had someone else found the veil?

She moved carefully, tried to put a decent amount of space
between them. Even as she did, he pulled her back, keeping
her close.

Why? Because he liked the feel of her as much as she liked
the feel of him? Or because he wanted to keep her from being
able to run away?

Though the first explanation was more appealing, she settled on the second, choosing logic over a flight of fancy.

His next words bore her out. "Since my father appears to
be well acquainted with your parents," he said, a thread of
steel creeping back into his deep, sexy voice, "perhaps I need
to meet them, as well."

For half a second, her heart stopped. Even as it resumed
beating, she shook her head. "That's not possible," she began.

"I want you to take me with you to your home," he continued, as though she hadn't even spoken.

The very idea was not only impossible, but ludicrous. "I can't do that," she said flatly. "Sorry. You had a bomb go off here recently. Isn't that enough to keep you occupied?"

"We know who set off the bomb. A group of extremists. My father has been searching for them for some time. He doesn't need me for that. Now a woman in my employ was brutally murdered and your mother's earring was stolen by someone who can only be one of your people." He tightened his grip on her arm, his hard body now appearing menacing, though still far too sexy. "You can, and you will."

Enough was enough. This time, Willow pulled away, shaking off his touch as though she found it not only distasteful, but repellent. And this time, he let her go.

Which, oddly enough, rankled. Calling herself all kinds of fool, she squared her shoulders and met his gaze, taking care not to let any hint of her thoughts show on her face. She'd watch for the first opportunity and then she'd simply disappear. Prince Ruben might search for her, but he'd never find her once she set foot across the veil.

Despite her best efforts, something of her thoughts must have come through her expression. Watching her, his dark eyes narrowed. "Guards," he called. "Come here, please."

She stiffened, wondering what he meant to do to her now. He wouldn't dare have her thrown into a dungeon, would he? Not with the king and queen in the area, she reassured herself. After all, even if Ruben didn't, King Leo knew who she was.

Down the hall, the king and queen and their retinue of guards exited Ruben's bedroom, moving toward them. The noise level must have drowned out Ruben's summons, because no one paid them any heed.

"Guard," Ruben called again, clearly annoyed at the delay. "Here. Now."

Immediately, one of the uniformed guards stepped closer. Ruben reached out and snagged a pair of metal handcuffs off the other man's belt. Then, as she gaped at him in disbelief, he snapped one around her wrist, the other around his.

"You can and you will," he repeated. "We cannot be separated now. Take me or you're not going home at all."

Dumbfounded, Willow looked toward his father for help, knowing he'd understand the dilemma. But King Leo was occupied with his semiconscious wife and the investigation going on with the murder scene. Still, she knew he would definitely not appreciate her taking his first born son across the veil into the land of the Sidhe. Who knew how much time might pass until his return?

"Your Highness," she called, pitching her voice to carry over the background noise. "Please. I need a moment of your time."

King Leo held up one finger, indicating he would be with her in a moment.

"Don't try and play on my father's sympathy." Expression like stone, Ruben tugged her toward the door. "Let's go," he ordered.

"Wait." She dug in her heels and again cast an entreating look toward Ruben's parents. "This is not a good idea at all. He can explain that to you."

"Why don't you explain and save us all time?" His voice silky smooth, he gave her a look that plainly said he was calling her bluff.

Once more she tried to make eye contact with the king. Instead of moving toward her, he'd actually moved farther back toward the room, conferring with several of his guards.

"Fine," she sighed, seeing no other way for it. "You can't come home with me. I come from another land, completely outside your realm."

"So?" Arms crossed, impatience made him seem both arrogant and wild, which called to her as all wild things did.

She took a deep breath and resisted. "Where I come from is a magical place."

"Which is why you claim time passes differently there than it does here?"

Pleased that he appeared to understand, she nodded. "Exactly. If I were to take you with me, even if it seemed like you were only gone days, you might return back to find a month or two had passed."

For a moment he only eyed her, as though trying to gage her sincerity. When her expression remained serious, he slowly shook his head. "Magic?"

She nodded.

"Another realm?"

Again, she shook her head yes.

"Are you telling me you're what—an…Elf?" Eyebrow raised, he looked as if he couldn't decide whether or not to laugh or grimace.

She couldn't help but smile at that. "Not exactly."

"Then what? A Fairy?" He said the word with such distaste that her smile widened.

"Neither. I'm a Sidhe. I come from the Court of the Bright."

"Right," he drawled. "And since we're telling truths, you might as well know about me. I'm a shape-shifting werewolf."

"I'm serious."

"So am I."

And stalemate. She didn't know how else she could get him to believe her. Maybe if he heard the truth from his father, he'd understand.

But no, once again Ruben began moving toward the stairs, tugging her along with him. As she had before, she dug in her heels, grabbing hold of a passing door frame to slow their progress.

To his credit, though Ruben could have moved her by

force, he did not. Why, she didn't know. Perhaps he didn't want to make a scene.

"Your sire knows the truth." This time, she allowed a thread of desperation in her voice. "Ask him. I guarantee he will not be happy if I take you to my land."

"Still sticking with your bizarre story?" He shook his head. "You should have tried something a bit more believable."

"It's the truth."

"Right." He gave her another tug. "Come on, let's go."

This time, he succeeded in yanking her a few feet down the hall. Since she had only one free hand to try and hold on, she knew if he gave her other arm one final, sharp tug, she'd be around the corner and away from the only other person who had a hope of making him understand.

To her relief, the king decided finally to come over.

"What's going on here?" he asked, clearly irritated at being interrupted.

Wordlessly, Willow raised her handcuffed arm, certain he'd order his son to set her free. To her chagrin, after a quick look, King Leo gave a booming laugh.

"What are you doing?" he asked Ruben.

"I've ordered her to take me to her home. If the killer has fled to her country as I believe he has, I can track him there and bring him back to face justice."

"Very good. But why the restraints?"

"She refused, so I did this to ensure that she would."

At this, the king's smile faded. "I see. She does have valid reasons for her refusal, you know."

"She says that time passes differently there, and more nonsense about being Sidhe—part of the Court of the Bright. She even mentioned magic."

King Leo scratched the back of his head. "Son, she told you the truth. It's not nonsense."

Ruben grimaced, clearly not wanting to argue with his

father. "She seemed to think you would mind if I went. But this killer must be caught."

"I agree. If the man we saw following her in the woods is the one who did this, then by all means travel to her land and find him."

Willow's heart sank. Not for one minute did she believe any of her people had traveled through the veil and murdered a human servant. Her people did not kill. At least, not like this. They used magic and spell and power, not physical brutality.

There had to be another explanation.

On top of that, whoever had done this had stolen her mother's magical earring, as well. She had to wonder if the thief even knew what he had. No one but Queen Millicent could use the magic contained in the jewelry. So it was worthless to anyone but her.

Willow wished she'd never borrowed the dratted things.

And now, when things couldn't get any worse, they were forcing her to bring a human into her realm?

Ruben dipped his head in gratitude. "Thank you, Father." He turned to her, his expression hardening once again. "I told you he'd feel the same way I do. Come on. We've delayed too long as it is. Let's go."

She waited until they'd traveled the rest of the long hallway. At the top of the stairs, she turned to him. "Are you sure you want to do this?" she asked softly. "Because you must cross the veil of your own free will."

His response was short and curt. "I don't have a choice now, do I?"

"You always have a choice."

When he didn't respond, she sighed and pressed him, well aware of the necessity, even if he wasn't. "One again, I'll ask you. Do you travel across the veil of your own free will?"

"I do," he answered grimly, not looking at her. She sensed

he had something to prove, something greater than finding a killer, though she couldn't imagine what that might be.

They didn't speak again until they were out in the forest.

Walking along the familiar path, tethered to a man whom the night before she'd found unbelievably attractive, Willow tried to imagine her family's reaction when she showed up with a human prince, even if his father had met her parents.

None of the scenarios she could picture were even remotely pleasant.

"I should warn you," she told him, hating the way the metal handcuff dug into her soft skin. "If these restraints are made of steel, they will not pass through the veil."

Despite his father's assurances that she spoke the truth, his skeptical expression told her Prince Ruben was not yet a believer.

"All right. If that happens, then you'll be free of me. We can each go our separate ways." He smiled. "Though I have to say I'm grateful that you trust me enough to leave me alone in your homeland. That is your plan, isn't it?"

Horrified, she swallowed hard. "Of course not. My people would eat you alive."

"Metaphorically or…"

Tempted to let him think the worst, she finally sighed. "You know what I meant. They'd mop the floor with you."

At this, he looked mildly interested. "Are your people great warriors then?"

"Some are." She shrugged to suggest that physical prowess was not important. "But more significantly, we have magic. There are great wizards and warlocks and sorceresses in the Land of the Bright."

"Wizards and Warlocks. I see." He gave her a skeptical look that told her he had decided to humor her rather than outright dispute what he plainly considered an outlandish claim.

"No, I don't think that you do." But that truly was not her

concern. If he persisted in this foolish request, he'd find out the truth soon enough.

If there was any chance, no matter how small, that she could dissuade him, she'd have to take it.

"I have an idea." Flashing him her brightest smile, well aware of what a pale imitation hers was compared to her sister's, she touched his arm. Again, she felt that sizzle, that spark. She swallowed and tried to ignore it, though she couldn't help but wonder if he felt it, too.

"Go ahead." Her smile, of course, appeared to have no impact on him.

"How about you let me go and I'll go home and see what I can learn about the killer? I can meet you back here in a week's time and fill you in?"

After one startled second, he tossed his head back and laughed. The masculine sound seemed to echo through the forest. "Right. And you'd definitely come back. I don't think so. Enough of your stalling tactics. Let's go."

Since there didn't seem to be any way out of it, she sighed. "All right then. Just remember, you asked for it." That said, she stepped toward the veil with him in tow.

## Chapter 8

Ruben didn't know what he expected. But whatever he'd believed Willow's story to be—fairy tale, delusion or the product of an extremely overactive imagination—he'd never in a million years supposed it to be real.

Yet, as they'd approached what Willow called the veil, he'd definitely felt a shift in pressure, a very noticeable change in the quality and composition of the air. His wolf felt it too and became restless. This time, Ruben let the beast have full rein, or as close as he could come without actually changing. He felt safer trusting his wolf's finely tuned senses and instincts. If Willow had looked into his eyes at that moment, he knew she'd have seen a hint of what he could become.

As they approached a small grove ringed by several tall aspen trees, she stopped yet again.

"We're here," she said, her amazing eyes troubled. "Please, I know you think I'm stalling, but you really should reconsider. This is your last chance to back out."

He lifted his wrist, the handcuff they shared causing her to do the same. When he saw the red marks on her creamy skin, he winced with guilt. "Sorry, but I have a killer to track down. I can't change my mind. Lead the way."

And so she did. Reluctantly, but he thought he detected a bit of mockery in the wry half smile she flashed.

"Come then. And don't say I didn't warn you."

As they walked forward, the pressure became more intense. His ears filled and he swallowed to pop them.

Though he squinted and tried hard to see—something, anything—the sunlit-dappled forest appeared unchanged. If there was magic—and the tingling along his skin told him there was—it remained invisible to the naked eye.

Just as the pressure became almost too intense to bear, it vanished. Ruben blinked and looked around. The forest from before was gone.

Instead, they stood at the edge of an unfamiliar wooded area. In the distance, rolling green hills danced toward a cerulean sky.

Dizzy, he staggered.

"Are you all right?" she asked.

"We've changed location," he said, feeling as though the ground had suddenly shifted right out from underneath his feet.

"Uh, yes. We've crossed the veil. It's in a different place on our side." One perfect brow raised, she eyed him. "Are you all right?"

Concentrating hard kept the world from spinning. He took another small step forward, dizzily feeling his way, and realized they were no longer tethered by the handcuffs.

Of course when she noticed the direction of his gaze, she smiled. "I told you they wouldn't transfer with us."

"Right." He swallowed, popping his ears again, and took another step, briefly closing his eyes and willing away the spinning. When he opened them again, everything seemed to have settled back into place.

"Where the hell are we?" he rasped. Inside, the part of him that was wolf still reeled, unable to regain his equilibrium.

Her smile widened. "Home. Welcome to SouthWard, land of the SouthWard Court of the Bright. My home."

Again he searched the horizon, reassured to note the sky had lightened somewhat. Though still darker than what he was used to, at least it had remained blue. "In the land of the…what? Fairies?"

Moving ahead of him at what honest-to-hounds looked like almost a skip, she shrugged. "Call it what you like. Elves, Fairies, Sprites, none of that matters to us. We are Sidhe. We exist in our own reality that closely mirrors yours."

Why he found this so surprising and difficult to digest, he didn't know. If anyone should understand the supernatural existed, as a shape-shifting member of the Pack, aka a werewolf, he should.

And he reminded himself, he was a prince among the royal house of Teslinko. Moving quickly and relieved to learn he'd regained his balance, he caught up with her.

"Where are we going?"

She cast him a sidelong glance, her expression serious. "I haven't quite figured that out. I'm not sure what I'm going to do with you."

"How about you present me to the court?"

She rolled her eyes at him. "Right."

"I don't think my request is all that unusual. I'm a prince, you're a princess. Protocol demands—"

"Forget protocol," she interrupted. "As much as I hate to be rude, shall I remind you that you're not a welcome guest? No one, and I can't emphasize that enough, is going to be happy to see you. Even if your father has met my parents."

He frowned, puzzled. "That doesn't make sense." Teslinko

was beloved among the countries of the world. Though small, the natural resources—diamonds, timber and miles of perfect white sandy beaches—made them a much sought after destination of tourists and celebrities alike.

"Doesn't it?" She stopped and faced him, hands on her hips. "No one here even knows that I travel to the human realm. And then, not only have I lost one of my mother's precious magical earrings, but I show up with a human when I'm supposed to be entertaining—"

"I'm not a human," he interrupted her this time. "Maybe that counts for something."

She shook her head, heaving a sigh. "Stop playing games. I'm serious."

"So am I."

Head cocked, she studied him. "Fine," she said at last. "I'll bite," she said, unaware of the irony. "If you're not human, then what are you?"

"I'm a Shape-shifter, just like my father."

When she said nothing, he continued.

"I can change into a wolf."

Now her eyes widened. "That explains why I saw…"

"What? You saw what?"

"A shimmering ghost of a wolf, surrounding you as though linked to your soul."

Dumbfounded, now it was his turn to stare. "You saw my aura? But only Shape-shifters can see that."

"Sorry." Her shrug told him she cared nothing for his preconceived ideas. "Maybe magic trumps shape-shifting. So if you're a werewolf, is your entire kingdom made up of werewolves?"

"Shape-shifters," he corrected, before he really thought about it. "Sorry. We prefer that term. And no, not everyone is like me. Teslinko has always been ruled by the Pack. I'm a prince of one of the oldest European Packs."

"Packs?"

"A grouping of wolves."

"I know what the term means," she snapped. "Though I guess I find it odd that you refer to yourself this way."

He shrugged. "How else would we refer to ourselves?"

To her credit, her steady gaze never wavered from his face.

He met her gaze with a straight face. "And as I said, not everyone in Teslinko is Pack. Like every other Pack, we co-exist with many ordinary humans all around our world. They have no idea such a thing as a Shape-shifter truly lives, apart from legends and old fairy tales."

She watched him in silence, mulling over his revelation. After a moment, to his surprise, she held out her hand, her caramel-colored eyes twinkling. "Truce, okay?"

Despite having absolutely no idea what she meant, he went ahead and shook. The instant they touched, electricity arced between them. Sizzling. He could tell from her wide eyes and the hitch in her breathing that she felt it, too.

Of course he found it incredibly difficult to let go of her soft hand.

"Do you believe me?" he finally asked, more to distract himself than anything else.

"I'm not sure." Lifting one shoulder in a delicate shrug, she looked away. "I guess you'll have to show me sometime."

Which meant, in her refusal to take things on faith, she was like him. "I will," he promised. "Though unless you like animals, you might not like what you see."

A shadow flitted across her mobile face. "I love animals."

"Good. Now will you present me to your court?"

Still considering, finally she laughed and nodded. "Yes, I think I will. Something tells me you can take care of yourself."

Relieved, he gave her a half bow, using his hand in flourish. He still had difficulty realizing the handcuffs had disappeared. "Then, please, lead the way."

When she smiled up at him, his heart skipped a beat. Unwillingly, he was reminded of how attracted he'd been to her when he'd first seen her at the ball. Was he still? He refused to allow himself to think about it.

"Let's go." Walking alongside her, he relaxed slightly as he took in the beautiful scenery. Here, he felt an amazing synergy between the earth and its inhabitants, as though Willow's people didn't rape the land and destroy nature for their own means as some humans did. His inner wolf approved. For a moment, the beast struggled to break free. Ruben subdued him with a promise of later. Soon.

Finally, they came up over a hill and a glittering golden castle came into sight. Even in the muted sunlight, the thing shone bright enough to hurt his eyes. Ruben couldn't decide whether it was beautiful or too much.

She'd stopped and stood silently watching him, no doubt to gauge his reaction. When he didn't comment, she began to move forward. "Most people around here like it. Personally, I think it's gaudy and garish."

Since her words so closely mirrored his own thoughts, he had to chuckle. "I didn't want to offend you by saying anything."

Her answering grin warmed his heart. "Don't worry, you won't. I should tell you, around here everyone is fond of glittery, loud and sparkly. Most times, so much gold gives me a headache."

He found himself grinning back. "Me, too. I much prefer nature."

Again she appeared startled, though he didn't understand why.

As they approached the golden structure, Ruben braced himself for when the guards stopped them. To his surprise, they weren't intercepted or even greeted. They proceeded into the castle unnoticed and unannounced.

Inside, everything—from the sparkling marble floor to the gilt-encrusted furnishings—carried over the bright golden theme. He even saw gold dust floating in the air.

They walked through a huge entryway, their footsteps echoing on the glittering floor. "This time of day, my parents hold court in the throne room," she murmured. "We'll go there and I'll try to present you."

Still no guards. He couldn't figure out if her people were extremely trusting or foolish. Finally, they reached a set of double doors, both of which appeared to be painted in pure gold.

"Are you ready?" she asked. Her neutral voice gave nothing away. But then, why should it? They were both royalty. It wasn't as if he'd never seen a throne room before.

He nodded and she pushed open the doors. Side by side they entered the room.

Instantly, Ruben realized this was nothing like home. Light reflected off every surface, so brilliant, so dazzling, the first impression brought pain. Too bright, in fact, the sharpness of it made him wish for sunglasses. Instead, he shaded his eyes and squinted as he looked around.

Where his family did not stand on ceremony, evidently here the king and queen did. Everyone wore formal attire, glittering gowns and equally dazzling suits. The court sat gathered around a raised dais that appeared to be made entirely from perfectly cut diamonds.

On the dais, two shining beings were seated on two equally glamorous thrones. Everyone watched as Willow led Ruben into the room. Temporarily blinded, he narrowed his eyes and struggled to see.

Willow dropped into a deep curtsy. "Mother, Father, may I present Prince Ruben of Teslinko?"

Still no one spoke. The king and queen eyed him with a regal intensity he would have been hard pressed to imitate. Though they possessed a beauty beyond words, he could tell from the disapproving set of their aquiline features that they found him utterly lacking. Too bad. He had more problems than pleasing them.

"I believe you have met my father," Ruben said. "King Leo of Teslinko sends his regards."

This seemed to do the trick. Though neither of the rulers moved, a subtle relaxing of the tension told him using his father's name had helped him somewhat.

Queen Millicent smiled. "Give him our regards, as well. He is a good man."

Ruben bowed his head. "I will."

"What do you want with us, human?" King Puck asked, his expression less austere.

"He's not—" Willow tried to interject. Ruben squeezed her wrist to silence her.

"I'm looking for a killer," Ruben announced, making his own tone equally chilly. He could go with courtly B.S. or try the direct approach. Considering the contempt with which this king eyed him, he figured he didn't have time to waste with hints and innuendos. "Someone from your kingdom traveled to my home and murdered one of my servants."

The instant he finished speaking, the room erupted in chatter. The king silenced them all with a single wave of his hand, an impressive feat. "You are mistaken," he said. "Our people do not kill."

The arrogance of the statement was not lost on Ruben.

"I've seen him. He followed your daughter from this land to mine. I happened to be in the woods when he did so."

"So? What proof do you have?"

"My mother saw him. She has described him perfectly,

right down to the violet eyes. Only one people have such a physical trait. Therefore, I know he's from here."

Again the crowd began to whisper and gossip. Once more, the king waved them to silence. "Why should I believe you?"

Ruben fought the urge to roll his eyes. "Why would I lie? I have nothing to gain and everything to lose, traveling to your realm in search of a killer."

The king frowned. "You say you've seen him?"

Ruben nodded.

"And would you recognize this man if you were to see him again?"

"Yes. I am sure of it." And he was. Even though the other man had looked exactly like most of the men present—tall, blond, with piercing violet or purple eyes—Ruben felt certain he could recognize his features.

"I see." Turning to the queen, the king spoke with her in a voice too low to be heard.

While he waited, Ruben realized how much this task meant to him. Not only would this search for the killer distract him from the approach of the madness he so greatly feared, but if he was successful, he might also succeed in banishing that completely. Here, he'd have no choice but to stay human.

Next to him, Ruben felt Willow tense. He glanced down at her to see why and realized her attention was fixed on a doorway midway between them and the throne.

Two people stood there, both elegantly beautiful, with shimmering blond hair and well-built physiques. After a quick glance at the man, Ruben's gaze was drawn to the female, the most amazing-looking woman he'd ever seen. With her lush figure draped in a bright red dress that wrapped around her like a caress, perfectly showcasing her curvy figure, she actually glowed with beauty. If that weren't enough, the exotic tilt to her violet eyes and her plump, bow-shaped lips completed the package.

Dazedly, he thought if Hollywood ever saw her, she'd be an instant sensation. No movie star or model could even hope to hold a candle to her.

"My sister, Tatiana," Willow drawled in a low voice. "And her fiancé, Prince Eric."

Though he nodded, he couldn't tear his gaze away from them long enough to respond.

As they advanced into the room, Ruben noticed an instant softening in both the king and queen. In contrast, Willow gripped his arm hard enough to draw his attention back to her.

"My darling," the queen all but cooed. "Come, join us." She held out one slender, regal hand, one side of her scarlet mouth turning up in a mocking smile. "Look at what your sister has done now."

Tatiana's tinkling laugh drifted through the room, making everyone smile in response. Everyone, that is, except Willow. She seemed resigned and apprehensive, an interesting combination. The undercurrents he sensed here would put his own royal court to shame.

Flanked by the tall blond man, Tatiana drifted closer in a cloud of exotic scent. His wolf twitched away from it, finding it distasteful. Part of Ruben agreed. The other part of him wanted to reach and touch her to make sure she was real.

"What have we here?" she purred, barely glancing at Willow as her bright purple gaze undressed him. Though she was undeniably gorgeous, Ruben knew her type. Man-eater, he thought. He'd do well to steer clear of this one.

Still eyeing him, Tatiana lifted one golden brow at her sister. "Willow, wherever did you find him? And tell me, dear sister," she said as she leaned close, her smile seeming almost a snarl up close, "when did you start associating with humans?"

Ruben's inner wolf growled. It took every ounce of willpower he possessed to keep from recoiling from her.

Willow straightened. She drew herself up to her full height which was, unfortunately, at least six inches shorter than her sister. "He's here for a reason." She pitched her voice loud enough to carry. "And that has absolutely nothing to do with me."

"You brought him through the veil," Queen Millicent pointed out, her dulcet tone dripping with malice. "Therefore, I would think his presence has everything to do with you."

"Not of my own free will," Willow answered.

At that, the entire room gasped.

"But he is here of his own free will?" the king asked, his tone making it plain the answer mattered.

Though Ruben decided he didn't much care, he knew Willow did. Taking a step forward, he distanced himself from both the pushy beauty and her quietly gorgeous sister. Willow released her hold on his arm.

"I am," he answered.

Crossing half the remaining distance to the throne, he wasn't surprised when six guards moved forward to intercept him. He stopped and spread his arms, addressing himself to the king and queen. "I mean no disrespect, your Highnesses."

The royal couple glared at him, but the king waved his hand, indicating he should be allowed to continue.

"I am Prince Ruben of Teslinko." Straightening his shoulders, Ruben brushed past the guards, aware his title should give him some special consideration, even though they'd chosen to ignore it when he'd been introduced. "I have come here to ask your leave to hunt down the killer and bring him back to my home for justice."

The king and queen exchanged looks. Neither expression revealed a clue as to their thoughts. Both focused their intent gazes on Ruben.

Every time they moved, the light shattered, sending shards of brilliance reflecting off everything else in the room. Willow hadn't been joking when she'd said her people favored bright and gaudy. Ruben's head began to hurt and again he longed for a pair of dark sunglasses.

"We will consider your request," King Puck said. "And we will talk more in private."

"Yes," Queen Millicent echoed. "We are very interested in learning about this crime, particularly how our daughter the Princess Willow came to be involved."

Tatiana laughed again. "Perhaps my sister's fiancé should stay closer to her. Eric, where is Prince Chad?"

Silent until now, the tall blond man at her side frowned. "I haven't seen him. I must find him and warn him about this interloper." With a sharp glare at Ruben, Eric strode off. Tatiana watched him go, the expression on her lovely face something akin to relief.

Beside him, Willow stirred restlessly.

As Ruben was about to speak, the king waved his hand. Just like that, they were dismissed. The guards surrounded them again and escorted them from the room. Willow went willingly, appearing both calm and happy. Ruben really couldn't blame her. His head ached.

On the way out, Ruben caught one more glimpse of Tatiana, as her gaze followed them with barely disguised dismay. He couldn't help but wonder why.

When they'd proceeded through a set of ornately carved double doors and into the hall, the guards finally left them, turning back the way they'd come.

"Phew," Willow let out her breath in a sigh. "Thank the stars that's over."

She said the words like she'd never attended court before. About to ask, he stopped himself. What did it matter? He was here to find a killer and prove his sanity, even if only to himself, not to make friends with Willow.

His wolf slinked close to the edge of his awareness. The

beast had retreated, repelled by Tatiana. Now that Ruben was alone with Willow, the wolf sidled near the surface, intrigued and attracted.

Ruben ignored it. He glanced at Willow. When he did, she quickly looked away.

Suddenly, he realized why. "You didn't tell me you were engaged."

Lifting one shoulder, she grimaced. "I'm not entirely sure I am. My parents are trying to arrange a marriage between me and Tatiana's fiancé's younger brother. Neither of us has committed to it."

The idea of her and another man rankled. Surprised and disturbed, he pushed the thought away. What Willow did with her life didn't matter to him. Finding the killer did.

"What now?" he asked, eager to begin his search. "I'm ready to go."

"You don't yet have permission," she reminded him, making him wonder how she'd known his thoughts. "Until you do, let me find you somewhere to stay." He couldn't help but notice that she still wouldn't look at him.

"Wait." He stopped her with a light touch on the shoulder. "What's wrong?"

"What's wrong? Honestly?" Bitterness tinged her tone. "Let's start with you handcuffing me and forcing me to bring you here. Which of course, brought me to the attention of my parents, especially my mother."

"Attention of…" This, he didn't understand. "You're a royal princess." He thought of his sister, and how often Alisa had complained about what to her had felt like constant scrutiny. Willow probably felt the same. "Surely they are well aware of your activities," he finished.

"I take pains to make certain they aren't," she said darkly. "Especially my mother."

He almost smiled at this, then remembered the strange,

almost vindictive way the queen had behaved a few moments ago. "Is she angry at you?"

"Perpetually." She grimaced. "Actually, she finds everything I do, including breathing, both humiliating and embarrassing."

In her tone he detected bewilderment and hurt. For the briefest of instants, he wanted to pull her close, hold her and tell her everything would be all right.

Of course he immediately pushed that thought away. She wouldn't appreciate his pity. "I want to apologize for involving you in this," he said, meaning it. "While my intention isn't to hurt you in any way, I don't see how I could have done this differently."

When she began to speak, he held up a hand to indicate he hadn't finished. "But you should understand, I really have no choice. Murder is not taken lightly among my people—among any people. I must find this killer and bring him to justice."

Her entire body, which had gone tense, relaxed slightly. "Follow me," she said, and turned away. He kept pace with her as they marched down one glittering hallway after another. The palace appeared so deserted, he began to wonder if they all were in the throne room holding court with the king and queen.

When they finally ran into a servant, Willow asked the golden coated footman to stop. Ruben stared in disbelief as the man ignored her, continuing on as though she hadn't spoken.

Stunned, Ruben cleared his throat. "Wait," he ordered.

Immediately the man froze in his tracks. Slowly, he turned and walked back to them. "Can I help you, sir?" he asked, addressing Ruben as if Willow didn't exist.

"Your princess called you," Ruben said, his cold tone letting the man know he'd better listen this time.

Willow stepped forward. "This is Prince Ruben. I need you to make sure a room is made ready for him."

The footman darted his gaze from her to Ruben and back again. Expression like stone, Ruben dared him to protest. He wasn't sure what exactly was going on here, but first impressions told him there wasn't anything friendly about this palace, especially toward Willow.

"Yes, my lady," the man finally said, the faintest sneer in his voice. Then, directing his gaze back at Ruben, he dipped his head. "Sir, if you'll follow me…"

Ruben glanced at Willow, who plainly had no intention of going with him. She waved him on, smiling slightly. "I'll meet you at the noon meal. Maybe by then, my parents will have made up their mind about you."

And then, her back straight, she walked away, leaving him without a backward glance.

## Chapter 9

About to enter the grand throne room right behind his brother and Princess Tatiana, some sixth sense had made Chad hang back. As he listened to the uproar from inside the room, he was very glad he'd stayed out.

Especially when he'd heard this Prince Ruben person state unequivocally that he would recognize the man who'd been following Willow through the forest.

How was this possible? He would have sworn no one had seen him. Clenching his fists, he swallowed back a rush of fury. This man, this human interloper, could identify him? This he could not allow to happen. If what he'd done was revealed, his family and the entire EastWard Court would have their reputations ruined. His parents would never forgive him and he'd be banished to live among the Shadows. With his Bright coloring, he knew he'd be lucky to survive a week.

In that instant, he knew what he'd have to do. Unless he was successful in disguising his appearance until he could return home, he might have to take extreme action and get rid of the only one who could identify him. This Prince Ruben would have to die. Soon. And if Willow got in the way, he'd kill her, too.

Once she'd taken her leave of Ruben, Willow hurried down the hallway. She knew she wouldn't be left alone for long. In fact, at any moment she expected Tatiana to come sailing around the corner. Or, even worse, her sister would find out where Ruben was staying and show up at his door, prepared to practice her considerable wiles on Ruben in order to learn everything she possibly could about Willow's involvement with him.

Stress tightened her chest. Either that or Prince Chad—who was conspicuously absent—would come looking for her, though he certainly hadn't seemed all that interested in staking a claim.

While she certainly didn't welcome either prospect, if given a choice, she'd take Chad over Tatiana any day. The man seemed to be harmless. Tatiana was less complicated, but her intentions as transparent as glass. Chad appeared reasonable. Normal, even.

By the time the bells were rung for the midday meal, she'd relaxed. To her astonishment, neither Tatiana nor Chad had sought her out. She'd had several hours on her own, time she'd used to shower and change into a dress her mother would consider suitable for court.

When the light tapping sounded on her door, she nearly jumped out of her skin. So much for relaxation. Heart pounding, she opened the door. Looking thoroughly annoyed, Prince Ruben stood in the hall.

"What is wrong with this place?" he asked, storming into her room. "I simply asked to be brought to your chambers. Everyone acted as though you don't even exist."

Mouth dry, she eyed his rugged, beautiful face and debated whether or not to tell him the truth. "Actually, to most of them, that's true. I don't exist. They take their cue from the king and queen. I think my parents actually wish I'd never been born."

She'd shocked him; she could tell from the way he recoiled. "Why would you say such a thing?"

"Because," she said sadly, "it's the truth. There are multiple reasons for this. It's rumored that my mother had an affair and I am the unfortunate result."

"That would be her fault, not yours," he said, making her feel warm at his fierce loyalty. "And the other reason?"

She sighed. "My appearance is distasteful to them. Here, two things are valued above all others. Beauty and magical powers. Because I have neither, I am considered worthless."

He frowned. "I don't know about magic, but you have beauty."

Unsure whether to laugh or blush, she considered him. Was he serious or was he making fun of her? Stars help her, she saw nothing but sincerity in his face.

"You really mean that?" she asked.

"Yes." He gave her shoulder a quick squeeze. "I'm not trying to hurt your feelings, but if we're going to work together, honesty is important, don't you think?"

Again, she heard only the important part. "Work together? Are we?"

"Of course. I need you to help me get home once I've completed my quest, remember?"

Just like that, her spirits deflated. "Oh, I don't think I'll be forgetting that any time soon," she said drily. "Are you ready to eat?"

Again she saw she'd startled him. Had he truly forgotten about the noon meal? Her stomach growled, letting him know she hadn't.

"Sorry." He flashed a rueful smile. "But if this place is what I think it is, I don't think I'm supposed to eat."

"Why not?"

"I remember reading something or hearing something." Scratching his head, he seemed sheepish. "About if you don't want to come under magic's spell or be trapped in the land of the Fairies forever, you shouldn't eat."

For a moment she was struck speechless, a major feat for her. A second later, she shook her head. "So tell me, do you howl at the full moon?"

He frowned. "Of course not." Then, as comprehension dawned, he grinned. "Are you saying the food thing is superstition?"

"Yep. It's only an old wives' tale." Taking his arm, she steered him in the direction of the dining hall. "Now let's go eat. I'm starving."

"I'm pretty hungry myself," he admitted.

Since the luncheon was usually served buffet style and they were early, they had the place to themselves. Willow went through the line, filling her plate with brightly colored fruit and fresh crispy vegetables. Ruben followed along behind her doing the same, but stopped when they reached the end of the long table.

"Where's the meat?" he asked, his voice pitched so low he sounded as if he was growling. In a way, he was. His wolf demanded meat, and plenty of it. "Beef or pork, or even chicken? Any of them would be fine."

"We don't eat meat," she began, stopping at the pained look of horror he gave her. For a second, she saw the wolf again, teeth bared in furious hunger. At least now that made sense.

"I'm a carnivore," he explained, unnecessarily.

Willow shuddered. "I'm sorry. You won't find animal flesh here."

Placing his plate on the nearest table, he dropped into a

chair. "I can exist on fruit and vegetables for a little while. But eventually, I need meat. My wolf needs it to survive."

She took a seat across from him. "If it's protein you need, there are various nuts and—"

"Trust me. It's not just the protein."

Deciding she didn't want to know, she ate her lunch quickly. When she finally looked up, she saw that he'd also finished his plate.

"It's perfectly okay if you want to get more," she said, smiling encouragingly.

"Maybe later." He pushed his empty plate away and leaned across the table. "I'm not familiar with your court procedures," he began. "But since it doesn't appear your parents need me for anything, at least immediately, I'm going to take off."

"Without permission?" Though part of her was stunned, most of her thrilled at the idea. He wasn't one of their subjects, but visiting royalty. Surely there was a different protocol in this sort of situation.

He shrugged, unconcerned. "I've got work to do."

By work, she knew he meant tracking down the killer. And suddenly, the idea of remaining trapped in her overly sparkly castle trying to trade witty remarks with a disinterested Prince Chad sounded about as appealing as jumping in a pit full of venomous spiders.

Quite clearly, she realized what she wanted to do. "I'm going with you," she said, crossing her arms and lifting her chin for emphasis.

He looked at her, his handsome face unreadable. "Why?"

At least he hadn't said an outright no. Encouraged, she leaned forward, too. "Because I feel responsible. This killer found your castle because of me. And you sent the maid to get my earring. So in a roundabout way, your maid got killed because of me. Honor demands that I help find the one who murdered her."

This last she'd just made up, but once the words were spoken, they rang true. She'd only said the truth. If she'd never traveled to Teslinko, hadn't attended the ball or borrowed her mother's magical earrings, none of this would have happened.

He frowned and she realized he was about to say no.

"I'm very well-liked here and my people won't talk to you without my assistance," she rushed on, fully aware that he had no idea exactly how unpopular she was with her people. Most of them thought she was a Shadow Changeling, hanging out in the land of the Bright with the intent to bring about mischief and mayhem.

Ruben knew none of this and for that reason he actually considered her words. "I do need a guide," he began.

"You've got one. Come on." Afraid he might change his mind, she stood, motioning him to follow her. Once he did, she began shepherding him down the hallway, aware she had to get him out of the open before Tatiana or Chad or someone sent by her parents found them.

To her surprise, he went with her willingly, apparently still mulling over her proposal. She knew on the surface, it made complete sense. And, since she wanted desperately to be part of something besides castle intrigues and fake civility, she hoped it would be enough for him to agree.

They reached her room unnoticed. Taking a deep breath— well aware of the repercussions of allowing a man in her room unattended—she opened the door and practically shoved him inside. Once she closed the door behind them, she locked it for good measure. She took a deep breath, turned and faced him. How she wished she didn't feel the pull of his masculinity so strongly.

"Have a seat," she told him, patting the bed. "We've got

plans to make and a lot to talk about. First up, I think we're going to need disguises."

He narrowed his eyes at her and waited.

"My people know me and you too easily stand out as a stranger," she said.

"And you think you can fix that with a change of clothing?"

"No." She grinned. "But with the right magical spell, we can fix anything."

Though he didn't relax his guarded expression, he did uncross his arms. "I thought you said... You can do magic?"

She felt her smile dim a bit. Then, realizing that even though she'd tried to tell him, he truly wasn't aware of how her people looked down on non-magical beings like her.

"No," she answered, managing to sound completely unapologetic. "But I know people who can. And with the right amount of coin..."

Jaw set, he considered. Then, apparently making a snap decision, he nodded. "Since I'd venture a guess that my money is worthless here, I'm assuming you can pay?"

Money was the one thing she had in droves, thanks to an untouchable and irrevocable trust fund her grandfather had left her. Since she rarely bought anything, she had a hefty amount available. Which was good, because any spell worth its salt didn't come cheap.

Keeping her voice low, just in case, she began to outline her case.

His nerves still thrummed from learning someone had seen him travel through the veil. Chad knew he had to do something, and quickly. Stalking off from the castle, he went bow hunting while he tried to weigh his options. The simplest solution, which also was the most boring, would be simply to leave now and go home, back to EastWard castle. If not, if he remained, he'd have to disguise his appearance while he was here so the human visitor didn't recognize him. And without arousing suspicion in the SouthWard Court.

That option and all the challenges it presented, made him grin savagely. Of course killing the human would remain on the table, especially since he secretly preferred this choice. For now, though, he would have much rather left no witnesses. The fact that he had, merely upped the game and sharpened the anticipation.

Life had suddenly become very, very good. No, more than good. Great. Awesome. Epic. Possibly even legendary.

And, he gloated, rubbing his hands together with glee, he hadn't even examined the magical earring yet. Since it belonged to Queen Millicent, he imagined it would have fantastical powers.

Stalking through the forest, tension building, he thought again of the way the maid had died. Even thinking about it brought him a buzz, better than the finest liquor.

He also felt a familiar restlessness, making him jumpy and uneasy. And angry.

With these emotions all roiling within him, he knew the only way to ease the tension and feel better would be to kill. Something. Anything.

He shot three rabbits in rapid succession and, disregarding every rule about hunting, left their bodies either to rot in the sun or to be savaged by other wild creatures.

This made him feel marginally better, at least able to face his brother again. Until he figured out a way to implement his disguise without the SouthWards noticing, he planned to avoid the rest of the royal family, especially Princess Willow and her human visitor.

When he reached the castle, he slipped into the back door and made his way unnoticed to his room. Once there, he closed the door and began pacing. Some of his rage had been quieted by the kills in the forest, but his problem still remained. That night, King Puck and Queen Millicent were throwing yet another ball to celebrate Eric and Tatiana's betrothal. Chad would be required to attend. Unless—he smiled grimly—he feigned an illness. A wretched, disgusting illness, the kind that couldn't be masked by a polite smile and a napkin over the mouth. His grin widened. Disgusting and gagging and nauseating. This, he could do. That would give him time to perfect a change in appearance so that the human wouldn't recognize him.

Now that he'd decided that, he took out the magical earring. Wiping it clean, he turned it over in the palm of his hand and began to try and learn its secrets.

Ruben listened as Willow outlined her case. He had to hand it to her. She sort of had a plan, and he definitely needed her help. She wanted to gather information, talk to people, see what they could find out. All in all, exactly what he had already planned to do.

The only problem he had was, despite his best efforts, every time he looked at her, he felt the strong tug of attraction. At the thought, his inner wolf grew restless. The beast wanted her, too—in other, more carnal ways.

As for his human self, Ruben admitted that her feminine vitality drew him on some instinctual level. He'd wanted her the very first time he'd seen her and his body craved her still.

But this he could control. He had an iron grip on his natural urges. Too bad the same couldn't be said for his wolf.

He'd let the animal part of himself have too much control for far too long. Therein lay grief and madness. The battle now, after the fact, felt futile. But he refused to admit defeat yet.

Willow provided a welcome distraction. Ruben didn't understand why, but the beast wanted this woman with a ferocity that defied all logic.

"Are you agreeable to us being a team?" she asked, watching him earnestly. "If so, we could get started immediately."

Slowly, he nodded, reaching a decision without giving it much thought. "Sure."

"Great." She took his hand, pulling him toward the door. "Then let's get out of here before someone comes looking for us."

Ignoring the shock her sudden touch sent through him, he let her lead the way. When they slipped through the kitchen and out of the castle through a back door, he was surprised. She headed into the wilderness rather than a road into town.

"Where are we going?"

"To get some answers," she said, smiling. "Since you are part wolf, you should feel at home here. Give it a minute and I think you'll understand.

They'd only gone a short distance when he heard a sound. The slightest of noises, but enough. Instantly, his wolf came alert. He sniffed the air, catching a scent. Then one more; no, two. More than that. There were others here, wolves. A wild pack, stalking them. Ruben glanced at Willow, who heedlessly continued crashing through the woods, the leaves rustling under her feet as loud as bells. Apparently unaware of the danger, she showed no fear.

He opened his mouth to warn her and heard a growl. His inner wolf responded in kind. He froze, the hair on his body standing on end as though electrified. Ahead, three large wolves stood, blocking their way.

Hellhounds. Always ready for a good fight, the wolf inside him struggled to be free. He knew if it came to a battle, he and Willow stood a much better chance if he let his beast loose. Shifters' wolves were easily twice as large as these animals, and much more ferocious. The aftermath would be brutal and bloody.

Wanting to avoid this at all costs, he kept his inner wolf at bay. After all, he'd never known a wild wolf to attack unprovoked, unless starving. A quick glance at these animals revealed they were well fed, with the glossy pelts of healthy beasts.

Unless he and Willow had inadvertently wandered onto their territory, the wolves had no reason to attack.

As he struggled with his inner beast, trying to formulate some sort of plan, Willow stepped forward. She moved with confidence and didn't appear to be afraid. She'd crossed half the distance separating them, dropped to her haunches and held out her arms, crooning in the wordless language one might use to an infant or a new puppy.

Had she lost her freaking mind? Disbelieving, he watched as the wild animals moved toward her, all trace of animosity gone from their demeanor. Like beloved pets, they rubbed up against her, allowing her to place her hands on them. She caressed their fur, still crooning, and their blissful reaction to her touch sent a nameless, wild ache through Ruben. This shook him to his core.

These animals, his Feral cousins, accepted Willow as if she was one of them, a pack-mate.

And she claimed she had no magic?

Looking up, she saw him watching and threw back her head in laughter. The sound, so full of joy and life, sent another kind of ache into his core.

"Come, meet my friends," she said, still smiling as she held out a hand for him.

But when he took a step toward her, the wild wolves' playful attitudes vanished. They formed a loose circle around Willow, letting Ruben know by their stiff stance and bared teeth that he wasn't welcome.

Another glance at Willow showed this puzzled her.

"They protect you," he said, the comment unnecessary, though he felt he had to say it. She looked from him to the wolves, her brow furrowed in puzzlement.

"I know," she said, her tone musing rather than worried. "Though our communications are only rudimentary, I can't seem to make them understand that you are not a threat."

That said, she rose to her feet in one fluid motion. Moving quickly across the few feet that separated them, when she reached Ruben, she wrapped her arms around him and snuggled close.

Then, once his heart started beating again, she began caressing him all over, much the same way as she had done with the wild wolves.

"I am attempting to show them," she murmured, her voice a throaty tickle against his ear. "By putting my scent on you, I'm letting them know you're part of me."

Despite himself, his body instantly responded. Desire flared, hitting so hard he quivered. Acting of their own accord, his arms came up and he let his hands explore her lush curves.

She gasped, thrusting herself against him as though shocked. This telling movement, however small, had his already aroused body strained nearly to breaking.

His wolf had gone quiet. Ruben barely noticed, so turned on he could scarcely think. He wanted to bury himself inside her, take her right there on the bed of dried leaves, with the wild wolf pack as his witness.

Inflamed, he nuzzled her, stroking her soft skin, lingering over the curve of her generous breasts. She pushed herself into him, groaning as his hand cupped her perfect behind.

When his mouth found hers, already drowning in sensation, the first crush of her lips against his sent a jolt of smoldering heat through him.

Reveling in the feeling as their tongues danced and mated, he realized he was dangerously close to losing control. He gasped, raised his head, struggling with his wolf, his desire, and most of all, with himself.

This was wrong. He couldn't let this happen.

As he saw the same awareness and realization flood her face, he realized the wolves had left them. Once again, he and Willow were alone.

Turning away, he desperately tried to think of something else, anything else, to dissipate his erection. He remembered his mother's horrible scream and the maid's lifeless body and his quest to find the killer. That did it.

When he could breathe again and speak normally, he turned to face her. She looked a bit tousled, though her serene expression told him she's also managed to put the incident from her.

"What just happened?" he asked, gesturing toward the spot where the wolf pack had been.

Willow flushed, proving her serenity was only an act. "I think we kissed."

"Yes, I know we did." Reaching out, he squeezed her shoulder, hoping she found his touch reassuring. He refused to analyze why he still felt the need to keep touching her. "I meant the wolves. I take it you managed to convince them that I was no threat?"

"Oh." Apparently at a loss for words, she squinted into the woods, gaze searching the shadows. "They left. They could sense your inner wolf. I think they thought you were staking a claim." Her blush deepened.

Staking a claim? Momentarily distracted, he found his gaze drawn to her mouth. Completely unintentional, but maybe he had, in a way. His inner wolf continued to prowl, somewhat mollified but not completely satisfied.

Ruben didn't like it. He'd kissed her but the beast wanted

more. Much more. At least he still had enough control over that part of himself to make sure human overruled beast.

Forcing his attention away from her soft, kissable mouth to the forest, he managed a savage smile. "What were the wolves doing here in the first place?"

"Um.…" Her chocolate eyes widened. "I guess I should have told you earlier. All the animals, whether here in the forest, or in town, seek me out. For some reason, I'm able to communicate with them in a rudimentary way."

Fascinated, he eyed her. "Are you serious?"

Slowly she nodded.

"Is that one of your magical abilities?"

"There's nothing magical about that," she said. "Is there?"

"Talking to animals seems pretty darn magical to me. Hellhounds, I'm a Shape-shifter and I even can't communicate much with wild wolves. What do your parents think?"

She looked down. "I haven't exactly told them."

He couldn't believe she didn't realize the magnitude of her ability, if it was true. "Why not? Surely they'd be proud of you."

"I don't think so." Crossing her arms, she shook her head and began walking, indicating the conversation was over. At least as far as she was concerned. He made a mental note to try and discuss it later.

For the next hour, they trudged southeast, sticking to uncultivated forest and eschewing anything that even remotely resembled a path or road. During that journey, Ruben witnessed the phenomena with Willow and the animals again and again. Deer and elk, rabbits and squirrels, hedgehogs and beavers—species didn't matter—they all came to greet her. Those that hunted and those who were prey, they came without regard for the danger.

With each and every one, she crouched low, petted and caressed, and appeared to confer softly and silently.

Keeping his distance, Ruben watched her, listening closely, trying to figure out if he had missed some little nuance, some trick. But he saw nothing other than the obvious—the animals came to Willow and she clearly adored them. It also appeared the feeling was mutual.

Finally, after another long stretch of walking, he decided to ask where they were heading.

"Nowhere, really." She shrugged. "I told you, I would ask some questions and get some answers. This is more of a fact-finding expedition than anything else."

"What?" He stopped, unable to believe he'd heard her correctly. "Fact-finding from whom?"

"The animals, of course." When she turned around and came back to him, he saw from the intent look on her face that she was serious. "That's why we haven't been following a path or a road."

*From the animals.* He decided to humor her. "And what have you learned so far?"

She eyed him, her expression so disappointed that he wondered if she could read his mind. "I've learned that we need to go back to the palace and start there. The animals saw the same person you did. Even worse, he's been here again since then. He killed several rabbits and left their carcasses to rot. They saw a man, tall and fair with light-colored eyes. They sensed something dark inside him."

"Perfect. Now all we need to do is find him."

"That's easier said than done," she finished glumly. "Unfortunately that description fits every single man in the South-Ward kingdom. EastWard, too."

He refused to be cowed. "Maybe so, but I'd recognize him if I saw him again."

"So would they." She gave a tired sigh. "It's just a matter of bringing him around them. Which, of course, would be impossible without knowing who he is."

"Let's go back." Holding out his arm, he told himself it was because he wanted to be gallant, not because he'd relish her touch. And when she took it and that same wild longing swept through him, he resolutely ignored it.

## Chapter 10

The kiss she'd shared with Ruben changed everything. Since Willow had never kissed anyone before, she didn't know if it was always like this. So intense. So powerful.

And when she'd felt his body swell with desire, her womanly parts had come alive. She'd wanted him, in a gut-wrenching, visceral way.

Apparently he hadn't felt the same.

The sense of loss that had come over her when he'd turned away had been shattering. Used to hiding her inner pain, she gathered her shredded dignity around her like a cloak, glad she was able to look calm and relatively normal when he'd finally turned back to her.

She'd let the peace of the woods surround her. As usual, the sounds and scents of the forest were calming, balm upon her troubled soul. The bold scree of the crow, the richness of damp earth and pine and maple, the way the dappled sunlight made shadows dance on the carpet of fallen leaves.

But her sense of tranquility was only fleeting as she forced herself to remember why they were here. Into this beauty, a killer had gone. Shaking her head, she tried to reconcile herself with the notion.

He'd been here only a short while ago, according to the wolves. His evil had left a taint and a blight upon the balance of the earth.

She wondered why she hadn't sensed it. No matter, because she knew it was true. The animals did not lie. The concept was foreign to them. They'd told her of the man who only minutes before had butchered small creatures for sport, leaving their carcasses to rot in the humid day. His actions had been more than cruel, they'd been insulted. He'd dishonored their lives.

The predatory ones, hawk and wolf and fox, who would not touch meat already dead, had skirted the area nervously. Finally, the carrion birds had come, big and black and awkward, their tattered feathers scattering as they fought over their spoils.

The perfect balance of life had been ruined. Evil had come to her woods. Jaw set, Willow sensed the evil putting tendrils of darkness through her forest. As they came upon the spot, the birds warned her. They didn't actually have to—the scent of death still hung acrid in the air.

"Shadows of Darkness," Willow muttered faintly. The edges of her vision faded to gray, as though she might pass out. Resolutely, she sucked in great gulps of air, steadying herself. She stopped and closed her eyes, unable to bear the bloody sight.

"What kind of man does such a thing?" Ruben asked, his tone hoarse as he surveyed the bloodbath—a churned up mess of bones and fur and blood. "Hunger or the need for a warm pelt, that makes sense. But to kill for no reason, other than taking cruel pleasure in the act of killing?"

Absurdly, she found herself thinking of her chores. Distraction, grounding her to normalcy. There were a hundred small duties she needed to be doing, back at the palace. Briefly, they crossed her mind, like a small, annoying dog nipping at her heels. She pushed them away, grounded once again and able to concentrate on the larger problem.

Her forest had been desecrated.

"Do you think this is the same man?" she asked. "The one who followed me and killed your maid?"

"Who else could it be?" Slowly turning, Ruben glared out into the shadowy woods as though by doing so he could will the offender to step forward and confess.

"We'll find him," she said, turning away lest her churning stomach heave. "We have to." She tried to sound certain.

At her words, his frown deepened. "I confess, I was doubtful. But someone who feels the need to kill for the act of taking a life, will feel this compulsion again. We just need to be near when he does. I would recognize him, I think."

He would kill again. Somehow, such a rational thought hadn't occurred to her. "Are my people in danger?" she asked, worried.

"They could be." His mouth tightened. "Now that he's killed a human, I don't think butchering animals will satisfy him any longer."

She'd wanted to leave the palace before. Venture out in a search for the villain. Now, she wasn't so sure. "If he's nearby, then we have no reason to travel to seek him out."

"Unless he leaves."

They exchanged glances, the unhappiness in his expression undoubtedly mirrored in hers.

"How will we know?" she asked finally. "I'm sure he won't be kind enough to give us notice."

"No." Grim-faced, he once again surveyed the damage. "The best way to track him is to follow the kills."

"And hope no other people get hurt," she said.

As she walked with Ruben back toward the castle, she covertly studied him. She'd always considered herself a good judge of character, able to read most people's inner psyche with one quick glance. Of course, she acknowledged with a rueful smile, most of the people she met were Brights and pretty darn transparent.

But Ruben was…different.

When she looked at him, his aura seemed cloudy, as though enveloped in a cloak of fog. Sometimes she saw his wolf more sharply than he, though the wolf hadn't yet manifested in corporeal form.

She put this down to the fact that he was a Shape-shifter. The only one she knew.

"What is it?" Ruben asked, startling her. Apparently, lost in thought, she'd been staring for far too long.

Deciding to be honest, she told him what she'd seen. The notion that his inner wolf had manifested in his aura clearly stunned him.

"You mentioned that before and I'm still trying to process that. Can everyone here see it?" he demanded. "Or is that one of your special skills?"

She didn't want to remind him again that she had no special skills. "I'm not sure. I'm thinking it might be due to my peculiar affinity with animals."

The tension in the set of his jaw relaxed somewhat. "Good. I'd rather not field a bunch of pointless questions."

That she could understand. "I think we need to come up with a way to make the killer reveal himself."

"But how? We know nothing about him other than his physical appearance. All we have is the fact that I've seen his face."

Which meant they had to hope Ruben saw his face again. Otherwise, they could prove nothing.

\* \* \*

Sickened and disgusted by the wasteful carnage he'd witnessed, Ruben needed to change the subject. Something else, anything else, to distract him from thoughts of the horrible scene.

He grabbed her hand. "Tell me about your land," he asked Willow. "You mentioned SouthWard, which is here, and EastWard. What about the other directions, North and West?"

"We, those of us who are SouthWard and EastWard, are the Brights. Your human legend calls us the Seelies. We are supposedly all good and wonderful and shoot rainbows out our—" She stopped, apparently horrified at what she'd almost revealed.

"Anyway," she continued in a much quieter voice. "Those of the NorthWard and WestWard are known as the Shadows, or the Unseelies. They are dark, both in nature and appearance. They are considered evil and dangerous. You'd do best to avoid them whenever possible."

He regarded her curiously. "And which are you, Willow? Because you don't resemble—"

"I know," she interrupted him, her expression resolute. "As I mentioned earlier, rumor and gossip have it that my mother, Queen Millicent, once had an affair with a NorthWard man. I am the result," she gestured with her free hand. "Which explains so many things, my appearance of course, and the loss of magical abilities. Light cancels out dark."

He studied her, suddenly understanding. "This also means—"

Again she cut him off, as though she'd heard the words too many times. "Yes, if it's true, then I truly am a bastard, not fit to be a royal heir. Believe me, that's another point my sister, Tatiana, never fails to make."

He gave a low whistle. "No wonder you sneak into Teslinko. This place is toxic."

"Yes." A trace of bitterness tainted her faint smile. "At least there no one looks at me as though I carry some horrible contagious disease."

He might have laughed at the apt description, but this was anything but funny.

"Why have you never traveled to NorthWard?" he asked, genuinely curious. "Confronted the man rumored to be your father and demanded to know if it was true?"

Immediately she tugged her hand free. The horrified look she gave him made him wonder why what he'd said was so awful.

"Do you think I have a death wish?" she asked, her gaze searching his face. "Our peoples are enemies. They would kill me the instant I set foot over the border between our lands. Not to mention what my own people would do to me if I were to somehow make it back unscathed."

"Kill you? Why?"

"Because I am a tangible reminder of what they don't want to believe." Earnestly, she took his arm, sending another violent shock through him. "I know you're an outsider and you don't know our ways. But believe me, my mere existence is a reminder, every single day, of my mother's foolish indiscretion. I'm amazed the king didn't smother me in my sleep."

Now it was his turn to be horrified. "Are you serious? I thought you said your people were the good ones in all this."

"Which is probably the only reason I'm still alive." Her tone changed, the abrupt flippantness telling him she had finished discussing the topic.

For now, he told himself. He was beginning to see why his father had wanted him to come here and learn these people's ways. Perhaps as an example of what not to do.

To be fair, his suggestion hadn't been anything she hadn't thought of doing herself, Willow realized as she and Ruben trudged back toward the castle. If King Puck wasn't her actual birth father, she wanted to meet the man who was. Unfortunately, she'd never been able to learn his name. She didn't dare ask her mother and, for all Tatiana's mean-spirited teasing, her sister didn't know, either. Without the name, Willow didn't even have a prayer of finding him.

Which was just as well. Because even if she knew who he was, traveling there to meet him would risk setting off an international incident. Assuming the man would even see her, never mind acknowledge her as his daughter.

Worse, she might be viewed as a danger. After all, she carried royal blood, a mixture of the Bright and the Shadows. As such, she could be seen as a visible symbol, proof that unity was possible between two such diverse groups. Therefore, she would be considered a threat to those who wished the two factions remain enemies.

Again, this was fine with her. She had no desire to become friends with any Shadows. Ever since she'd been a small child, like all the other Bright children, she'd been threatened with them whenever she'd misbehaved. They were like the monsters that lurked in the mist.

Now, as an adult, she knew they were just people. A lot like the Brights, but different, too, in many fundamental ways. She had no doubt that they'd harm her if she were careless or foolish enough to wander into their territory.

The Shadows Court was rumored to be menacing, full of intrigue and deadly magic of the type that would drift into one's room at night and steal the very breath from your lungs. The thought made her shiver.

Despite her appearance, which assured she'd fit in, she didn't believe she possessed an evil bone in her body. She could no more pass as a Shadow than one of them could pass as a Bright.

She could never go there. Nor, she told herself as she had on many sleepless nights growing up, did she want to.

Ruben made a sound, bringing her back to the present. They'd made it to the top of a small rise in the land, enabling a grand view in many directions. Flowers and green, as far as the eye could see.

"I thought by now we'd be able to see the palace," he said, sounding perplexed.

"We're almost there," she said, making her voice sunny and cheerful, as befitted a Bright. Then, feeling Ruben's curious gaze on her, she tugged him toward the castle, already regretting telling him anything even remotely personal.

She knew virtually nothing about him. He claimed to be a Shape-shifter, able to change into a wolf at will. Her wild animals, from smallest chipmunk to ferocious wolf, hadn't recognized him as anything but a man.

Except, she reflected silently, the wolves.

Maybe she should demand proof, ask him to become a wolf in front of her, so she could see if he'd spoken truth, once and for all.

They were almost within sight of the castle. If she was going to finally work up the nerve to ask him, she needed to do it quickly.

There were several things Ruben hadn't expected when he'd handcuffed himself to Willow. First and foremost, he hadn't expected her story to be true. The entire notion of a veil or passageway, between worlds, had seemed way too surreal.

Then, while he was still reeling from the shock of realizing she'd told the truth, he'd been surprised at how beautiful—if garish—her home actually was.

From then on, Willow had been a veritable wellspring of surprises. Her story, her family, the unabashed gaudiness of her home, each new revelation came completely and utterly from left field.

And, just when he thought he'd heard it all, she hit him with something new. Talking to wild animals? Seeing his wolf in his aura? He began to wonder if he'd wake up in a few hours, only to realize all of this had been a dream.

When they'd happened upon the blood scene of the slaughter, he'd known she'd been telling the truth. The animals had told her this man had killed. Now they'd witnessed proof.

It was a little difficult to swallow. Had it only been a day since he'd stood in the abandoned tower and wondered if his life could possibly get any worse?

"Are you all right?" Willow asked him, her voice curious. "You look as though you're a million miles away."

He had to grin at her apt description. "In a way, I was. All of this is so unreal. I keep wondering what's going to happen next."

"Okay, listen to me." Stopping, she tugged on his arm, making him look at her. The earnestness in her expression made her appear far more vulnerable than he'd ever seen her.

"You need to watch your back," she continued. "I don't know how things are in Teslinko, but the court here is a dangerous place. Anyone, my parents, my sister—"

"Your sister?" He remembered the glorious, man-eating creature he'd met earlier and nodded. "Never mind."

Eyes narrowed, Willow watched him. "Look, I know she's beautiful, but Tatiana cares about herself more than anything else. She won't hesitate to betray you if she'll get something out of it."

"You don't trust her?" As the youngest of four, Ruben had three sisters. He was closest to Alisa, the one who'd recently married and moved to America. He'd trust any of them with his life and knew they felt the same about him.

"No," Willow responded simply. "I don't trust her at all."

"What about her fiancé, that giant blond guy?"

"Eric?" She shrugged. "I don't know enough about him to say, but he seems pretty self-absorbed. If those two marry, they'll have to figure out a way to take turns admiring each other." She made a face. "For now I plan to avoid them both as much as possible."

"And your fiancé?" He found himself holding his breath for her answer. Once he realized this, of course he immediately released it.

"I've already told you, nothing's been agreed upon," she said crossly. "And yes, we should try to avoid him, as well."

"Then we need to vamoose."

Her blank expression told him she wasn't familiar with the word. He opened his mouth to explain, but before he could she asked him something else.

"Will you shape-shift for me?" she asked, her voice casual, as though the question was completely normal. "I'd like to see what you look like when you become wolf."

Stunned, he thought about how to reply, not sure what to say. He opened his mouth to answer her, and then something happened. Something completely and totally unexpected and out of his realm of experience.

Right in front of her, he could feel his body begin to change without him initiating it. Of course. Now he'd lost control of that, too? Worse, seeing an opening, his wolf chose that moment to mount a fast and furious attack, taking an already off-balance Ruben completely by surprise. Before he even had time to mount a defense, the wolf began the process of shape-shifting, forcing him to change. Wolf. Human. Wolf. Ruben struggled, gripping his rapidly shredding humanity and trying like hell to hold on. If he let the wolf win, even once, what little tenuous hold he had on his sanity would be gone.

He could not let the beast win.

As he battled for his sanity, his life, a horrible sound burst from his throat. Snarl, howl and part moan. He heard this dimly, as though from a great distance, even as he felt another cry bubble up inside him.

An uneven fight, this. In prime condition, the wolf had watched and waited, with the perfect patience of its kind. And when Ruben had let down his guard, his attention focused on Willow, the animal had struck.

Payback time.

"Ruben?" Willow's voice, sweet and worried and curious. "What's wrong? Are you okay?"

He could no more answer her than he could let the wolf win. But when she reached out and placed her soft hand on his arm, his inner wolf roared.

Even now, the beast craved her.

Even now, so did the man.

The momentary distraction was enough. Ruthless, Ruben fought back the wolf, penning it into a mental cage and locking the door. Then, exhausted and breathing heavily, he opened his eyes to find Willow surveying him as though she feared he'd become possessed.

In a way, that's exactly what he'd been.

"Are you all right?" she repeated.

Temporarily unable to speak, he nodded. Because he feared at any moment his legs would give out from under him, he let himself sink to the floor.

"I'm going to call for help," Willow said.

"No," he croaked. "Please. Just sit with me."

Looking alarmed, she slowly and reluctantly did as he'd asked, dropping to the ground alongside him. "What just happened? Was that normal?"

As he tried to catch his breath, he also gathered his thoughts, attempting to figure out some sort of cohesive explanation.

"My wolf wanted out," he finally told her.

She leaned close, searching his face. "You mean you were about to actually shape-shift into a wolf?"

"Sort of." Closing his eyes so he couldn't see her expression, he sighed. "I know you wanted to see what it was like, but that change wouldn't have been a good one. Sometimes my inner wolf tries to gain control."

"And you have to be the one who is in command of it?"

"Yes. Otherwise it's...dangerous. I have to fight him for the right to remain human." He wondered if she'd really understand what this meant.

"Is shape-shifting like that for every Shifter?"

Wordlessly, he shook his head.

"I see," she said, making him wonder if she really did. "What happens if you lose?"

"Good question. I don't know. So far that hasn't happened." He shuddered, thinking about the repercussions were such a thing to become reality. "And I don't want it to."

"I'm sorry." She sounded sincere. "I shouldn't have asked you to become a wolf like you're a performer in a circus or something. I promise you, it won't happen again."

"That's okay." He didn't bother to keep the exhaustion out of his voice. "My wolf and I battle constantly. It could have happened regardless."

Again that pause, as though she was holding her breath. He made the mistake of opening his eyes, to find her much closer than was prudent.

"I have to wonder," she murmured, her gaze fixed on his mouth. "What would happen if you let the wolf win, just once?"

Temptation, both the woman and the thought. He knew an instant's fierce aching, a wild flash of need, before he shoved the notion away. Partly because he didn't want her to know the truth, and partly because he'd fought enough battles for one day, he gave in to one temptation, at least. The lesser of two evils.

The instant he covered her lips with his, he knew he'd made the right choice.

Kissing her was like coming home. And more. Arousal and sanity were commingled in her mouth and as she wrapped her arms around his neck and pushed closer, he thought he might never want to leave.

And that, he knew, carried yet another chance of dangerous madness. Yet this was a risk he was willing to take.

# Chapter 11

They fit together like separate halves of a whole. Soft where Ruben was hard, she smelled of flowers and the pine scent of the forest. The kiss went on and on, a lingering embrace, neither willing to break apart. Finally, aroused and aching and much wearier than he should be, Ruben gently set her apart. He might be many things, but he knew he didn't have the right to do this. No matter what he wanted.

She sighed and snuggled into his side, smiling happily. Contentment radiated from her and he fought a virulent urge to change that contentment to desire.

No.

He took a moment to regain control, eyeing her with something akin to wonder. She looked beautiful and sexy, with her rumpled hair, flushed cheeks and swollen mouth. Chest tight, he gazed at her, wondering how one small dark woman could affect him so strongly.

so softly that at first, Willow wasn't certain she'd heard him correctly.

"Wrong about what?" She forced herself to pay attention to the man her parents wanted her to marry. It wasn't his fault that she couldn't stop thinking about Ruben.

"You." Lightly he moved his hand from her shoulder, skimming her neck and tracing the side of her face. "You're absolutely lovely, you know."

Shocked, she tilted her head, wondering what he'd been drinking. "Uh, thank you."

A smile tugging at one corner of his sensuous mouth, he moved closer, stroking her hair with a reverence that suggested he'd never seen locks so lovely.

Though everyone in SouthWard abhorred her hair, apparently he liked the color. Still, something about him made her uneasy.

While he cupped her chin, she could think of nothing else but how badly she wanted to move away. Instead, she forced herself to hold still, curious to see where he was going with this.

"You smell like lilacs," he murmured. His eyes had drifted half closed, as though sensory awareness of her had overwhelmed him. "And something else. Maybe vanilla."

Skepticism warred with fascination as he moved his hand from her face to her hair. From her brief experience with Ruben, she imagined he would want to kiss her soon.

At the thought, she found to her surprise that she wanted to giggle. With a major effort of will, she kept her expression serious, focusing on the handsome Bright man who had moved even closer still.

He was handsome and muscular and well-proportioned. Well-bred and polite and oozing with masculine charm. Yet he couldn't hold a candle to Ruben.

Again, she pushed the unwelcome thought away. Accord-

ing to her parents, she was to marry this man. She might as
well see if his kiss affected her as strongly as Ruben's had.

If not, she would be in for a world of trouble.

Encouraged by her stillness, Chad cupped the back of her
head. Gazing into her eyes, he tilted his head and hesitated,
as though asking for permission or waiting for her to make
the first move. She wasn't sure how she was supposed to respond, so she decided to take matters into her own hands
and kiss him first.

She pulled him to her, letting him crush her mouth with
his. The instant his lips began to move greedily over hers,
she realized she'd made a mistake. *Blech.*

Unfortunately, Chad apparently didn't feel the same.

Deepening the kiss, he crushed her to him, letting her feel
the strength of his formidable arousal as he ground his hips
against hers.

Starshades. Not what she wanted. Not what she wanted at
all. She struggled then, attempting to push him away, which
only seemed to inflame him even more.

When he attempted to ram his tongue down her throat,
making her gag, she brought her knee up in reflex, jamming
it into his man parts so hard he staggered backward. Then,
as he doubled over, gasping and groaning, she pulled away,
uncertain if she should apologize or not.

The shudders wracking him indicated her move had caused
him great pain. She hadn't meant to hurt him, only discour-
age him.

"I'm so sorry," she told him, reaching to touch his shoulder. Unsurprised when he recoiled from her, she doggedly
continued. "I didn't mean to hurt you. It's just—"

"Enough," he snarled. When he raised his head, the rage
blazing from his eyes hit her hard enough to send her stag-
gering back. Then, as he struggled to regain his equilibrium,
he stumbled toward her. He opened his mouth to speak, and

she felt the familiar sizzle of magic. She might be in serious danger. Though all of her people had been trained to put up shields to protect against magical attacks, Willow didn't even have enough magic for this.

Praying Chad didn't know about her serious lack of power, she raised her hand and waved it slowly in front of her, as though building a magical wall. "Don't do this," she ordered, relieved her voice sounded strong and sure, the exact opposite of the true way she felt with her insides quaking.

He narrowed his eyes. "Give me one good reason why not?"

"Because I am a princess of the royal house of SouthWard and your intended betrothed. I meant you no harm. My actions were those of a foolish, scared virgin," she told him, hating the way something else, something even darker, flared in his eyes at the word *virgin*.

Nevertheless, she kept her shoulders back and her spine straight as she continued. "I was frightened and lashed out without thinking. I didn't mean to hurt you."

All of a sudden he became all smiles. "I understand," he said, though his eyes remained cold. "I wasn't aware of your untouched state. I confess, I'm a bit surprised, especially given the way you kissed me."

"Are you?" She crossed her arms, cocking her head and wishing she could find a way to let him know, subtly of course, that she was no fool. "You of all people should know princesses are expected to be pure."

He laughed. "Now you're trying to tell me Tatiana is a virgin? Please. How stupid do you think I am?"

Though she blushed, she wanted to keep the topic on track. "Tatiana is not my concern. We are talking about me and the fact that because of one kiss, you thought you could take liberties with me? Might I remind you that you are a guest in our palace and my father would not take kindly to the thought of you trying to force yourself on his little girl?"

As if her father would care. She had a painful suspicion that both her parents would forgive just about anything if it ensured they could get their youngest daughter married off and thus out of their hair.

The color had mostly returned to Chad's face. Straightening, he grimaced and swept his hand through his hair. "Let's walk," he said, managing to sound both menacing and soothing all at once.

Warily, she started off. She hoped he couldn't sense her revulsion as he fell into place at her side.

"Tell me about this human friend of yours," he asked casually.

Instantly she was inexplicably suspicious. "He's not a friend, actually. More like an acquaintance."

"I heard you brought him to your parents for an audience." Still he sounded merely curious, nothing more. Briefly, she wondered if he was jealous, then discounted the idea. If she'd been as beautiful as her sister, maybe. But she knew there was no way someone as attractive as Chad would be jealous of her.

"I did bring him to see them," she agreed. "I couldn't just let him roam around without acknowledgment. He is royalty, after all."

"Human royalty." The way he said the words put them on a level with horse dung.

She nearly laughed. "Yes, human royalty." She saw no reason to mention the Shape-shifter aspect, either.

Prince Chad turned the full wattage of his purple-violet gaze on her. "What does he want?"

She blinked. "He's here on a quest and I've promised to help him in any way I can."

"A quest? What does he hope to find?"

Just like that, her lighthearted mood evaporated. "A killer," she said grimly. "Someone killed one of his servants."

"Servants?" He raised one golden brow.

"Yes, one of his palace maids was murdered."

"Hmm," Chad mused. "He values his servants that highly?"

Stunned at his callousness, she opened her mouth and then closed it. Chad didn't appear to notice.

"Has he offered you gold?" he asked.

This question startled her. "Gold?"

"For your magic," he said, sounding slightly impatient.

She realized he truly didn't know that she had no magic. She also had no reason to tell him the truth, at least not yet. If it came down to the fact they both became serious about their nuptials, then of course she'd fill him in. She wouldn't be so cruel as to let him marry her believing she'd been gifted with magical ability.

For now, she'd play it safe. She did have a moment of wonder that she felt such a thing necessary with the man whom she might be spending the rest of her life.

"No gold." Smiling to take any potential sting off the words, she slipped her arm through his. Trying not to notice the way her skin crawled, she pretended to be honored to be accompanying him.

A moment later, as they rounded the corner and headed toward the sweeping staircase, she began to worry how she would extricate herself. If only Chad wanted to go downstairs, she could excuse herself and head up to her room. Every man understood a woman's need to refresh herself.

But then Tatiana appeared. Her sister took one look at Willow and Chad and fell to the floor in a dead faint.

The instant she'd seen Willow gazing up so adoringly at the altered Prince Chad of EastWard, Tatiana had known something drastic had to be done. So of course, she'd pushed aside the sharp bitterness of jealousy and called on her well-skilled acting abilities to pretend to pass out.

Willow bought it hook, line and sinker. Tatiana couldn't tell about Chad. Watching through her eyelashes as her younger sister fussed around her, she could barely make out Chad, standing stiffly several feet away, a bored look on his chiseled features. Briefly, she noted the shimmering hint of glamour, and wondered what he'd done to himself, then decided she'd examine it more closely as soon as she got the chance.

Whether he suspected she was a fraud or simply didn't care, either way, she'd won. She'd managed to break up their little tête-à-tête.

What the shades was Willow thinking? Tatiana believed she'd been quite clear in communicating to the twit what she wanted. Chad. She'd practically ordered Willow to focus on Eric. He would be easily won over with just the right amount of awe and hero worship. Which Willow would actually owe him, especially if she could get someone as beautiful as Eric to fall in love with a woman who looked like her.

In love. Right. With an effort, Tatiana kept from snorting out loud. As if such a foolish emotion even existed. And if it did, Eric would never fall for someone as homely as Willow. No, that plan was doomed to fail even before implemented. Still, she didn't actually care what Eric did. As long as it wasn't with her.

Again she eyed Chad. Though he'd used a spell to dull his looks, he was still tall, bright and handsome. And the secretive side to his nature appealed to her more than anything else. Bright men were…boring. Transparent, uncomplicated and, well, *Bright*.

She finally understood why her mother had taken a lover among the Shadows. She'd do exactly the same, if given a chance. Meanwhile, she'd work with what she had at hand.

Chad. To think she hadn't believed he'd be much of a challenge.

The glint in his bright purple eyes told her he was aware
of what she was doing. He played his own little game, using
his own set of rules.

Even better. She wanted to rub her hands together with
glee. Nothing got her blood boiling like a rousing game of
cunning. Of course, among the Brights, it never was any sort
of contest. She always won.

Willow glanced at her, flashing an uncertain smile. Tatiana smiled back, letting her sister know not to consider herself the winner here.

Of course, what could she do? She'd need to get rid of her
younger sister and coax Chad into her bed chamber. Once
she'd succeeded in seducing him, she could make sure his
older brother found out, thus effectively ending that engagement and setting herself up for a new one with Chad.

Who, she was willing to bet, would be much easier to manage than that overconfident bag of wind, Eric. Even if Chad
wasn't as beautiful, there was much to be said for the benefit
of having a willing adoring slave.

Tatiana hadn't a doubt she would win. She always did.

Meanwhile, her foolish, gullible sister still crouched in
front of her.

"Speak to me," Willow pleaded, her brown eyes full of
concern. "Please, Tati. Are you all right?"

*Tati.* A nickname from their childhood. Tatiana almost
softened and took pity on her younger sister. But just as she
was about to sit up, open her eyes all the way and assure Willow she was, in fact, fine, Chad spoke.

"Maybe we should give her some space," he drawled, cynicism coloring his voice. "You never know what delirious
people might do."

*Delirious?* She wasn't…silently seething, she realized

Chad knew this and was baiting her. Fine. All part of the game.

Spine stiff, she forced herself to lie still a moment longer. Only by using a major force of will was she able to keep a secretive smile from curving her lips. She loved a good challenge.

"Move." Using the same bored tone, Chad nudged Willow aside. He bent down, causing Tatiana to flutter her eyelashes oh-so-delicately as she heaved a dramatic sigh, sending her awesome breasts quivering. Of course he noticed them— how could he not?

"Up and at 'em," Chad said, hauling her up brusquely. She sagged against him, as though her legs wouldn't support her, taking pleasure in pressing her ample breasts into his hard chest.

She felt the hitch in his breath, the immediate hardening at the front of his body. He might think he didn't like her, but his arousal said otherwise. Proving what she already knew. There wasn't a man alive who could resist her.

Satisfied, Tatiana stretched and slowly opened her eyes. She let her gaze travel slowly down his body, coming to rest of the swell of his arousal. Impressive.

"Glad to see me?" she murmured.

Bracing herself as she half expected him to drop her, she was relieved and gratified when he did the exact opposite, snuggling her close as though he couldn't help himself.

Right in front of Willow. Fantastic.

She sagged even heavier against Chad, taking pains to make sure her woman parts pressed against his rock-solid body.

Good lights! His obvious arousal was getting her going, as well. She let a tiny moan escape her lips.

At the sound, Chad's eyes narrowed to slits, but his erection continued to swell against her unabated. If they'd been alone, she knew she could have pulled him into one of the empty rooms for a round of hot and heavy sex.

Except…completely unaware, Willow watched with wide eyes. She looked from Chad to Tatiana, her expression troubled. Concern was written all over her rather drab features and even her dusky skin had gone pale.

"Where's your human friend?" Tatiana drawled, hoping her sister would get the hint and leave her and Chad alone.

"He's resting before the evening meal," Willow answered. Apparently she had no intention of going anywhere. Too bad.

Smiling, Tatiana snuggled closer, privately thrilled when Chad's already aroused body grew even larger. If she hadn't needed to play this complicated game, she'd drag him into the first available room and let him use that magnificent tool.

All she needed to do was get rid of Willow.

## Chapter 12

For his part, Chad hadn't decided whether or not to let Tatiana seduce him. Right now, though she'd done an excellent job arousing him, he wasn't all that interested. For one thing, she was not even remotely a challenge and, for another, having sex with her could really mess things up if Willow found out. And Willow was definitely a challenge.

So, even though his libido was ready, willing and eager, he tamped down hard on his arousal. Ever conscious of Willow's watchful gaze, he knew exactly how to play it. Cool, calm and collected.

First, he shifted her weight so Tatiana rested on his hip rather than his front. Secondly, he staggered slightly, as though he no longer had the strength to support her weight.

"Willow," he entreated, managing to look both repulsed and in desperate need of assistance. "Will you please help me with your sister? I'm afraid I might drop her."

After a moment of stunned shock, Willow sprang to action. She reached out and pried one of Tatiana's arms from her death grip around his neck. "Here, Tati, lean on me."

"Lean on you?" Tatiana sputtered. She pushed away and sprang up perfectly straight on her own two feet, her violet gaze shooting sparks at both of them.

From the look on Willow's face, her sister's dramatic recovery hadn't been entirely unexpected. In fact, Tatiana was rather predictable. Chad yawned discreetly, making sure Tatiana saw.

Willow, meanwhile, was still focused on her older sister. "You're better now?" she asked, her voice an intriguing combination of concern and disgust.

"Leave me alone," Tatiana snarled, whirling away from her. "I'm fine. Thanks for your concern."

Amused, Chad stepped back. Already his very visible arousal had begun to go down.

Tatiana's smirk made him realize she had definitely noticed. Her magical power rolled off her in waves, carefully banked, but enough to let him know it was there. If the two of them were to join, they'd be unstoppable. Not only could they rule the Brights, but the entire realm.

He nodded at Tatiana in acknowledgment.

"Are you sure you're all right?" Willow pressed, treating her older sister as though she expected her to keel over at any moment. Either that, or haul off and slap her. Though he had to say, Willow looked as though she could defend herself just fine.

"Yes." Tatiana waved her away. "I'm great. Fabulous. Fantastic."

If she noticed her self-descriptive adjective came off as conceited, she didn't show it.

"Good," Chad said. "I'm glad to hear it. Now if you'll excuse us…" He held out his arm to Willow, who immediately took it. "We're on our way to have lunch."

"Oh, I'll go with you," Tatiana immediately trilled.

"I don't think so." Looking down his nose at her, Chad frowned. "Your sister and I would like some time alone together. We need to get to know each other so we can decide whether or not to follow you and Eric's example and become engaged."

He didn't miss Willow's relieved smile or Tatiana's heightened color.

"But—" Tatiana began, narrow eyed with anger.

"No buts," he said, rather cheerfully. "Why don't you go find your own fiancé and spend some time with him? I'm sure Eric would love to get to know you."

Delivering that final dig almost set her off. He saw it from the tightening of her lush mouth and the flash of rage that crossed her face. She even took a step toward them, fists clenched. To do…what? But at the last moment, she reined herself in and managed to smile back, the calculating look on her face promising retribution.

Good. He looked forward to that.

"Tatiana?" Willow began, sounding uncertain. "What is it? What's wrong?"

Even more interesting, Chad thought, watching her. He'd bet three bricks of gold that Willow knew exactly what was going on with her sister. Like the rest of them, she was playing her own little game.

Of the two sisters, he had a feeling she was the most like him.

"Nothing's wrong," Tatiana snapped. Then, apparently realizing the crushed look on Willow's expressive face didn't reflect well on her people skills, Tatiana reached out and awkwardly patted Willow's shoulder.

"Sorry. I'm a bit shook up, that's all. I'm all right, really."

Willow looked doubtful. "Are you sure?"

"I'm positive. Now run on off and have your lunch. Have

fun then, you two!" Tatiana said, the gaiety in her voice ringing utterly false with the malice shimmering in her violet eyes.

Chad flashed an equally fake smile. "We will. Say hello to my brother for me, will you?"

"Of course." Grumbling something else under her breath, Tatiana moved away.

"Well done," Willow said quietly. "You are aware of what she was angling for, aren't you?"

"Of course," he answered smoothly. "She is very competitive with you for men's attention, is she not?"

Willow swallowed hard. When she spoke, he noticed that she didn't answer the question. "Most men would have taken the time to enjoy my sister's ample charms."

Giving her a tender smile, he put an arm around her shoulder and pulled her close. "Most men haven't already found the woman they want."

Then, as she blushed delicately, he went in for the coup de grace. He kissed her lightly on the side of her cheek. A gentleman's kiss, but one that promised much, much more.

"Chad," she turned to face him. "I'm not sure I—"

"Ahem." Behind them, someone cleared a masculine throat.

Willow stiffened, moving away from Chad so quickly he wondered if he'd caught fire or something. Then, as he saw who had intruded, he had to force himself to relax. He'd worked his glamour to ensure the human wouldn't recognize him. He'd also taken pains to dress differently than he had earlier.

This was the best he could work out without wearing a mask, which would be way too obvious. The moment of truth had come. Would the human recognize him? If so, he prepared himself to deal with the consequences.

"Ruben!" Willow said, her blush deepening as she stepped

away from Chad. "You haven't met Prince Chad. Chad, this is Prince Ruben of Teslinko."

Now or never. Turning slowly, Chad kept his expression casually friendly. He held out his hand, all the while holding his breath while he waited to see if a glint of recognition would show in the other man's face.

To his immense relief, he saw only pleasant politeness and curiosity as they shook.

"Pleased to meet you," Ruben drawled, glancing from Willow to Chad and back again.

"Yes, indeed," Chad drawled right back. Victory? Or was, as Chad suspected, Ruben actually toying with him?

But he saw nothing in the human's rugged face to indicate recognition. And what would be the point of pretending? None, none at all. No, he suspected Ruben would be the sort to have him immediately arrested and brought before the king and queen.

"Where were you two going?" Ruben asked, studying Willow's flushed face before looking at Chad.

"We were just about to head down for lunch," Willow said, still sounding breathless. And glad, Chad noted. Definitely glad. "Come with us."

Ruben considered.

Chad waited for the other man to decline. Surely even one as obtuse as he could tell Chad and Willow wanted to be alone.

Instead, Ruben nodded. "Great. I'm starving. Lead the way."

The happy smile that blossomed on Willow's face infuriated Chad. He moved closer to her, placing a proprietary arm across her shoulders.

"Maybe I should have let Tatiana come with us," he put in, reminding her not-so-subtly that he'd earlier declined her sister's blatant invitation because he had wanted to spend time alone with her.

At his comment, her blush deepened, though she made no move to tell Ruben not to come. Interesting. Glancing from Ruben to Willow, he filed the information away for later. He couldn't help but wonder how he might use this to his advantage. But he would, somehow.

"I'm sorry," Willow finally stammered, low enough that he knew she didn't want Ruben to hear. "I didn't think... That is..."

Apparently oblivious to the undercurrents, Ruben kept pace with them, looking straight ahead. Chad guessed the other man was lost in his own thoughts. Briefly, he wondered what those might be.

"Any luck on finding your murderer?" Chad asked, keeping his tone mildly curious.

Ruben's head came up and his amber eyes narrowed. "Not yet. But we're still waiting for the king and queen to give us permission to go out among their subjects."

"We're? Us?" Chad looked at Willow, who suddenly became very interested in her feet. "Are you helping him with this?"

"No." Her answer came too quickly, which meant she was lying. "Of course not."

At the same time, Ruben shook his head. "I asked her to help me, but she's refused." Also lying. Hmm.

"I'll be happy to help," Chad offered. What a perfect solution. That way, he'd be right there on top of the investigation and would know if anything happened to point to him.

"You?" Ruben frowned. "I thought you were a visitor here, just like me."

"Not exactly. My kingdom is about one hundred miles east of here."

"But you're not from SouthWard," Willow pointed out, annoyingly.

"No, but I am a Bright," Chad shot back. "And EastWard is an equally possible destination for this madman."

Ruben studied him, his look assessing. "You know what? If I don't find the killer here in SouthWard and I have to go to your kingdom, I'll take you up on that."

"Done," Chad said promptly, well aware that no matter how hard Ruben searched, he'd never find the one he sought among the SouthWard men. Actually, since Chad planned to ingratiate himself into the investigation, if Ruben even so much as displayed the smallest suspicion, he'd be a dead man.

As they entered the banquet hall, Chad made certain to stick close to Willow's side. It annoyed and amused him that Ruben did the same.

Many of the nobility had already arrived and made their way down the banquet line. Willow stood on her toes, trying to see over the crush of people.

"It looks like some sort of fish today," she said, smiling. "Though we don't eat meat, we make an exception for creatures of the sea."

Preoccupied again, Ruben nodded, then raised his head to meet Chad's intent stare.

"What?" he asked, sounding mildly curious rather than irritated.

Chad decided to test him further. "Nothing. It's just that you look awfully familiar. I don't know why or how that could be, since I've never traveled across the veil, but something about your face…"

Letting the words trail off, he waited to see how Ruben responded.

"Really?" Ruben turned away and sounded completely disinterested. "You don't look familiar to me at all."

Though he had no reason to doubt him, Chad suspected the other man was not telling the truth.

The truth of the matter was, Ruben didn't like Chad. At all. Something about the other prince made his wolf's hackles rise. He couldn't imagine why Willow would want to marry a man like that, but then again, what did he know about what women wanted in their men?

Though if he knew his sisters, they'd agree with his assessment of the blond prince.

And when Chad had mentioned seeing him before, he'd been lying. For whatever reason. Though now that he mentioned it, Ruben wondered if the other man's face *did* seem familiar. Despite the fact that he didn't have the same aristocratic features, was it possible he actually was the man Ruben and his father had seen following Willow?

The instant he thought this, he knew it made no sense. If Chad had used magic to alter his appearance, Willow would have commented on it, wouldn't she?

When they reached the stack of plates, Ruben grabbed one and eyed the food trays. His family rarely served meals buffet style, preferring instead a more formal service and a sit-down sort of elegance. To each his own.

As he studied each food, Willow kept up a running commentary about where it had come from and how it was prepared. From what he'd seen of her, she must have really been nervous to chatter so much. His admittedly limited experience around her had revealed her to be a quieter, introspective sort.

Nervous about what? He glanced at her, noticing the way her gaze occasionally darted to Chad. The man her parents wished her to marry?

While they were finishing up their lunch, which was eaten in blessed silence, they were summoned to the throne room.

The page that had come to fetch them glanced at Willow anxiously and swallowed.

"Best hurry," she whispered, loud enough for Ruben to hear. "Your mother is in one of those moods."

Willow blanched. Again, Ruben found himself wanting to comfort her.

On her other side, Chad raised a brow. "What's this about?"

Though Ruben felt a sudden urge to tell the other man to mind his own business, he answered cordially, "I'm sure they've reached a decision as to what they want to do with me," he said. He couldn't help but wonder what it was about the other man that made him feel so competitive. Willow? That would be extremely foolish.

Willow sighed and placed her napkin on top of her plate. "Did they ask for me only, or Ruben, also?"

"Both of you." Waiting, the page dropped her eyes.

"That's what I thought." She stood, motioning to Ruben, who rose also. Chad, he noted, remained seated.

As they followed the page, Willow leaned close. "I'm worried about this. Whatever you do, don't ask if I can go with you."

Surprised, he cocked a brow. "Why not?"

"Because I don't want them to forbid me. I'm going anyway and I'd rather not have to openly defy them."

"Makes sense," he said, even though to him, it did not. But then he thought of his sister Alisa. She'd done whatever she wanted, consequences be damned, and had nearly gotten killed in the process.

He couldn't take the risk of that happening to Willow. "You know, I've been rethinking the idea of your accompanying me," he said. "Maybe I should take Chad instead."

That got her attention. She stopped, crossing her arms and glaring at him. "You can't be that obtuse. Chad is the last person you'd want to trust to have your back."

So she had sensed something about Chad. "Why do you say that?" he asked, hoping she'd elaborate.

"I don't know. But something about him reminds me of my sister," she said darkly.

The page, having proceeded several feet without them, turned and waited impatiently for them to catch up.

At the door to the throne room, she left them, whispering a quick "Good luck" to Willow, who winced.

"Are you ready?" Willow asked, the slight tremor in her voice the only hint of her agitation.

He nodded and they stepped inside.

Once inside the space she privately thought of as the display room, Willow marched up the carpet—red, of course—with Ruben at her side. Though she would have liked nothing better than to take his hand in hers as a visible show of support, she knew such a gesture could be viewed in a wrong way. She didn't want to take a chance of doing anything that could jeopardize Ruben's position.

"We have given thought to your request to be allowed to question our people," King Puck intoned.

Willow noted how her mother's smile dripped with malice and stiffened. This was so not going to be pleasant.

"I have decided to allow you, Prince Ruben of Teslinko, to conduct your investigation," the king continued. "You may search not only in the lands that immediately surround our castle, but all of our lands, all the way to those that border the four directions."

So far so good. Again, Willow glanced at her mother. The queen looked positively gleeful.

"Thank you, your Highness." Ruben executed a perfect bow. "If I may, I'll start with your castle this very night. I should be done before dawn, at which point, if I've found nothing here, I'll make ready to get on my way."

"I'm not finished," King Puck said, his arrogant tone grating on Willow's nerves. "I will allow you to proceed with some conditions. First, our visiting EastWard prince, Prince Chad, has asked that he be allowed to accompany you once you go outside the castle. I have also decided to honor his request."

Chad? What in the shades...? Willow exchanged a glance with Ruben. Judging from the hard set of his jaw, he was as displeased—and shocked—as she was.

Chad had outplayed them. The question was, why would Chad even want to accompany them? Willow looked up to find Queen Millicent watching her closely, her bright violet eyes glinting with spite. As she surveyed her mother, Willow realized the woman knew she'd planned to go along with Ruben.

Even so, why Chad?

And what of Chad? Glancing over her shoulder, she saw him standing in the back of the room, stone-faced, arms crossed, his dimmed-down beauty looking slightly out of place despite his tanned skin and purple eyes.

For the first time, she realized what others saw when they looked at her. Even though her eyes were brown and her skin dusky, she must look out of place to all the fair-haired, violet-eyed Brights.

As she met his gaze, he dropped his gaze. She couldn't read his expression so she had no way of knowing what he was thinking. Since they'd just run into him a short while ago and he hadn't seen fit to mention this, she had to think he had some other reason for asking to accompany Ruben.

Did he know she planned to go, too? Was his sudden desire to assist Ruben based in a fear that he'd lose her?

Somehow she doubted that. The one thing she sensed Chad had in abundance was confidence.

"I'd be happy to accept all the assistance you are willing to offer," Ruben said.

The king shook his head. "I have asked him to keep an eye on you. You are an outsider in our land and I know your father would want us to make sure you stay safe."

From the back of the room, someone made a sound. Everyone turned, only to see Tatiana striding up the red carpet as though on a mission.

As Willow watched Tatiana storm to the front of the room, she wondered what else could go wrong.

When she reached the front of the room, Tatiana stopped a respectful distance from the dais. "I request permission to go, too," she declared.

Narrow eyed, the queen tilted her head. "What nonsense is this? You have too much to do planning your wedding to indulge in such foolishness."

Since her sister was not used to being denied anything, Willow braced herself for the fireworks.

"Mother, the wedding is not for another year," Tatiana pleaded. "Allow me one final adventure before I settle down to a life of married bliss."

Willow began chewing her thumbnail before she realized and forced her hand back down. The old habit, a relic from childhood, had been expressly forbidden by her mother.

Tatiana and the queen locked gazes. Willow couldn't believe it. Shadows help her, but her parents appeared to be seriously considering Tatiana's request.

No way in Darkness. If Queen Millicent allowed Tatiana to go, then Ruben would never find the killer. Her sister would prove not only distracting, but a major inconvenience. Out among her own people Tatiana would expect to be treated with all the status a visiting member of royalty should receive.

Plus, Tatiana would drive Willow absolutely crazy.

Glancing sideways at Ruben, Willow prayed he'd speak

up. He swallowed, opening his mouth, and then Chad interrupted him.

"A manhunt is no place for a woman," Chad declared.

Willow nearly groaned out loud. Making such a statement in her mother's presence nearly guaranteed Tatiana would be allowed to attend.

"Not just that," Chad continued, apparently unaware of the dangerous ground he now tread. "But from what I've seen of your lovely daughter, she is used to the finest delicacies and a life of luxury. As she should be. This journey will be arduous and lacking in those very things."

"I agree," King Puck began.

"I do not." Standing, Queen Millicent placed her hands on her hips and glared, first at her husband, then Chad and finally Ruben. "I feel we should let her go. This will be a character-building exercise for our precious daughter."

A character-building exercise? What?

A hush fell over the room while the king deliberated. Willow knew how much they valued her sister, so she doubted they'd give in to Tatiana's request. Would they?

Queen Millicent shot her husband a glowering look and Willow's heart sank. She knew what that meant. The king had better give in or his wife would spend the next several weeks making sure his life was a living hell.

Yet why would the queen risk her precious first born? Unless…she had ulterior motives. Did she have some sort of plan?

"Tatiana may go," the king declared.

The queen flashed a brilliant smile. "I agree. As long as Prince Eric goes, as well."

Just like that, Tatiana's triumphant grin faded as she realized her mother had something up her sleeve.

"Eric?" she echoed, sounding dazed. "I'm sure he—"

"Would welcome the opportunity to go on such a heroic

quest," Chad put in smoothly. "I feel quite certain that I can speak for my brother here. He will be delighted to accompany Prince Ruben."

Obviously Queen Millicent had noted Tatiana's apparent reluctance to be around her fiancé. She'd made sure they'd spend time together, increasing the odds of cementing the deal.

And so it was accomplished. Nothing was mentioned about Willow, but then nothing had to be. Plainly, no one cared whether or not she tagged along with the others. Dejected, she nonetheless straightened her shoulders and hurried out of the throne room, right behind Ruben.

"Ruben, wait. We need to talk," she said, pitching her voice low so that it wouldn't carry. She glanced around, making sure there were no eavesdroppers. "Quickly."

Ruben appeared dazed and waited until she caught him. She grabbed his sleeve, tugging him along after her to a small alcove filled with two overstuffed golden chairs and an enormous arrangement of yellow and orange flowers.

"Please, sit." She indicated one of the chairs.

"What's wrong?" he asked, remaining standing and sounding impatient. "Not only do I need to begin my search of the castle, but I've got to go pack. Though I said morning, I'd really like to leave before nightfall."

"What's wrong?" she asked, stunned that he didn't see. "First off, it's going to take you more than a few hours to search the castle."

"Not really. Most of your people have attended every single audience with your parents. I've been looking through them all and have seen no one who resembles the man I saw following you."

"Even so." She took a deep breath. "Once we leave the castle, we have to take Chad and Tatiana with us. That's what's wrong. Do you have any idea how awful this is going to be? My sister is…" Words failed her.

Rather than agreeing with her, he glared at her. The cold set of his handsome features made him look aristocratic and unapproachable. "I fail to see how having them help out will be any worse than simply you and I. I need Chad."

"Why?"

"Manpower," he answered shortly. "And magic. Though I don't know this Eric, I'm glad to have him, too."

*Magic.* The instant he had said the word—in truth—she realized he was right. He did need Chad and Eric and Tatiana more than he needed her. She had absolutely no magic. They did.

Before she could tell him that he was right, he grimaced. "If I have to worry about protecting you women, I'll need all the help I can get. At least this way, you can entertain your sister and vice versa."

She was unable to believe what she'd just heard and gaped at him for a moment. "Me? Entertain Tatiana?" She snorted, beyond caring if she sounded ladylike or not. "That's not going to happen. I'd rather ride into a hive of angry bees."

Surprise registered on his face before he thought to school his expression back to completely emotionless. That's when she realized the truth. Ruben was trying awfully hard to stay uninvolved.

Proving it, he shrugged carelessly. "Yeah, but that's life. If I had my choice, I'd prefer to do this alone."

Even though she understood his reasoning, his words hurt, to a point. She faced him, and a tiny flash of anger blossomed. "You would? Well, you know what? Good luck with Chad and my sister. I'm going to wash my hands of both you and your expedition."

With that, she walked away, leaving him to his fate.

## Chapter 13

The instant he so callously dismissed Willow, Ruben realized he'd made a mistake. He saw how his cold words had wounded her and wished he could call them back.

Why had he hurt her? The bigger question was *how?* Had it been because of the kiss they'd shared? Even so, she barely knew him. Why did she care what he thought?

Watching her as she strode away, her back ramrod straight, he shook his head. Though he got an uneasy feeling around the other man, the truth of the matter was he felt Chad would be a much bigger help than Willow or her older sister. In fact, he planned to grab Chad and make arrangements to leave the castle post haste, without Tatiana. Or Willow, for that matter.

Though his decision sat like a rock in his gut, he'd stick by it. Thus completely sure of his fate, he did nothing to stop Willow as she stormed away.

Oddly enough, he missed her. Which was, of course, ridiculous.

An hour later, packed and ready, he went out in search of Chad. Despite petitioning the king to accompany him, the EastWard prince seemed to have disappeared. Ruben chanced upon Tatiana and Eric, who were engaged in a vigorous debate over the merits of their little adventure, as Eric put it. Apparently Eric wanted to travel with his full retinue while Tatiana wanted to rough it.

Would wonders never cease? Ruben would have expected the opposite. They were so involved in their bickering that neither one noticed him.

Wisely, he backed away, taking care to remain unnoticed. He realized perhaps he'd been a bit hasty in his thinking of who would make good traveling companions. If he could only find Chad, they might have a chance of conducting a quick but thorough search of the castle and still getting away without Eric and Tatiana.

But Chad had vanished. In fact, the large glittering castle appeared surprisingly empty. Ruben didn't know if everyone was still in the dining hall or had gone to the throne room, but he didn't care. The less people, the less likelihood that he'd be stopped before he made it out.

Of course the later the hour grew, the more likely it appeared he'd have to leave in the morning.

Well into his search for Chad, he finally located the other prince, alone with Willow in a secluded arbor. Seated side by side on a stone bench, surrounded by roses, and their heads together, they looked up in unison as he approached.

A brief uneasiness settled in his stomach as he wondered what they'd been discussing. The sky had taken on that dusky glow of evening. Too late now to leave. Resigned, he realized he'd have to finish the search of the castle tonight, and attempt to travel as close to dawn as possible.

"A word?" Ruben asked, motioning Chad over. The other

man's patrician expression revealed nothing as he excused himself from Willow and strolled over.

Ruben ignored his inner wolf's visceral reaction to Chad. Once he had the other prince alone, he spoke quickly, outlining his revised plan.

"Leave Willow?" Chad said, deliberately speaking in his normal voice, which would undoubtedly carry to Willow's ears. Ruben winced. With the way she straightened, he knew she'd heard what he'd said.

"She tried to tell me she's staying, but that's not going to happen," Chad stated, still pitching his voice so she could hear. Ruben wondered what he was up to. Obviously, Chad had his own agenda. Again, suspicion crawled along his spine. He'd have to watch the other man closely.

Either way, he had no time for theatrics, especially from the last person he'd expected to have them.

"Look, I'm beginning the search in the morning," Ruben finally said, abandoning all efforts at keeping the conversation private. "Willow's already said she is staying here. If you want to go with me, meet me outside in front of the gate at dawn. Otherwise, I'm leaving without you."

He left quickly, not waiting to hear Chad or Willow's response. He'd do one last check of the castle before he left, then try and get a good night's rest.

Searching the castle alone, Ruben wondered when the war between his beast and himself had deteriorated to the point where even the wholly human part of him was at war. He'd used to pride himself on trusting his gut and right now, he was deliberately ignoring all of his instincts. He felt confidence in Willow. Could he say the same for Chad and Eric?

Again he questioned whether or not he'd be better off if he went alone. The advantage of having a guide might well be outweighed by the inconvenience of dealing with a prima donna. He pushed the thought away. He had a castle to search.

Once more he visited the throne room, still packed with people. He slipped unnoticed among the crowd, searched faces, but failed to locate his quarry there.

After, he roamed the castle halls, breaking up more than one secret tryst in a deserted hallway. The investigation took longer than he'd expected and the middle of the night had arrived before he made it back to his room. He finally climbed into his bed and fell into a fitful sleep.

When he returned to the rose arbor just before sunrise, he wasn't surprised to find Willow there, waiting alone. Holding the reins of two sturdy horses, she wore jeans and boots and what appeared to be a down vest. He noted she had already placed her packed bag onto the horse's saddle.

Contemplating her, his inner disquiet finally settled. Interesting.

"Where's Chad?" he asked, just to be sure.

She shrugged. "I have no idea." She wouldn't meet his gaze, making him wonder if she'd done something to delay the other man.

Then she raised her head and their gazes locked. Again feeling that insistent tug of attraction, Ruben stared down at her, his heart pounding. He said the first thing that came to mind. "I thought you weren't going to come with me."

Finally, she dropped her gaze and he found he could breathe again.

"I changed my mind," she said, smiling slightly. "I wouldn't miss this for the world."

"What do you mean?" he started to ask, about to make it clear to her that his plans did not include her sister and fiancé. But before he could, Chad and Eric strolled into the clearing, accompanied by four packhorses, all loaded to capacity. Behind them, tripped Tatiana, all decked out in her brightest, most sparkly gown. Though she looked gorgeous, she also shone like a beacon, visible from a mile away.

With great difficulty, Ruben kept from rolling his eyes. He glanced at the two EastWard princes, expecting to see, at the very least, sympathy. Instead Eric pouted, apparently mutinous. Judging from Chad's heightened color, he'd already had words with the other two and was completely disgruntled.

Upon seeing her sister, Willow turned away so no one could see her laughing. Only the silent shaking of her shoulders gave her away.

"Well?" Tatiana trilled. "I'm here. What are we waiting for?"

"You can't ride with us wearing that," Ruben finally said. "You need to dress more like your sister."

At his words, Tatiana's face froze into a regal impression of horror. "How dare you insult me so. I will not dress like Willow. Ever."

Willow's face burned as everyone turned to look at her. Ruben thought she'd dressed exactly right for this expedition and opened his mouth to say so. But before he could, to his surprise, Eric jumped in to her rescue.

"Willow looks very practical," he said. "You'd do well to emulate her, Tatiana."

Chad grinned as Tatiana huffed. Studying the two brothers, one so handsome he seemed fake and the other much more normal-looking, Ruben wondered again what was off with the other man's appearance—his features seemed misshapen somehow. Maybe he'd recently broken his nose? Whatever, Chad's face lacked the perfect symmetry of all the other Brights. Even his hair appeared dull.

"Shall we wait while Tatiana goes to change?" Willow asked, the sparkle in her voice letting him know that the instant her sister disappeared from sight, they'd be riding off.

"I'm not changing," Tatiana put in.

"I thought you wanted to rough it."

She shrugged. "I did, at first. But then Eric insisted that

we ride with every luxury, as befits the heirs of the Brights. Therefore, I need my best team hooked up to my day coach. Willow can ride with me if she likes."

Willow seemed properly horrified. Ruben and Chad exchanged glances while Eric studied his perfectly manicured fingernails.

Meanwhile, Ruben's patience ran out. "Listen up," he said, his voice ringing with authority. "We're not taking a coach. Tatiana, either go change or be ready to be left behind."

Eric raised his head as if to argue. Glaring at the other man, Ruben let part of his wolf self show as he dared the other man to say anything.

Immediately, Eric looked away. "Do whatever he says, Tatiana. Hurry."

Golden brow furrowed, Tatiana glanced from one to the other before flouncing away.

"Now," Willow said, swinging her leg up over her horse's back. "Let's ride."

Grinning at the mischief in her voice, Ruben mounted. So did Chad. Only Eric continued standing, jaw rigid as he glanced from Ruben to Chad. "We can't just leave her."

"Yes, we can," Willow put in.

"I don't want to wait." Ruben spurred his horse toward the gate. "If she wants to catch up with us later, more power to her. Otherwise, let's go."

"Raise the gate," Willow shouted, effectively cutting off whatever protest the other man had been about to make.

Slowly, the massive gate began to rise. Watching as it creaked slowly to the top, Ruben wondered if they used rope and pulleys to raise it, rather than electronics. Another question he made a mental note to ask Willow about later.

Finally, with the gate all the way up, they rode out. After taking his time tying up Tatiana's horse, Eric brought up the rear, riding slowly, apparently lingering in the hope that Tatiana would reappear. Ruben had to admire Eric's devotion to his new wife-to-be.

"Do you think she'll make it?" Chad asked no one in particular.

"I doubt it. She takes hours to change clothes," Willow answered, sounding relieved.

But just as they'd cleared the castle and the gate had begun to lower again, they heard a feminine screech.

Ruben winced, scratching the back of his neck. He exchanged a look with Chad, who shrugged.

Willow grimaced. "That sounds like my sister."

A moment later, Tatiana came into view, leading her horse. "Wait!"

With a sigh, Ruben signaled and they all reined to a halt. Tatiana vaulted gracefully onto her horse's back and spurred the animal into a gallop. She caught up with them quickly, her color high and fury sparking from her bright violet eyes.

Ruben braced himself for a tantrum. But, instead of spewing invectives, Tatiana smiled a completely insincere, falsely sweet smile. "Shall we go, gentlemen?" she asked, completely ignoring Willow.

Without answering, Ruben nudged his horse forward.

Though the idea had been to visit several villages outside of the castle proper, the landscape kept shifting. The first time it happened, Ruben halted, studying their surroundings distrustfully. His wolf snarled, uneasy, as well.

The others looked at him curiously. They didn't seem to notice the swirling landscape.

"Did none of you see that?" he finally asked. "The horizon keeps changing. One minute I see mountains, the next a great distance of flat plains. There are trees now but if I look away and then back, I will see rock cliffs."

Chad laughed. "I forgot you were mortal. It's only magic. Don't worry about it."

Ruben eyed him in disbelief. "Don't worry about it? How will we know where we're going, never mind if we'll ever arrive there?"

"Because," Eric broke in, using the exceedingly patient voice one might use to explain to a child. "We can see through the magic."

"I can't." Though he might be stating the obvious, Ruben didn't understand how they could hope to reach a particular destination when everything kept shifting. "We've been riding an hour and I see no signs of any town or village. How far is this place anyway?"

This time Chad and Eric exchanged glances, making Ruben uneasy. Had the two of them hatched up some sort of plan to get rid of him? If so, what did they plan to do with Willow and Tatiana?

Since the others all had magic to help them, he realized he and Willow were severely outnumbered. Still, at this point, there was nothing he could do about it.

When had he become so paranoid? Was this yet another sign of approaching insanity?

They continued to ride, Ruben doing his best to concentrate only on the path directly in front of them.

As darkness settled over the treetops, Willow brought up the subject of finding a place to camp for the night. Tatiana agreed with her, surprising everyone, Willow most of all, judging by the startled look on her face.

Riding slightly off the path, Chad returned a few minutes later. "I've found a level clearing that would be a good place to camp."

And so it was decided. They began to make camp. As they pitched tents and dug a fire pit, he saw the way Willow kept watching him, as though she expected him to grow claws and fur at any moment. His skin crawled with energy, and he knew his beast lurked just below the surface, ready at any moment, to wrest control and break free.

This had become his daily existence. As often happened these days, he wasn't sure which was his true nature—man or beast.

Later, after a completely unsatisfying meal of nuts and dried berries—again, Ruben had managed to forget that the Brights did not eat meat—they allowed the fire to smolder into embers and prepared to bunk down.

Letting the women share one tent and the two brothers share another, Ruben had staked his bedroll near a group of sturdy trees, ensuring he had some kind of protection at his back.

The others retired to their tents, the horses tied nearby. Quiet stole over the clearing, though out in the forest the night animals had begun to stir.

Ruben's stomach growled as he thought of roasting a plump rabbit. But when he imagined the horrified looks on his companion's faces, he knew if he was to eat the meat necessary to sustain him, he'd have to do it as wolf.

And there, he'd have to be very, very careful. Closing his eyes, he settled down to rest.

Though the Pack scoffed at the human legends about werewolves, sleeping outside under a velvet sky and a full moon always made Ruben feel a bit…odd. Out of sorts, uncomfortable in his own skin. He supposed there had to be some shred of truth in the old legends; most fables were born this way, from a long-ago occurrence combined with centuries of embellishment.

That night, Ruben's wolf came to him in a dream, trying yet another method to win dominance over his corporal body. Though he had prepared himself for just this eventuality, this time he'd been so involved in a pleasant dream involving Willow and kisses, he nearly missed the danger when it presented itself.

Where before his inner beast had fought him using traditional means, this night the wolf snuck up quietly, not making him aware of its presence until the last possible moment. Then—ambush! The beast attacked.

Half asleep, still in the throes of an absolutely wonderful dream, at first, Ruben couldn't muster the wits to fight back.

Then, as his bones began to lengthen and change, he lost. There, in the middle of the forest, surrounded by slumbering Sidhe, he became wolf.

Once the change had completely finished, he took a few steps and paused. In a world where scent ruled, at first the wolf was confused. These people smelled nothing like Pack or humans, but still their scents enticed.

With what little bit of human self-control he had left, Ruben forced the beast to leave the encampment and travel deep into the forest to hunt.

Filtered through the eyes of his beast, Ruben took great pleasure in the hunt. Since the Sidhe, or at least the Brights, were all apparently vegetarians, the forest was full of plump game. He caught a rabbit and a pheasant and devoured them both, glorying in his power and the renewed strength the meat-based protein brought.

Finally sated, he roamed the woods, thrilling to the feel of the damp and fertile earth under all four of his powerful paws.

He ran, just for the pleasure of it, enjoying the way the lesser animals scattered in blind panic as he approached. Tearing through the forest, heedless of the noise he made, he circled around the encampment, always staying within a mile, just in case anyone needed him.

Finally exhausted, he slowed to a walk, then let his familiar furry body sink to the forest floor, panting. He lay in the undergrowth, loving life, happy for the first time he could remember.

He hadn't been truly happy—alive, in the moment—since the last time he'd been wolf. Other than, some part of him whispered, when he'd kissed Willow. Immediately, he shoved the thought away.

The human part of him, still sentient, though relegated to only a small part of the wolf's brain, knew he eventually would have to shift back to human. He knew also that the wolf would fight this and the battle would be tremendous.

But to remain wolf—as his soul longed to do—was to become mad. Feral. He'd heard stories of Ferals flinging themselves from cliffs or dashing in front of semi-trucks, all in a bid to escape madness.

However tempting remaining wolf might seem, the short life of a Feral was not a fate he wished for himself.

Gradually, the moon sank lower, vanishing behind the treetops on its trip toward the horizon. Ruben-as-wolf finally pushed to his feet and Ruben-the-man made the first attempt to force the change.

As expected, the wolf resisted.

Thrashing, biting at an external enemy that only existed within, anyone watching would have guessed the animal mad. In a way, there was a kernel of truth; the wolf's desire to remain in corporeal shape hovered right at the precipice of insanity.

And the man knew he had to win, at all costs, at any cost.

The horizon flushed pink as the darkness lightened. Still Ruben and the wolf fought its solitary/dual battle, rolling and snapping, growling and biting at an unseen enemy as well as itself.

Any other time he would have sensed her. Any other time, the soft sound of her footsteps on the carpet of leaves wouldn't have been silent enough. He would have detected her scent, which he'd always recognize as individually hers, long before she reached him.

Instead, preoccupied with the battle to change/not to change, Willow was nearly on top of him before he realized. Apparently unafraid, she reached out to him and stroked his fur.

The wolf's first impulse was to snap. With a supreme effort of will, Ruben kept the beast from biting her.

Willow, crooning softly, reaching out to gather the crazed animal close to her breast.

Ruben thought his heart would stop beating. Even the wolf, now uncertain, confused, held its breath.

As she caressed his fur, the animal began to relax. Though he didn't want to shock her, Ruben seized this moment and initiated the change back to human. Taken by surprise, the wolf couldn't muster enough strength to fight.

Ruben became man again, right there in Willow's arms.

One thing all Shifters knew was that the moment they changed back to flesh, adrenaline blazed through the veins like lightning. The human body reacted with instant arousal. This would become glaringly obvious the instant the change was finished.

As the animal changed shape with her soft hands still buried in its fur, Willow let out a soft cry. To her credit, she didn't try to jump up or dislodge the beast rapidly shifting from wolf to man.

"Ruben?" she asked, sounding uncertain but markedly unafraid.

At first he could not speak; still locked within the throes of the change, he could only growl.

As his bones settled back into place and the fur disappeared, he tried again to force words past his still evolving throat.

Then. Man. Completely.

With one swift motion, he rolled away from her, landing on his soft human belly in the cushioning leaves. His powerful erection under him, hard and aching.

Though he knew she had to have seen it, at least he could lay this way, breathing the scent of the wild forest, until his arousal subsided. Breathing hard, he closed his eyes and willed her to go away, to leave him to come to grips with the act of being human once again.

This time, the horrible sense of loss he always felt seemed to have vanished. Puzzled, he tried to understand, but though the wolf normally lurked just under the surface, the beast appeared to have retreated further into the dark recesses of Ruben's psyche.

"Ruben?" she said again. "Are you all right?"

Evidently she wasn't going away until he answered her.

"I'm fine," he ground out, his body pulsing with need. "Please. Go back to your tent."

"But—"

"Go. Away."

If he expected her to comply, he was more delusional than he'd realized. Instead, she did the opposite, crawling across the pine needles and dead leaves until she reached him. This time, she tangled her hand in his hair rather than his pelt. This time, she pressed her body close as she stroked and caressed the man rather than the wolf.

And this time, when she pressed her soft lips against his jaw, he lost all control.

He rolled, pulling her down on top of him, pressing himself into her. She let out a soft cry, one of encouragement rather than fear, and impossibly he felt himself grow even larger, even harder.

He locked her in his arms. Now fully man, they gazed into each other's eyes. Naked, his skin tingled where she touched him, and he dimly realized her clothing was a barrier that would have to go.

As if she had the exact same thought, she pulled her sleeping shift over her head, letting it drop to the forest floor. Naked, her full breasts gleamed in the predawn light, her dusky pebbled nipples inviting his tongue.

Her grip tightened as he took her into his mouth. She arched her back, making a soft sound of pleasure. Though he wouldn't have believed he could get harder, the sudden surge of desire had him stretching to huge dimensions, throbbing.

When she closed her small hand around the hard length of him, he jolted, nearly losing his already tenuous control. Her fingers seared him, the movement hot and sensuous, pleasure and pain combining in her touch.

Just when he thought he could bear no more, she rose up and settled over him, taking him deep inside her. The moist heat of her body surrounded him, welcome and titillating.

He writhed beneath her, pushing deeper. Her hands came up, tangled in his hair as she pulled him to her. He crushed her mouth with his, blazing hot, his tongue mimicking the movements of his body.

Flesh silky against flesh, they moved together in exquisite harmony. Blazing, a bright torch soaring in an explosion of need and desire.

When she shattered, her climax pulsing around him, he gasped in agony, trying to hold on to the last shreds of his control. Failing, he crested on the wave of a release so powerful he swore the earth moved under his body.

Panting, they clung to each other, wordless and awestruck. He didn't pretend not to know what this met—his kind found their true mate only once.

But Willow? She was Sidhe, neither human nor Pack, and she came from a place that existed in another space and time.

Shoving away his disquieting thoughts, he kissed the

smooth swell of her shoulder. She made a sound, a quiet murmur of contentment, then reached for her sleep shift. Smoothing the garment, she dropped it over her head and smiled at him.

"I brought you peace," she said. "Your wolf is very troubled. I can help him, I think, if you'll let me."

Whatever he'd expected, it hadn't been this. He opened and closed his mouth, biting back the instinctively harsh words he'd been about to say.

He didn't need her help. He hadn't asked for it, and for her to offer... With a sigh, he dropped his head.

This was something that would require thought. For now, he had other, more pressing issues.

Pushing to his feet, conscious of his nakedness, he held out his hand to help her up. "Come on. We'd better get back to camp before we're missed."

Eyes huge in her heart-shaped face, she bit her lip but did as he'd asked.

They walked a few feet, the silence feeling absurdly loud, before he found the right words to say.

"I'm sorry," he told her. "I hope I didn't hurt you."

"Not with your body," she quipped, sounding almost angry. "I came to you of my own free will. But your refusal to let me help you—that's another story. I heal wounded animals. That's what I do. And I can help you, I sense it." Her voice trembled, dancing around on the edge of tears.

Chest tight, he stopped and turned to face her. "Despite the fact that I think you mean your offer with sincerity, I'm not a charity case," he said. "I'm here only to find this killer and bring him to justice. Nothing more, nothing less."

Slowly she nodded, the unhappiness that shadowed her beautiful face making him want to kiss her again and drive every bit of the darkness away.

Instead, he squeezed her shoulder. "I may just take you up on that offer some day."

"I bet you will," she said, the bitterness in her tone muffled but still discernible. Ruben didn't comment on it as he walked her back to her tent. He waited until she was safely inside before returning to his pallet and dressing as he prepared to meet the day.

# Chapter 14

Chad heard Ruben leave the camp. In fact he was up getting dressed in preparation of following him when he saw the huge wolf skulking in the shadows where the human prince had been. Rubbing his eyes to clear them, he blinked and looked again. The beast was gone. Magic? He stood still, searching for the familiar tingle of skin and raising of hair. Instead, he felt nothing.

Not magic then. He debated going off into the woods to see what Ruben was up to, but the thought of that huge wolf roaming nearby was deterrent enough.

Instead, he waited.

Bored after about thirty minutes, Chad considered giving up his watch and going to sleep. Just as he was about to push to his feet, Willow exited her tent. With her slender shape silhouetted in the moonlight, she looked ethereal and beautiful. He watched her and felt a powerful stirring in his loins.

Unaware of him watching, she gazed off into the woods,

head tilted as though listening. When she began to move, he stood. And when she disappeared into the trees, he went after her.

Back in her tent, Willow sat down hard, then winced at the unexpected soreness. Her body felt tender in places she hadn't even known it was possible to hurt. But more than that—her soul felt wounded.

Meanwhile, Tatiana continued to sleep, snoring softly.

Now at last, she knew what it was about Ruben that drew her to him. She'd always been drawn to wounded things. A bird with a broken wing, a mountain lion cub too timid to hunt. Whether of the body or the psyche, she'd always been able to heal with a single touch.

When she'd been a child, she'd regarded this gift as her magic. Until she'd tried to tell her mother and Millicent had scornfully told her what she claimed to be able to do was absolutely *not* magic. In fact, Willow had been told in no uncertain terms never to mention this again.

That didn't matter to her. The wild creatures of the forest and the plains had come to her with their needs. She'd always been able to sense their pain.

And never, until today, had she been turned away.

But then, Ruben wasn't all animal. The wolf was only half of his nature. The human had refused her help, not the beast.

That didn't make it hurt any less.

Outside, she heard sounds of others stirring about. The sunrise had begun to lighten the sky. With a sigh, she checked her clothing and smoothed down her hair.

"Tatiana," she said softly, bracing herself for the backlash. Her sister had never been a morning person.

"Wake up. We're going to be breaking camp soon."

"Go away." Without opening her eyes, Tatiana waved her hand in the air as though warding off a mosquito.

From past experience, Willow knew how this went. Instead of putting herself through it, she left the tent and went in search of Eric. He could deal with waking his fiancée.

She found him wandering around in search of his brother Chad. Eyes still dazed with sleep, he reminded her of her sister. Completely nonfunctional.

Perfect.

Taking his arm, she steered him in the direction of Tatiana's tent. "I need your assistance," she said, fluttering her eyelashes. "Will you help me?"

Either too befuddled with sleep or too unobservant to notice how unlike herself she was acting, Eric gave a slow nod. "What do you want?"

"Help me wake Tatiana up." She gave him a small shove in the direction of the entrance to the tent.

He frowned and looked perplexed. "I think it'd be better if you—"

"I can't." She put on her best poor-pitiful-me face. "I have too much to do." Taking a deep breath, she dashed off in the direction of the horses, as though she had to make sure they were fed and watered.

When she glanced back over her shoulder, Eric was just ducking into the tent. She braced herself for the scream that was sure to follow. Any minute now...

Instead, she heard only silence. And Eric didn't pop back out like she'd expected. Interesting. Maybe theirs would actually be the one arranged marriage that would work.

Humming to herself, she checked on the horses, making sure they were feeling well and had enough to eat and drink. As a group, they had appeared pretty well satisfied, glad to have been able to escape their humdrum lives inside the palace stables.

Now, something had changed. The horses were uneasy.

Willow tried to calm them and attempted to find out what had gotten them so spooked.

Their answer so shocked her that at first she only stood, fixated on nothing in the distance, trying to think.

They were terrified of two people. Ruben and Chad.

In Ruben, they sensed his inner wolf, a predator toward their kind. She did her best to communicate the truth—that Ruben was no danger to them, whether in human form or lupine.

Chad however, was a different story. The horses feared him a hundred times more than any wolf. They considered him a monster.

Moving slowly, she cast a casual look back in the direction of the tents. Chad sat alone close to the fire, working on a piece of wood with his knife. Tatiana and Eric had not reappeared. And Ruben had gone into the woods. Since he was the only one who ate meat, he had to hunt his own. He'd gone off in search of fresh game.

Again she studied Chad. He looked ordinary and calm, his masculine beauty more subdued and somehow reassuring. Not at all like the monster that the horses believed him to be. Chad. Are you sure, she asked the animals silently. Are you certain about him?

The horses couldn't use words so instead they gave her images instead. According to them, Chad was capable of a thousand subtle cruelties. Too tight reins, held in such a way that the bit cut into the horse's mouth. A whip used indiscriminately, and in the same place so that it caused welts. The animals sensed violence in him, and claimed they feared the day when it would erupt.

What about Ruben, she asked, thinking of the huge wolf he could become. Such a beast was a natural enemy of the horse.

Oddly enough, they preferred Ruben and his wolf. The lupine beast was familiar and would act in ways that were in accord with nature. Though the wolf had sharp teeth and claws, he did not kill for pleasure but only for food.

The horses believed Chad enjoyed violence.

She knew what she must do. Tell Ruben. He'd know what to do.

Leaving the horses with a promise to do what she could, she strolled with studied casualness back to the camp. Since it wasn't safe to go out in the woods in search of a hunter, she'd have to wait until Ruben returned. She took a seat on a fallen log well away from Chad and sighed.

"Good morning."

Chad. She turned slowly, to give herself time to hide her instinctive—and unwarranted—reaction. "Good morning."

"How are you feeling today?" He sat down next to her, close enough that their shoulders bumped. Too close.

She scooted away before answering. "Why do you ask?"

"That's not an answer," he chided, the way his voice purred sending a shiver of revulsion through her. "I ask because I'm worried about you. You look a little pale."

"Do I?" She doubted that. Perhaps it was best to play along. "Now that you mention it, I do feel a tiny bit fatigued."

"Perhaps you should imitate your sister and take a nap," he suggested, the hint of slyness in his smile telling her he knew she'd do no such thing. Especially since they both knew Eric was still in the tent with Tatiana.

Chad placed his hand lightly on Willow's shoulder, making her tense up so much that he couldn't help but feel it. Shrugging off his hand, she stood and stepped away from him. To her dismay, he stood, as well.

"Let's walk," he suggested, both his voice and his expression oozing friendliness.

"Oh, I can't," she demurred. "I really have a lot to do before we ride out."

He grabbed her arm. This time, his grip felt more forceful than friendly. "I think we should."

Futilely, she tried to pull away. "Chad—"

"I saw you last night."

She froze, though her heart skipped a beat. "I see." How much had he seen? No doubt enough to break their tentative betrothal. She couldn't blame him, either. If the situation were reversed, she'd do exactly the same thing.

She opened her mouth, but nothing came out.

"I think we have something to talk about, don't you?" he asked, flashing his teeth in what appeared more grimace than smile.

Of course she went with him. After all, what choice did she have? She had to find out what exactly Chad had seen and worse, what he intended to do with that knowledge.

For a moment, they walked without speaking. Surrounded by birdsong and the sounds of the morning forest, to anyone watching they would have appeared simply as a young couple out for a stroll.

Only the tension that had Willow holding herself stiffly would have told an astute observer a different story.

Finally, Chad broke the silence. "I saw you playing with a giant wolf."

Swallowing hard, Willow nodded. "I have an affinity for wild animals. I always have."

This time, when he flashed a smile, he didn't bother to hide his ferocity. "And wild men? Do you have an affinity for them, as well?"

Had he seen Ruben change from wolf to human? Worse, had he been watching as they made love? If he had, it would be more than an appalling intrusion of privacy. It would be… desecration of something sacred.

"What exactly do you mean?" she asked carefully.

"Ruben," he said, still smiling that same fierce smile. "I mean Ruben. When I said I saw you, I meant I saw you with him."

Eric raised his head as they approached. His petulant expression spoke of his dissatisfaction.

"What's going on?" Eric asked, using the booming voice of a king-to-be. He stood, shoulders back, head up, turning in a slow circle. "Whoever has done this to us, I demand you show yourselves immediately."

*"Demand?"* A bodiless voice spoke.

Again that feeling of electrical current arcing through the air. A quick glance at the others showed they felt it, too.

"Magic," Willow mouthed, looking apprehensive. The other three Brights appeared focused, as though by concentrating they could pinpoint the source.

A small man, his hair and skin the color of midnight, materialized in front of them. With his dark twinkling eyes and boisterous energy, he appeared both young and old. As they stared at him, his countenance changed from wizened to youthful and back again.

"Welcome," he said, sounding anything but hospitable.

Ruben and Willow exchanged a glance. "Where are we?" Ruben asked, keeping his tone respectful just in case.

"You have reached the Land of the Shadows," the little man intoned, his entire body beginning to shimmer in a way that reminded Ruben of the moment before shape-shifting. Sparkles of light danced in the breeze. "We brought you here. There is one in whom we have much interest."

"Who?" Eric demanded, the expression on his face showing he was positive it was him. "Which of us is the one and why?"

The glimmers of color grew brighter, so bright that it hurt to gaze upon them and Ruben had to look away. When he looked back, the man had vanished.

Everyone stood still, stunned speechless.

Eric cleared his throat, about to speak again. Chad shook

his head, stopping him, before looking at Ruben and then Willow.

"Now what?" he asked sullenly. "This was your expedition. Somehow, you've managed to land us in the middle of enemy territory."

Ruben didn't bother to point out that the other men were supposed to have been his guides. "According to that man, we were brought here. I can only assume by magic. Since we're here, does anyone have any suggestions?" he asked carefully.

Expression shuttered, Chad shook his head. Eric appeared to be considering his question. "Whoever captured us brought us here, tied and hooded. That was a poor use of magical ability. Then they released us and sent someone to make sure we understand where we are. For what purpose? What do they hope to gain?"

"Maybe they want to help us find Ruben's killer," Chad put in nastily. "Any Bright who sought refuge here would stick out like a sore thumb." He gave Willow a pointed look to underscore his point.

"Like I did at home?" Willow asked, sounding amused rather than hurt. "If you're going to insult me, Chad, you'd better try a more direct approach."

When Chad opened his mouth to reply, Ruben stepped in. "We don't have time for squabbling. I'm sure they had their reasons, even if we don't know what they are."

"I think I know," Willow grimaced. "I think they didn't want us to see the location of their portal."

"Portal? You mean like the magical doorway you used to get to my world?"

She nodded. "Exactly. Because the Shadow lands are nowhere near my family's. The only way they could get us here this quickly has to be with a portal."

"Thus the hoods and the bonds," Eric finished. "At least now all of this makes sense."

"Except for one thing." Chad glanced from Willow to Ruben, his expression pensive. "We still don't know why."

"I have a feeling we're about to find out," Ruben told him. "We've got to get moving. At least they left us our horses. That's something."

"Yes, but it'd be even better if we knew the way back to the portal. It's a long ride home without it," Willow put in.

Chad made a rude snort. "I'm sure you can find it. You seem to have a knack for such things."

Tatiana, who until now had been uncharacteristically silent, yawned. "I don't know about the rest of you, but I think we need to ride for the nearest castle. Royalty carries privileges."

"Not with Shadows," Chad said.

"How do you know?" Tatiana rounded on him. "Have you ever dealt with them before?"

"No," he admitted.

"I didn't think so," she rushed on, before he could ask if she had. "Royals don't turn away other royals. I'm heir to SouthWard and he is heir of EastWard," she said, jerking her head to indicate Eric. "That ought to count for something."

"Maybe in your world," Chad began.

Tatiana silenced him with a regal wave and a harsh glare. "You, like my sister, are not directly in line for the throne. Since you aren't an heir, you know nothing."

As Chad's expression darkened, Eric finally moved to intervene. Apparently worried there would be an all-out war, he clapped his hand on his brother's shoulder and pulled him close, murmuring something too low for the rest of them to hear.

When Eric moved away, Chad once again wore his familiar bored expression. "What do you want to do?" he asked Ruben, only the ice glittering in his brilliant purple eyes giving him away.

Deliberately Ruben smiled. "I agree with Tatiana. Let's ride for the first castle we see."

Without waiting for their replies, he strode over to their horses and located his mount. After checking to make sure the saddle was still cinched tightly, he untied the gelding and swung his leg up over the animal's broad back.

Next to him, Willow did the same. He sensed her curiosity, the tentative desire to at least meet those people whom she was said to resemble.

To his surprise, Tatiana was the next to come forward. She untied her horse and mounted with the same easy grace that seemed part of her nature. "Are you coming?" she asked the two EastWard brothers.

Eric looked from Chad to Tatiana and back again. "I still don't understand how we ended up in Shadow Territory," he groused. "The boundaries are definitely not within one or two days' riding distance. Even though they attacked us and knocked us out, there's no way one man had enough magic to transport us. This never should have happened."

"Unless he, whoever he might be, has stronger magic than any we've ever known. Or more than one Shadow was involved," Chad drawled. "That has to be the case."

"I would have sensed it." Of course Tatiana dismissed his statement, even though it was the only realistic solution. "We all would have."

Shifting his weight uneasily, Rubin flashed the other man a flat smile. Chad remained stone-faced. Neither he nor Eric had budged.

Finally, Ruben shrugged. "Fine. Stay here or come with us. Either way, we're riding out."

Ruben turned his horse and began to ride off. Willow was at his side and Tatiana right behind them. He kept an eye on the other men, glancing over his shoulder, to make sure they didn't try any tricks.

Finally, the two brothers moved. Side by side, they retrieved their horses and climbed aboard, keeping to a fair distance behind the others. Tatiana glanced back, then slowed her horse so they could catch up with her. She maneuvered into a position in between them, smiling prettily.

"Is that true?" Ruben asked Willow. "Can you sense when magic is being used?"

"Most times, yes." She glanced warily at the others when she answered. "However, we know nothing about the parameters of Shadows and their magic. It might be completely different for them."

She'd barely finished speaking when they heard a loud clap, like thunder. They all glanced up at the misty gray sky.

When they looked back down, they found they'd been surrounded by armed guards on horseback, and judging from the hostile expression they wore, they weren't friendly.

Eric raised his chin and opened his mouth, no doubt to spew some sort of haughty orders. Exchanging a quick look with Ruben, Chad nudged his mount sideways into Eric, knocking him off balance and effectively silencing him.

While Eric was momentarily distracted, Ruben spoke for the group. "What have we done?"

"You've trespassed on royal land," the apparent leader said. "We're here to escort you to see the king."

"We didn't trespass willingly," Ruben told them. "Someone attacked us, knocked us out and when we came to, we found ourselves here."

If the leader believed them, he gave no sign. "We will ride with you until we reach the castle," he said.

Then, herding Ruben's little band like sheep, they moved out.

# Chapter 15

A good half hour passed while they rode in silence, the horses' hoof beats on the moist earth the only sound.

Ruben and Willow kept close, almost within touching distance, while the other three rode behind them. Surrounded on all four sides by the armed guards, they couldn't have made a break if they wanted to.

And, though he had no magic to speak of, Ruben did have his gut instinct. Right now, his gut was telling him that whatever was about to happen would be a good thing for Willow, possibly not so great for the others.

"I have no desire to interact with Shadows," Eric intoned imperiously.

"They probably have no desire to interact with you either," Tatiana said, surprising Ruben. Glancing back, he saw from the speculative expression Chad wore that she'd surprised him, as well. Even Willow cracked a half smile.

"Are you ready to meet some Shadows?" Ruben asked Willow.

No, she wasn't, he could tell by the flicker of panic that crossed her mobile face. "I guess so." She sounded miserable.

Ruben studied her, stunned anew by the overwhelming urge to comfort her. "It might not be so bad, you know. It could be a great experience, getting to know your people. Despite how you've been raised, half of your heritage is here with them."

"What do you two keep whispering about up there?" Tatiana asked, the edge of her irritation making her voice whiny.

"They're probably talking about you," Eric sneered. Then he kicked his horse and rode ahead of her, leaving Chad at her side. Grimacing, Chad glared at his brother before shooting Tatiana a look daring her to speak. He made no secret about being unhappy about this situation.

"Come on," the guard captain ordered, nudging his horse into a jog. Reluctantly, they all followed suit. The farther they went into the valley, the heavier the fog grew.

Ruben's skin pricked with unease. Soon, the mist was so thick he could scarcely see five feet in front of him. If not for the group of guards behind them, if they let the leaders get too far ahead, they'd lose sight of them and it'd be a simple matter of vanishing into the mist. Even if they'd been able to do this, Ruben doubted it would work. He knew from experience that life was anything but simple.

It seemed the Land of the Shadows truly was…in the shadows. And mist. Damp, dreary, chilly mist. He would much rather have ridden in the rain.

Before too long, they were all soaked. The horses were spooked, ears twitching and eyes wide, ready to spook at the slightest provocation. He glanced at Willow, who nodded, letting him know her mount had told her in no uncertain terms that she did not like this place. The horse and all her companion animals longed for wide-open meadows, fresh-cut hay and the warm sunlight of home.

Ruben could definitely relate to that. The sense of uneasiness wasn't confined only to the horses. Everyone seemed jumpy, jittery. Ruben took deep breaths, calming himself. Beside him, he noticed Willow doing the same.

As they proceeded cautiously forward, gradually faint sounds drifted toward them in the mist.

As they inched along, Ruben listened carefully. Music and snatches of laughter. He reached over and touched Willow's arm. "Do you hear that?"

She nodded. "What is it?"

"Sounds like we're getting close to a town."

"You know what? Though I know this is going to sound ridiculous, that floors me. For some reason I hadn't expected the people of the Shadows to live regular, normal lives similar to the Brights."

"What had you expected? Them to live in caves and underground, only emerging in starlight to cast their wicked spells?"

Expression sheepish, she looked down. "Put that way, it sounds even sillier."

"So do you think it's possible that they are, as Tatiana thought, exactly like the Brights, with gilded palaces and thrones draped in precious metals?"

"I don't know." She shrugged. "To be honest, when I thought of them, I'd always pictured them as savages, content to live in dark squalor, full of evil intent and with below-average intelligence."

"Why?" he asked, stunned.

"Because that's what we're taught as children. The Shadows are our Boogeymen." She swallowed hard, her pained expression revealing she'd faced a bitter truth. "I'm stunned that I, who'd always prided myself on my open mind, could be so bigoted and so close-minded."

"Especially about your own people," Tatiana put in nastily, letting them know she'd been eavesdropping. "I mean really, Willow. If the rumors are true, you're half Shadow. You're not like that, so why should they be?"

"Point taken, Tatiana," Willow said quietly. "Clearly, I was wrong."

Her sister found that funny, which made Ruben want to lash out at her. But watching Willow wallow in her own misery made him bite his tongue.

When she realized Ruben studied her intently, Willow blushed. He nudged his horse so close to hers that his leg brushed against hers. "Don't worry so much about the small stuff," he murmured. "We all learn lessons as we go along. You're no different."

At first, she only nodded, still lost in her thoughts. He stayed by her side, keeping her in his sights and marveling at her quiet beauty. Finally, she glanced at him, appearing a bit surprised to find him staring.

"What?" she asked, smiling slightly and making him wish he could kiss her.

"Something just occurred to me, thanks to your sister," he said. "Since everyone seems to think you're part Shadow, do you want to try and find your father while we're here?"

"Find my...?" Various emotions chased themselves across her features. At first, dumbfounded and shocked and appalled, all she could do was stand with her mouth open. "I hadn't even thought of..."

"Of course you have," he continued, relentless. "How could you not? We're here, in his land. You have to wonder who he is, what he's like. It's human nature."

"Maybe it is but," she reminded him, "I'm not human."

"Even so," he persisted. "You must be curious."

"Maybe a little. But I'm more interested in helping you find the killer."

"The killer isn't here," he told her. "We all know that. We'd have to go back to SouthWard to find him."

Stunned, she asked, "Then why are we still here?"

Flashing a wry smile, he touched her arm. "It's not like we had a choice, remember?"

To his surprise, she grinned back. "You do have a point."

"About your father?"

Her smile faded. "I'll have to think about it."

He took that as promising, especially since she hadn't refused outright.

Surrounded by soldiers, they were led on a silent march, down a path into a murky valley, where even the flowers seemed mere spirits of actual plants. A low mist shrouded everything—sky and forest and earth—and seemed almost tangible, as though conjured to life by a spell from a long-dead sorcerer.

Despite the gloomy appearance, Ruben did not sense true evil or danger. But then again, he reflected ruefully, he was not only without the magic these people took for granted, but he was damaged. A wounded Shifter, afraid to trust the senses of either half of his dual nature.

The mood among his little group grew bleaker. Even the horses appeared listless, as though their energy had been leached by the overwhelming dreariness of the landscape.

When the castle appeared, seeming to spring from the earth in a maelstrom of blackness, someone gasped. Not Willow, who despite everything had remained resolutely at his side. A quick glance over his shoulder showed Tatiana, clinging to a disinterested Chad, eyes wide, practically quivering from fear.

The closer they came, the more menacing the place seemed. The breeze even smelled differently. He swore he detected the salty scent of the sea mingled with the ever-present cloyingly damp mist. The ocean smell reminded him of Teslinko, though his home had been sunny and warm, and he felt a sharp pang of homesickness.

Willow shivered, wrapping her arms around herself in a futile attempt to get warm. Because of the moisture in the air, their clothing had grown soaked and remained that way, no matter how far they rode or how the breeze gusted and blew. Unhappiness hung over them like a miserable black cloud and their physical discomfort only strengthened it.

And he was no closer to finding the killer. Again, Ruben sighed. He didn't really need to be here; in fact, he was wasting precious time wandering these dark lands. The one who'd traveled to Teslinko and murdered a servant was one of the Brights. He didn't believe the killer would be so foolish as to travel here, where his golden hair would stick out like a sore thumb.

Again, he thought of Chad. Mentally, he reviewed his memories of the man he'd seen briefly in the woods, following Willow. Tall, golden hair, purple eyes. An arrogant, chiseled face.

Could that have been Chad? Was it possible Chad actually was the one Ruben hunted?

A quick glance at the other man, and he decided no. No killer would be foolish enough to attach himself to the one who hunted him, placing himself constantly in contact with someone who might recognize him.

Therefore, Chad could not be the killer. Ruben must continue to search until he found him.

In any other situation, Ruben would have found a way to escape and gone on about his task. Instead, he'd remain here for one reason and one reason only. Willow. She'd been so transparent with her need to connect, to have people, a family of her own, despite vehement denials. This he could never refuse her. He suspected the others were intrigued, which explained while they hadn't yet rebelled.

"Don't worry," Willow murmured, tugging on his sleeve. "I'm really good at sensing danger. Right now, I sense nothing."

No doubt, she thought he was afraid. Gazing down at her, he allowed himself to be distracted by her soft, kissable lips. Then, as her eyes widened and her pupils dilated, he swallowed, bringing himself back to the situation at hand. He nodded, unsure of whether or not to trust her instincts.

A screech came from above them, loud and piercing and shocking. Tatiana let out a little yelp, as though she'd been stung. Even Ruben and Chad jumped. Only Willow remained perfectly calm and steady.

She lifted one arm, bracing her small body as a huge bird of prey landed on her, exactly as if she'd summoned it.

The hawk swiveled its head, fierce and wild and glorious. Inside, Ruben's wolf strained against invisible bonds, wanting to snap at the bird.

All watched in stunned silence at Willow stroked the bird's feathers, crooning wordless, nonsensical sounds in a soothing voice.

When the hawk nestled in close, delicately moving Willow's hair with its fierce beak, several of the guards began to mutter. Neither Willow nor her winged friend paid any heed. In fact, as she and the bird interacted, Ruben knew she was doing her thing and communicating with the hawk.

One of the soldiers raised his bow and fitted it with an arrow.

"No," the captain barked an order. "Stand down."

Instead, the soldier pulled back the bow. Ruben didn't think—he launched himself at the man, connecting in time to send the arrow harmlessly into the sky.

The hawk screeched. Huge wings flapping, it launched itself up, the force of its flight knocking Willow off her horse onto her back on the forest floor. She writhed in pain, the breath knocked out of her.

Cursing, Ruben pushed himself off of the stunned soldier, shoving the man away and leaving him for his commander to deal with. He rushed to Willow's side and helped her to her feet. At first she hunched over, heaving as she struggled to draw her breath. Gradually, she straightened, her cough subsiding. She wiped at her streaming eyes and sniffed.

"Are you all right?" he asked, brushing the leaves and pine needles from her hair.

Eyes huge and face far too pale, she nodded.

Chad made a rude sound and sauntered over, Tatiana still clinging to him like a leech.

"What the shades was that?" he asked, glancing up at the stars as though he expected an attack from above. "That bird acted like your personal hawk. Is that your form of magic?"

Tatiana laughed. "My sister has no magic," she said, her mocking tone cutting. "Not even enough to call a wild bird."

Chad narrowed his gaze, looking from one sister to the other. "Is that true?" he asked, his tone demanding.

Willow just smiled sadly and turned away. When she began moving forward again, the entire armed escort snapped to attention. Then, as if she'd given a verbal command, they fell into place, surrounding the three Brights and Ruben on their way to the castle.

Whatever secrets the hawk had divulged to Willow, apparently she now felt compelled to continue on to the dark castle. Despite the fact that he had no hope of finding the killer here—the suspect was Bright, after all—Ruben knew he had to keep her safe.

The closer they got to the castle, the grimmer it appeared. If King Puck and Queen Millicent's palace had been over-the-top glitz, this castle could be considered the polar opposite. Where everything had sparkled and shone at the home of the Bright, here the absence of light was what made the place notable. The grim stone appeared to devour anything bright or shiny. What little light there was seemed to sink into its inky blackness.

At the thought, Ruben glanced at Willow and her sister, hoping that didn't apply to Sidhe, as well. Surely, the palace wouldn't devour them.

They rode to a stop and at a signal, the entire regiment of guards dismounted. They motioned to Ruben and his party to do the same.

Slowly, they all followed suit. As soon as everyone's feet were on the ground, black-clad groomsmen appeared and led their horses away.

Meanwhile, their armed escorts continued to look straight ahead, unblinking. Ruben began to wonder if some sort of magic compelled or hypnotized them.

No sooner had he finished the thought when the massive obsidian doors swung open. Inside, a yawning hole of blackness. Of course.

"Don't you people use any kind of light?" Ruben asked, directing his question at the captain of the guard. Predictably, the soldier didn't answer. In fact, each and every one of them continued to stand at stiff attention, though their faces had regained some color and motion. They waited as though they expected someone to exit the castle and inspect their ranks. Which meant, no doubt, that someone would.

A sense of expectation hung in the air, nearly visible.

Willow gripped his arm. He saw she had the same rapt expectation on her lovely face. A quick glance showed everyone, from the soldiers to Eric and Chad, had the exact same look.

A moment later, he saw why. A tall man, hair as black as the night sky, strode out of the mouth of the castle. Dressed all in black, the only spot of color was the blood red lining of his long cloak.

At the sight of him, Ruben's wolf growled. Their soldier escort immediately dropped to their knees. Only Willow, Ruben, Chad and Tatiana remained standing.

Ruben braced himself for a fight. A quick glance at Chad showed the Bright man had also adopted battle stance.

Willow stood frozen, in obvious shock. Her sister however, was not so bold. After one quick look at the dark man, Tatiana dropped to the ground in a dead faint.

Though brave Willow trembled violently, she held her ground. As the Shadow king approached, she held her head high, like a queen about to receive a supplicant.

Ruben admired her courage even as he feared for her safety. He tried to go to her, shocked when he found himself unable to move. When he glanced over at Chad and Eric, he noticed they both struggled futilely beside him. Whatever magical spell had gripped him had touched them, as well.

He did not care. He would not give in. This was Willow, and he would not abandon her when she needed him most. With a huge shudder, he pushed through, feeling the very atmosphere tear as he broke free.

Before the dark king reached her, Ruben stepped in front, placing himself squarely between Willow and danger.

To his shock and disbelief, Willow pushed her way around him, so that she once again stood, alone and unprotected, to wait for their enemy's approach.

"He is not our enemy," Willow said, again as though she'd read his mind. Her beautiful dark eyes glinted—with unshed tears?

Ruben looked more closely at the Shadow king. Something about him seemed familiar, but it wasn't until he compared his features with Willow's that he realized what he saw. Similarity. Willow had the same chin, the same skin tone and the same almond-shaped eyes.

Howling hounds. Was this man Willow's birth father? He hadn't expected it to be this soon or this easy. Stepping back, he decided to wait and see.

Willow stared at the man who had sent the hawk to find her and who, also according to the hawk, had sired her. She waited for a jolt of recognition. But when she met the tall man's caramel-colored eyes, so like her own, she felt...nothing. No immediate sense of kinship, no feeling that fate had somehow worked a miracle by bringing them together. Not even the lurking sense of completeness that she'd half hoped would finally click into place.

The king glanced once at the others, then his cryptic gaze settled finally on her.

"Welcome to NorthWard," the tall man said, his aristocratic features showing no hint that he knew who she was. "It's been many long years since a Bright has graced our shores."

Shores? For the first time she realized they must be near an ocean. As she was about to speak, Eric and Tatiana snapped out of their trance. They jostled each other while rushing forward, vying to claim recognition as the head of their respective families.

They both began speaking at once, their words tumbling over each other in a jumble. The dark king waited one heartbeat, two, then raised his hand and silenced them as effectively as if they'd been gagged.

"Someone will show you to your rooms," he told the others. Once again he looked at Willow and this time, he held out his arm for her to take. "Walk with me," he said.

Hesitating briefly, she placed her hand on his arm and went with him.

As they walked, he talked. He spoke of nothing of conse-
quence; rather he described his gardens to her in such lush
and lavish detail she could almost smell the blooms. She got
a sense he was testing her, sounding her out as though a short
conversation would give him an insight into her soul.

She played along, nodding and smiling politely, though
she volunteered nothing about herself. They strolled down
long, empty hallways, eerily similar to those in her home
except for the stark lack of color. After his garden, he spoke
of pets and land and horses. Finally, he got around to telling
her about his family.

He and his queen had three children, two boys and a girl.
The eldest and heir had recently married and his wife was
expecting a child in a few months. Willow caught her breath
at the thought that she might have half brothers and a half
sister, but until this man broached the subject, she wouldn't
even allow herself to consider the possibility.

Finally, he stopped in front of a door. It was, like all the
others, constructed from a single piece of black obsidian.

"This is your room," he said, smiling slightly. "I'll leave
you here to rest and freshen up. Someone will come and get
you for a more formal audience, at which time you may meet
the rest of my family, if you like."

Taking a deep breath, she wished she had the courage to
finally ask if they were her family, too.

Instead, she smiled back and thanked him, then entered
the room she'd been given, letting the door close softly behind her.

Alone, she realized her hands were shaking. She didn't
know what to think. Was this man, this king, her father, as the
hawk had claimed? If so, why did he not acknowledge who
they were to each other? Was he testing her for some reason?

Finally she turned and studied her room. The bed, despite
the unrelenting black of the fluffy comforter, looked soft and

warm. Too tired to think straight, she crawled between the sheets and let the welcome oblivion of sleep claim her.

Ruben was too keyed up to sleep, so he decided to explore the castle. He hadn't been given strict instructions to remain in his room or anything. He found a flowing cloak with a hood and settled it around his shoulders. Since Willow had once told him that the Brights would not welcome him in their land, he could only imagine how the Shadows would feel.

The empty hallways had an eerie feel to them, enhanced by the monochromatic coloring. No stranger to palace life, he kept expecting to encounter someone, anyone. A harried servant, a bored socialite, the requisite drunk uncle. Instead, his footsteps echoed off the granite walls, reinforcing his solitude.

With each turn, the endless expanse of hallway stretched out before him, dark walls studded by black doors. Finally, he came to a landing with a massive, two-sided staircase. He could either go up or down.

He chose down. And as he took the steps two at a time, gradually the hum of voices came to him, letting them know there was a part of this castle still full of life.

When he reached another landing, he realized the sounds came from still another level down. The curve of the massive staircase made it impossible to see below, so he continued on. Once he stepped onto the next landing, he saw a crush of people gathered around a set of double doors at the end of yet another infernally long hallway. He hurried to join them, not certain what they were doing, but curious nonetheless.

Though several cast him curious glances, no one questioned him as he took his place in the line of people pressing through the doors. The tide of bodies carried him inside, disgorging him as everyone headed in their own direction.

He glanced around and realized he was in the throne room. He thought of the one at home, remembering how he'd compared it to the SouthWard room. Then, he'd believed that difference to be great, but the difference between Teslinko and SouthWard was nothing compared to this.

The Shadows' throne room, like everything else in the palace, was dark, very nearly sinister, whereas the Brights' had been over-the-top, glittering, gaudily, bright. The sharp contrast between the two throne rooms was as remarkable as the difference in the castle itself. Lit solely by giant iron candelabras, the black marble floors gleamed, reflecting back the candlelight which gave the room a gloomy, surreal appearance.

Trying to blend in with the others would be an exercise in futility, especially since he wore trousers of a soft fawn color and his shirt was a pale blue. The entire court wore dark colors—deep maroon, navy, purple and the ever-present black.

Despite their proclivity to drabness, by contrast the people appeared happy, wearing bright smiles and joyous expressions as they chatted with their neighbors. No one seemed to take notice of him, standing alone and feeling out of place on the edge of several large groups of people.

There was no dais; rather the enormous black obsidian throne sat beside an immense fireplace where only embers smoldered.

The king, dressed all in black, waited regally for his subjects to approach. Briefly, Ruben wondered why his queen didn't hold court with him, then as King Drem began to shimmer right in front of his gaze, he forgot about the question. The king faded and reappeared, solid one moment and ethereal the next. He and the chair appeared to merge, becoming one. Only when he flashed his white smile did people begin to move.

Again, there appeared to be no orderly process. As far as Ruben could tell, if one wished to speak to the king, he or she took their place in line and waited patiently for their chance.

Since he had absolutely nothing to lose, Ruben got in line and mentally prepared to appeal to the king.

When he reached the front of the line, he stepped forward. Taking his cue from the men who'd gone before him, he dropped to one knee in a gesture of respect.

"Welcome again, Prince Ruben of Teslinko," King Drem boomed. "What can I help you with on this glorious day?"

"I need to get back to the land of the Brights," Ruben said, the urgency in his tone making it no less respectful.

"Are you certain?" King Drem regarded him curiously. "What do you seek there that cannot be found here?"

Ruben hoped the tight set of his jaw didn't betray the fact that the Shadow king acted as though he might have to stay here forever. He had to tread carefully, so he drew himself up and looked the other man in the eye. "I hunt a murderer, a killer who crossed from that land to mine and brutally slay one of my servants."

King Drem's dark brows rose in surprise. "A murderer? Among our people? We are not killers, whether Shadow or Bright. That does not seem possible."

"I assure you that it is."

"And you're certain."

"Very certain. My servant is dead. And I saw the man cross the veil. A magical artifact is also missing."

At his words, the king's expression grew pensive. "And the one you seek—is he Bright or Shadow?"

"Bright. The man had golden hair and purple eyes. He was tall, broad shouldered and athletic."

"Like the SouthWard princes?" the Shadow ruler asked, glancing at them.

Eric and Chad, who stood with a group of admiring women, were oblivious.

"Yes," Ruben answered. "Like them. Though something is off with the younger brother."

The king frowned, studying them. "He uses some sort of magical glamour, dulling his appearance."

"Dulling it? Would that change his appearance very much?" Enough to ensure that Ruben would not recognize him? Suspicion and anger burned in his chest.

"It's possible." King Drem shrugged. "Did you think to ask him why?"

"Willow told me. I think it was his peculiar way of courting her."

"Courting? He wishes to marry her?"

"Her parents arranged the match."

"Millicent and that…" Anger flashed across his aristocratic features. "They've arranged for my…for their daughter to marry a man of the East?"

"My mother has little use for me," Willow put in, startling Ruben, who hadn't been aware she'd arrived.

Coincidence? Or had she been summoned? He turned to look at her, crossing his arms to keep from reaching out to her as she took a step closer to the throne.

"I think my existence reminds her of things she'd rather forget," Willow continued. She took a deep breath and raised her chin in that cute way she had, letting Ruben know she was about to do something that, for her, was very brave.

"I need to know something, your Highness," she said, her voice barely quivering. "When you sent word to my room that you wanted to see me, I came willingly, because I must ask you a question."

The king nodded. "Go ahead."

Quickly glancing around at the packed room, she frowned. "Perhaps we should speak in private?"

"I don't see the need." He smiled, making Ruben wonder if he already knew what Willow meant to ask.

"I have no secrets from my people," the king said. "Please. Ask your question."

"Very well." She took a deep breath. "I would like to know if you are my birth father."

## Chapter 16

Abruptly the room went utterly silent. Whispers died down, everyone making no secret of their rapt attention. Willow kept her gaze fixed on the king and told herself that she didn't care. These were not her people. Not yet, at least.

Back straight, heart in her throat, she faced down the man who, for whatever reason, had not only failed to acknowledge her parentage, but had done his best to pretend as if she'd never been born.

It shouldn't have hurt so badly.

He bent his head, his expression pensive. Again, he didn't appear to be ready to give her a direct answer. That was all right. She'd waited her entire life. She could wait a few more minutes. But no more than that.

"I loved your mother once. Twice," King Drem mused, his tone pensive. "And I believed she loved me. We made plans to wed, but right before our wedding, she told me she would be marrying King Puck instead. She wasn't royalty then and to her it was a heady thing, to be made queen of her own people."

Shocked, Willow took pains to conceal it. This was news to her. She'd always believed her mother had come from minor royalty. But then, since Millicent was extremely tight-lipped, Willow hadn't actually known anything of her mother's history, nor she suspected, did Tatiana. Her mother had always been very secretive of her past. Now Willow understood why.

For a moment, an old pain flashed across King Drem's autocratic features. "I loved her," he repeated, his low voice breaking. He looked away, obviously gathering his composure. Out of respect, Willow glanced down at her feet, waiting until he spoke again.

Finally, he cleared his throat. "She had a choice," he continued. "True love and ruling over my people or…her own people. She chose to remain among the Brights."

Eyeing her blankly as though he didn't really see her, the Shadow king appeared lost in thought and memories. His obvious grief, even after all these years, made Willow's chest ache.

She glared at the court, willing them to converse. She hated that they were so bold as to intrude on such a private moment. Everyone in the room strained to listen with no shame.

"That was her reasoning?" Willow asked, pitching her voice as low as she could to keep it from carrying. "The desire to rule the Brights meant more to her than her true love?"

Of course, knowing her mother as she did, Willow could easily imagine this scenario. What she couldn't picture was her mother actually loving someone other than herself. Though, the more King Drem spoke, the more it sounded like she hadn't.

"Millicent didn't want even to try to overcome the prejudices of our two peoples against each other. She would have been an outsider here."

Raising his head, he sighed, gazing off into the distance. "So she chose Puck instead. They married amid great celebration, or so I hear. I, of course, was not invited to the wedding."

"But this was all too long ago to have resulted in my birth," she protested. She fell silent when King Drem raised his hand.

"You have no concept of how difficult this was for her," he said. Though privately Willow doubted that, she nodded and kept her mouth shut.

"Were your two people enemies then?" Ruben asked. He'd come up beside her and, to her surprise, took her hand, wrapping his fingers around hers.

"Not enemies," King Drem said sadly. "We weren't friends, either, but we did do a fair bit of trading between our lands. That has completely stopped these days."

Willow nodded. Though many years had passed, and Shadow handicrafts were few and far between; their knives were valued for their craftsmanship and beauty.

This was all very well and good, but didn't even begin to answer her question. Again, Willow faced the king, drawing strength from Ruben's fingers intertwined with hers.

"If this is the case, did you ever see my mother again?" she asked. "Obviously, you must have."

Focusing on her, slowly King Drem nodded. "I did."

"When?" she persisted, wishing he'd just come out and say she was his daughter.

"Years had passed and Millicent had been married to Puck several years. She had already borne her husband a daughter when she sought me out. She was unhappy and wanted to see if what we'd once had still burned as bright." His throat worked as he swallowed. "I, of course, could never refuse her anything."

So it was true. She waited for a sense of joy that never came.

The king smiled sadly. "Obviously, you were the result of

that union. Foolishly, I thought she'd stay. But her husband wooed her back with jewels and honeyed promises."

She couldn't help but notice he didn't mention the baby she'd been. Willow squared her shoulders and braced herself to hear the rest. She'd come here for the truth and the truth she would have. No matter how much it hurt. "Weren't you curious about me? Did you truly have no desire to see the child you helped create?"

His dark brows came together in a thunderous frown. "Your mother didn't tell you?"

She shook her head. "Tell me what?"

He sighed. "I wondered if you knew. I was forbidden to contact you, as long as you remained in your land. King Puck said he would wage war on NorthWard if I tried to see you or get in touch with you in any way. So I did not."

Her knees almost buckled. Now at last, she understood everything. She felt a rush of anger toward the woman who'd raised her. All these years. Teased by her classmates and her sister, gossiped about by her own people and shunned by the man she'd believed to be her father. All the while wondering why.

And now she knew.

Something of her thoughts must have shown in her face. Leaning forward in his massive black chair, King Drem studied her. "You didn't know?" he asked quietly.

Still gripping Ruben's hand, she took a step closer, bringing him with her. "No. I suspected, when I first met you. But then why were we bound and made to wear hoods? We were brought to you, then. Did you not order this?"

He smiled, looking anything but regretful. "I did not. My closest advisor took it upon himself to do this, as a gift to me."

"I don't understand…"

"Years ago, when I located a portal that led to your lands, I've routinely sent men to check on you and report back to me. This time, you and your friends were riding so close to the portal that he couldn't resist. You were bound and hooded so he could bring you through, without giving away the location."

So she'd been right.

"Do you not worry about my parents' retribution for this?"

Again he smiled. "I don't think they'll be so eager to pursue that now. As far as they will know, unless you tell them differently, you came to me."

She nodded, agreeing silently. "So you did send the hawk—" Horrified at what she'd almost revealed, she bit back the rest of her words.

But the king looked pleased. "You've inherited my gift then, daughter. I too can communicate with wild things."

Stunned, she felt tears well up in her eyes. Not only had he called her *daughter,* but they shared the same abilities. She couldn't believe she was no longer an outcast, no longer alone.

"Come here," King Drem ordered, opening his arms wide. "Come here, my child, my girl."

Letting go of Ruben's hand, she walked into her father's arms.

As she watched from the back of the room, Tatiana took care to remain hidden. She'd found one of the drab dresses favored by the Shadows and hidden her bright golden hair under a hood. With this disguise in place, she'd not only managed to avoid Eric and Chad, but move around the palace unnoticed.

Jealousy gnawed at her as she saw the way the human prince supported her younger sister. Here, Willow was no longer an oddity. Among her own people, she was not ugly but beautiful. Here, she fit right in.

For the first time in Tatiana's life, she was made to feel outcast, undesirable and alone. For this she hated Willow, but when she saw the Shadow king take her sister in his arms and proclaim her *daughter* to his entire court, she almost lost control. Digging her nails into her palms, she clamped her mouth shut to keep from screaming. She wanted to rush forward, rip Willow out of King Drem's embrace and fling her across the room.

"Do I detect a bit of rage in the set of your jaw?" Chad drawled from beside her.

She almost snapped at him for startling her. Instead, she gulped in a deep breath of air and, when she was certain she had her emotions under control, turned to him.

"How did you recognize me?"

His leering smile widened. "Such beauty shines beyond any disguise."

"A compliment?" She didn't even smile. "Tell me, what are you doing here?" Though her tone was silky, she let him hear hints of her anger. "I thought you were with your brother, being fawned over by admiring women."

"Tsk, tsk. Jealousy and anger do not become you."

"I believe this is an emotion you're familiar with," she said smugly. "You despise Eric as much as I loathe Willow."

He grabbed her arm and pulled her out of the room. Stumbling after him, she allowed him to pull her down the hallway. Her heart racing, her blood pounded.

No one stopped them.

Chad shoved open a door and yanked her in after him. Thoroughly aroused, she went willingly, though she feigned a token protest. Chad kicked the door shut behind him and pushed her onto the bed. Panting, she lay on her back, gazing up at him. His expression was cruel as he tore her dress, yanked down his trousers and climbed on top of her.

Thrilled, she clawed at him. Her last coherent thought as he pushed himself into her ready body was that she'd finally found The One. They were two of a kind.

Later, pleasantly sore, she gazed up at Chad as he adjusted

his clothing. His handsome features were austere, as though they hadn't just shared a savagely brutal sexual encounter.

She stretched, grinning. "I get to be the one in charge next time," she said.

He blinked, gazing down at her as though he had no idea what she meant. "Next time?"

Unable to resist boasting, she pushed up on her elbows, well aware that her enormous breasts were on full display. The better to tempt him. "Honey, with me there's always a next time. Unless I don't wish it, that is."

Chad scowled but didn't respond. She couldn't help but smile. He'd already proved he was powerless to resist her.

Watching Willow reunite with the father she'd never known brought mixed emotions. Poignant, true, but Ruben also felt a sense of loss. She'd found what she'd unknowingly been seeking, while he…had failed on all levels. So far. He refused to admit defeat yet.

He finally understood the dual nature of his task. Yes, he had to find the murderer and bring him to justice. But he also needed to find a way to heal his fractured psyche, to learn to coexist with the wolf inside him. If he did not, he knew he'd either go completely mad or he'd die.

One thing he did know for certain. He wasn't going to find anything he sought here. And while he'd let himself hope that Willow would be part of his journey, now that she'd reconnected with her past, he wouldn't blame her if she wanted to stay here.

He wished he knew what she wanted. She hadn't shared this with him. She took visible delight in her new family, and their apparent acceptance of her was like balm on her troubled soul. He hadn't seen much of her the last few days and the fact that she'd been willing to walk with him both relieved and worried him.

She'd changed in many small, subtle ways. He felt as if she were slipping away from him. Not that she'd ever been his to begin with, but he was no longer certain she'd even go back to SouthWard with him and the others.

No matter. The sense of urgency had returned full force. A killer had yet to be caught. Restless, Ruben knew he'd soon have to be moving on. Tatiana, Eric and Chad had made no secret of their readiness to return home.

Willow, however, was less easy to read. Either way, it was time for him to leave. With or without her. He only wished the thought of leaving her behind didn't feel like his heart had been ripped from his chest.

So he bided his time and let her enjoy her new family. He roamed the palace, waiting. The few times he had encountered Willow, she had seemed like a ghost, clearly no longer interested in anything but her newfound family.

Finally, he'd had enough. By his reckoning, nearly a week had gone by. Time wasted that he could have been spending hunting the murderer. Eric, Tatiana and Chad also kept to themselves, so he didn't even have them to discuss this with.

He knew he could wait no longer. When he did see Willow again, it was by chance. Returning from yet another solitary stroll in the woods, he'd made up his mind to seek out the others, learn what they wanted to do, before finding King Drem and informing him of his plans to leave.

Willow was first on his list.

As if his thoughts had summoned her, he saw her hurrying down the path toward the meadow. She carried a small bouquet of flowers. How beautiful she looked, as though the mist and rain agreed with her, her dusky skin glowing with health.

"Willow," he shouted. She turned and waved, the joyous expression on her face warming his heart as she hurried over.

"I've missed you," she said, hugging him. Chest aching,

he hugged her back, before setting her apart. Cocking his head, he studied her.

Though she colored prettily, she continued to hold his gaze. "It's been so long since I've seen you," she finally said, breathless.

He nodded, momentarily unable to speak over the lump in his throat.

"How much time has passed since we've been here?" he finally asked her. "I mean in my world. I remember you said time passes differently here."

She frowned, looking up from her contemplation of a particularly dark rose, as scarlet as blood. "I'm not sure. Why?"

He resisted the urge to touch her and smiled gently. "Because I've got to go back to your land, the land of the Brights. I've got a killer to catch, remember?"

The look she gave him told him that she had, in fact, managed to forget. This saddened him more than he could express.

As she rearranged her expression back to one of bland vagueness, he reflected that the woman standing before him was nothing like the Willow he'd come to know and care for.

Maybe there was a good reason why this was so.

"Willow." He cleared his throat, smiling slightly to lessen the sting. "Are you all right?"

She gave him a quizzical look. "Of course. Are you?"

"You seem different. I've got to ask. Are you under some kind of spell?"

"What?" She recoiled, blinking rapidly. "No. A spell? Why would you say such a thing?"

She'd barely finished speaking when the blankness crept back into her expression. He swore he could see it take over her eyes, much like a storm sweeping across a previously cloudless sky.

Curling his hands into fists to keep from touching her, he

sighed. "Because you've been acting differently, completely unlike the Willow I'd begun to know."

Her face was expressionless as she replied, "I don't know what you're talking about."

Again, the toneless voice. Unable to take anymore, he grabbed her shoulders and pulled her close. Expression unchanged, she allowed this.

"Willow, where are you?" he said, choking as he searched her face. When she didn't react, he cupped her face with one hand and brushed his lips across her mouth.

Still she didn't react.

So he deepened the kiss, forcing open her lips with his tongue and kissing her deeply, devouring her sweetness.

Finally, she melted against him, kissing him back, making desire sing in his veins. He felt their souls join—surely she had to feel this, too—and he knew he had his Willow back. He only hoped he could keep her.

Finally, he stepped back, breathing heavily. "Willow?" he asked, praying she wouldn't disappear inside herself again.

Intense astonishment raced across her face, as she stiffened in shock. "What just happened?" she asked faintly. "Where am I?"

Still holding her as close as he dared, he stroked her hair as he explained. When he finished, her shoulders sagged and she gave a sheepish smile.

"I've felt like I've been living a dream," she admitted. "I'm not sure if I should be angry or worried. Who did this to me?"

"Your father?" he guessed. "Probably out of some misguided attempt to keep you here, with him."

She sighed. "You're probably right. It's been hard on him, not being able to contact me. But to do this? That's wrong on so many levels."

"I'm not sure it would accomplish anything to speak with him about it."

"Oh, I don't know." She rubbed the back of her neck. "He needs to understand he can't go around doing things like this."

"You were acting like a ghost," he told her, more relieved than he'd care to admit, even to himself.

She buried her face against his throat. He held her, his heart thumping in his chest, so hard it almost hurt. How could he even think of going on without this woman, when she was his best friend?

At the thought, the wolf part of him snarled. More than that, he realized. His heart, his…*mate?*

No. He felt like he'd taken a blow in the gut. That wasn't possible. Straightening, he gently moved her away. Not his mate. He had no right even to think such a thing, no right to claim anyone as his mate. Not until he completed his quest and figured out whether or not he was well along the winding path to insanity. Here, he thought, the magic might be affecting him, much like a drug. Taking off the rough edges and keeping everything on an even keel.

While he liked this, he wasn't sure what would happen when he returned home. Would he be better or worse?

"Still battling yourself, I see," she said wryly, her lips curving at the corners, making him want to kiss her again.

"Sorry," he told her, meaning it. "I'll eventually figure everything out. But first, I've got to find this killer."

She nodded, her gaze becoming slightly remote, making him worry until she sighed and met his gaze. "I suppose we do have to go back. I'm so different now. I don't know how I'll do back home."

"Different how?"

"I don't know. It's all been very, very strange. I can't believe I have an entire family. Though we were completely unknown to each other, they all seem to care about me very much. And I've come to care about them, too."

Taking a deep breath, he asked the question he knew he had to ask. "Do you want to stay?"

"Here?" She tilted her head, seriously considering the question and looking so beautiful she made his chest ache. "I hadn't really thought about it."

"Come on," he prodded, needing to be certain. "You can't tell me the idea has never crossed your mind."

Turning away, she was silent for so long, his soul began to hurt. Even though they'd made no promises to each other, he would feel as if he'd lost his heart if she chose to remain here. More than his best friend. With the possibilities stretching endlessly in front of them, he would lose his future, as well.

For the first time he realized he needed to think about what it would feel like when he finally got back to his home, to Teslinko. Without her. He just couldn't see that happening.

Pushing the thought away, he forced himself to focus on his task. "I'm going to find the others and see what they want to do. Then I'm going to meet with King Drem."

"When?"

"Before the end of the day." He was unable to keep from touching her and took her hand. "Please let me know your decision as soon as you can."

"My decision?" She frowned. "Surely you don't really believe I'd stay here with the Shadows. Though they feel like family, this is not my home. Plus…"

"Plus?"

Her entire face turned pink. "There's you," she said quietly. "At some point we'll need to talk about that. But for now, I'm going with you."

Relieved, he kissed the top of her head. "I'm glad."

Moving away, she tilted her head, watching him. "You know I plan to help you find whoever murdered your servant. But it's really like trying to locate a needle in a huge haystack. We don't even have a single suspect."

"Actually, I do. I've begun to wonder about Chad."

"Chad?" Considering, she finally nodded, apparently agreeing to exactly what he meant without him having to say the words. "The animals fear him and he has done things that…" She swallowed hard, aware of the war she'd start if she told Ruben all that Chad had done to her. "He gives me a weird feeling, as well." Understatement of the century.

"The animals?"

She nodded again. "Yes. I suspect he has more issues than he lets on."

Crossing his arms, he waited for her to continue. When she did not, he prodded gently. "Care to elaborate?"

"The horses do not like him," she confessed, the worry in her caramel-colored eyes making him want to pull her close and comfort her again. "They believe him to be cruel and violent."

"Are horses usually a good judge of character?"

She nodded. "All animals are. Ask the wolf inside you. He'll have insights that may surprise you."

The wolf inside him. Ruben carefully considered her words. Had he been so involved with making sure his wolf self didn't take over his life that he'd missed using a valuable part of his intuition? For far too long he'd regarded his beast as the enemy. What would happen if he actually began to consider it his friend?

Shocked, he realized he actually didn't know. It had been forever since he'd tried.

"You might be right," he said slowly. "Next time, I'll test out your theory."

The brilliance of her smile warmed him all the way to the core. His wolf, sleeping until now, rumbled his approval.

"As a matter of fact," she mused, "Chad's the last person I spoke with before this…fugue. Though I can't imagine why he'd do such a thing, it's entirely possible he put the spell on me that made me forget."

With a flash of insight, Ruben understood. If Chad actually was the killer, it would be to his advantage to have Willow want to stay here in NorthWard indefinitely. The longer they remained here, the less likely they were to be successful in the hunt.

He said as much to Willow.

"Do you truly think he's the one?" she asked.

"It's entirely possible. That would be one reason why he used this glamour to change his appearance."

She nodded. "At first I thought he did it to make me like him more. But you're right. We need to watch him more closely. Especially on the ride back home."

A feeling of foreboding settled over him. "Maybe we should confront him here."

Her eyes widened. "Safety in numbers?"

"Something like that." Jamming his hands into his pockets to keep from touching her, he gazed off into the forest. "Let me come up with a plan. Once I have one, I'll talk to King Drem."

She nodded then crossed the space between them. Standing on tiptoe, she kissed him. Her scent, lilac and fresh air, made him shiver with desire.

"Thank you." Smiling, she stepped away. "And your wolf is saying he needs a run before we leave. Make sure you take care of him, all right?"

Then, leaving him staring at her in astonishment, she walked away.

## Chapter 17

That night, as they all gathered in the banquet hall for dinner, Chad sat with his brother on one side and Tatiana on the other, clenching his teeth while suppressing the urge to snarl at his brother's fiancée to stop her incessant chatter.

"Look," Eric said, jabbing him in the side. "The human prince and Willow are heading our way."

One glance showed Chad that the minor spell he'd used on Willow had been broken. How? The only way to break such a spell would be with love's true kiss.

Shadefire. Chad kept his hands in his lap, fists clenched. The other man had kissed her and worse, Willow believed Ruben to be her one true love. He'd wondered when Ruben would wake up and remember he had a hunt to complete. Apparently he had and had somehow grown wise to the fact that Willow had been ensorcelled to make her forget.

Very shrewd of him. Chad gave Ruben points for that

move. The fact that he was too blind to realize the killer had found him was simply icing on the cake.

Sometimes, Chad thought Ruben knew. A couple times he'd caught the other man eying him with barely disguised speculation. He supposed Ruben's innate sense of fairness was the only thing holding him back from outright accusation.

Perhaps Chad would send a small clue his way, to liven things up. There was nothing he loved more than a game of cat and mouse. Except ending the game, that is.

What fun that would be. A bloody finale. He could hardly wait for the moment when both Ruben and Willow realized Chad was behind it all. Both the murder and the theft of Millicent's earring, which was a worthless bauble as far as he'd been able to tell. If it had magic behind it, he hadn't been able to discern the spell.

Patting his pocket to make sure it was still there, he vowed to either unlock its secrets or return it to Queen Millicent, painting Ruben as the villainous thief who'd dared steal from her. A fitting end. He'd be a hero for killing the miscreant human. And, since he felt pretty certain no one in the South-Ward Court cared about Willow, the fact that she'd been killed in the cross fire wouldn't cause anyone sorrow.

Smiling and nodding as Ruben outlined his plan to ride out in the morning, Chad gripped Eric's arm to keep him from protesting. His brother liked to play the leader and he couldn't take a chance that the idiot would try to call the shots and somehow manage to change Ruben's mind.

Understanding, Eric jerked away but kept his mouth shut. Tatiana, to Chad's surprise, expressed a desire to get back home to her family. The twit claimed to have had enough adventure.

Chad agreed to meet Ruben and Willow in the courtyard at sunrise, pending of course, the king's approval, and watched them stroll away.

Something had changed. Considering the human prince carefully, Chad tried to figure out what. He saw how close Willow stayed to the other man, noticed too the many small touches and smiling looks the two shared on their way to seek out King Drem.

They looked like a couple. Like lovers.

Narrowing his eyes, he pushed back the rush of red hot rage. Though he hadn't made up his mind yet to marry her, he still considered Willow his. His possession, to do with as he pleased. Including kill, of course.

He did not accept the idea of her and Ruben becoming a team. Willow and Ruben had clearly made some sort of emotional connection. That was—he clenched his jaw and tried not to grind his teeth—unacceptable. Completely untenable. Even though she'd already released him from the betrothal, he still considered her his possession.

Until now, he'd simply fantasized about the moment when he'd kill Ruben of Teslinko. Now, he knew with certainty the other man would have to die sooner than he'd originally planned.

And—his heart began to race as savage joy filled him—so would Willow. She deserved a slow, excruciatingly painful death. She'd betrayed him with the foolish human prince.

As he pondered the best way to commence, he gazed at his older brother. Eric truly wasn't fit to sit upon the East-Ward throne. Maybe he'd have to kill Eric and Tatiana, as well. He'd be doing the world a great service.

A massacre, much easier to explain when he was the only witness. He could always say they'd been set upon by a band of renegade Shadows who were deeply unhappy that King Drem had acknowledged Willow as his offspring.

Decision made, Chad began to plot the where and how. This was all part of the fun. So much so, the temptation to drag it out would be great. But this time, he couldn't afford to wait too long.

He'd do it on the way back to SouthWard. Perils of the journey and all that. The trick would be to keep Eric and Tatiana in the dark.

Rubbing his hands together with glee, he backed out of the banquet hall and returned to his room to plot and plan and pack.

King Drem listened quietly as Ruben expressed their plans to leave. He turned to Willow and held out his hand.

Taking it, she felt a surge of fondness.

"I promise to visit more often," she said, smiling even though her eyes filled with tears.

He kissed her forehead lightly and then released her. "I'll hold you to that promise."

Chest tight, she nodded. Though she'd only known him a short time, she truly would miss him.

"I would also ask you to consider marriage to one of my people," he said, surprising her. "We have many fine young men to choose from. Such a marriage would go far in repairing the chasm between our two people."

Instinctively she glanced at Ruben and caught him glowering at her father. His harsh expression softened as he met her gaze, but he did not protest.

King Drem laughed. "So that's the way it is. I understand." Waving away her sputtering attempt to protest, he laughed again. "I'll have the kitchen prepare some supplies to take with you. Now go and shades speed."

Face flaming, she ignored Ruben as she turned to go. He caught up to her when they'd exited the room.

"Are you all right?" he asked gently, taking her arm.

She shook her head, going with part of the truth. "I'm

going to miss him. It's difficult to finally locate my other family and have to give them up so soon."

He kissed her cheek, making her smile reluctantly.

"I still stand with what I said. If you want to stay here longer, I can come back for you after I find the murderer."

"No." She'd started shaking her head even before he'd finished speaking. "We've already covered all this. I'm not leaving you."

Pulling her close, he simply held her. She wrapped her arms around him and placed her head on his chest, loving the solid steady sound of his heartbeat.

Just being so close sent desire, slow and sweet, cascading through her veins. Though she knew she could seduce him with a look, she realized they all needed to be rested for the journey ahead.

Pulling away, she feigned a yawn. "I don't know about you, but I'm turning in early so I can get a good night's sleep. You really should consider doing the same."

And she left him, hurrying off before he could see how her entire body quaked.

Only when she'd reached the corridor leading to her room, did she slow down. Fumbling with the handle to her door, she realized her hands were shaking so badly she could barely function.

She wanted him, but more than that…

She loved him.

She loved Ruben. With every fiber of her being, heart and soul and mind. She wanted to spend the rest of her life with him by her side. And she didn't even know his last name.

Once inside her room, she let herself sink slowly down onto the bed. She didn't know whether to laugh or cry. How Tatiana would chortle if she knew—which she wouldn't. No one must ever find out, including Eric and Chad—especially Chad. The man her parents wished her to marry.

Instead, she was in love with a human man who shape-shifted into a wolf. Perfect.

How in the shades had this happened? Head in her hands, she tried not to weep while she attempted to figure out what to do.

Instead of heading to his room to rest, Ruben went outside, intent on changing and letting his wolf have one last run in the forest.

What Willow had said to him earlier kept replaying inside his mind. For the first time he could remember, he felt a glimmer of hope.

Acceptance? Was that the key? Had he been too busy fighting his inner wolf that he'd never learned to accept it? They were both parts of the whole. He was wolf and wolf was human. One remained subservient to the other, depending on who had control of the body.

He was wolf and...wolf was him.

Stunned, Ruben dropped back onto his haunches, inhaling deeply of the damp forest earth. The wolf, uncharacteristically still, whined. Just once, but the pathos in the sound ripped at his heart. He'd been so busy trying to shut down the wolf that he'd shut that part of himself off completely.

How had he been so blind?

Perhaps, he thought, feeling hope for the first time in far too long, he wasn't going mad after all. If there was a chance, even the smallest one, of him having a future, he'd grasp it with both hands and never let it go.

He pushed to his feet, a tentative joy blossoming inside him. Hurrying deeper in the forest to let his wolf out, he found himself grinning savagely at nothing in particular. So focused was he on his task, he nearly collided with Chad on the way into the trees.

"Slow down." Hands on his shoulder, Chad regarded him curiously. "Where are you going in such a hurry?"

Ruben's wolf lunged at the other man, teeth bared. Containing the beast, Ruben moved away from Chad. He realized the wolf was right. Something about the EastWard man was off, like milk that had curdled from being left too long in the sun.

Again he considered the fact that he might have known the murderer from the very beginning.

Careful to keep his face expressionless, Ruben crossed his arms and studied the Bright man. Had it been him all along— the killer, the one he hunted in an effort to bring him in to stand trial for his crimes?

"Well?" Chad asked again, impatient arrogance coloring his voice. "Are you going to tell me where you're going or not?"

"Not." Not caring if he was rude, Ruben began to move away. "I'm not in the mood to talk to you right now. I've got—"

"Better things to do?" Chad interrupted snidely. Ruben didn't see him move, but somehow he did, blocking Ruben's path into the forest.

Only vampires moved that fast and Ruben knew for sure that Chad was no vampire. Therefore, he must have used magic.

Sensing a threat, Ruben studied the other man, noting that he wore a sheathed knife and a coiled rope on his belt.

"What do you want?" Ruben asked. His wolf snarled, making Ruben twist his mouth in a grimace. Chad's presence infuriated the beast and Ruben needed a clear head to deal with him.

"Why, I want to help you in your search for the one who killed your servant." Chad's smile was a terrible thing.

"I thought that's what you've been doing," Ruben said.

"Not really." Still Chad continued to smile, his violet eyes full of frost. "But I'll make it easy for you. I confess to the crime."

Stunned, Ruben remained silent.

Chad withdrew a small object from his pocket. "I even have the earring I stole. Worthless piece of junk, as far as I'm concerned." He tossed the pearl into the bushes.

"You know I'm going to have to bring you in to face trial," Ruben told him, wishing like hell his weapon had transferred from his world to this with him. He hated being unarmed, especially when he knew the other man had other magical weapons at his disposal.

"I'd like to see you try." Chad sounded smug. "But first, we have unfinished business, you and I." He waved his hand and Ruben felt the electricity that always signaled magic.

Intuition told him this wasn't going to be good.

"What the hell are you doing?" Ruben snarled, abandoning all pretense at civility.

Regarding him with malice shining from his purple eyes, Chad's smile widened. The terribleness of his expression chilled Ruben all the way into his bones.

"I'm going to do what I should have done a long time ago." Waving his arms again, Chad began muttering words in some archaic language. "This spell will keep you still while I gut you. But don't worry," he said with fierce merriment. "You'll still feel everything. And then when your body parts are spread all over this clearing, maybe some wild animals will come to feast on you. Because of my spell, you'll feel that, too."

Narrowing his eyes, Ruben struggled to free words from his throat. "Why?" he managed.

But instead of answering, Chad grinned at him, the lopsided grin of a madman. "Why not?" he countered. "Don't try to tell me you haven't realized I'm the one you've been hunting all along."

Still smiling, he muttered more nonsensical words, brandishing a wicked-looking knife.

Though he knew nothing about magic, Ruben swore he could see the dark tentacles of this spell swirling, wrapping him in ropelike layers.

He couldn't move—not his feet nor his arms. In fact he could scarcely breathe.

Inside, his panicked wolf snarled, pacing and occasionally launching an all-out attack in an attempt to break free.

The knife flashed in the dim light as Chad raised it.

Suddenly, Ruben knew. Changing into wolf might be the only way to fight this madman. For the first time ever, his wolf might be his only hope.

Releasing his mental hold on his inner beast, Ruben took a deep breath. And then he set his wolf free.

The change ripped through him, breaking the magic's hold on him and pushing him to his knees. His clothing shredded, his skin bled as the fur took over. He bit his tongue to keep from crying out as his bones changed shape, slamming him from human to wolf in one heartbeat, two, the sheer ferocity of it sharply painful.

Wolf now, his animal self reacted without thought, teeth bared, leaping at the man who still chanted his useless magic.

Chad staggered backward, taken by surprise. Dropping the knife, he went down, arm up in reflex to protect his neck and face. Otherwise, wolf-Ruben would have ripped out his throat without hesitation.

Instead, he tore open Chad's arm, laying the bone bare. Completely abandoning his attempt at completing the spell, Chad shrieked and tried to crawl away. Enraged, wolf-Ruben held fast, fury driving him to sink his teeth in deeper. The next bite would be at Chad's throat.

"Stop," a voice said from behind him, the air of command as clear as a bell.

Willow. Surprised, wolf-Ruben let Chad go.

"Get him off me, get him away from me," Chad babbled, struggling to staunch the flow as his life's blood gushed away into the dirt.

Ruben snarled, baring his teeth. He shook the injured man, wanting him dead. The coppery smell of blood further enraged his beast.

"Ruben." Willow's hand in his fur. He froze, his human aspect dimly realizing what he'd almost done.

"Leave him alone," she said sternly. Then, apparently trusting a wild beast to follow her orders, she went to Chad. Dropping to her knees, she used pieces of Ruben's torn clothing to tie a rudimentary tourniquet.

"We'll get you some help," she murmured. "Try to focus. You're in shock."

Once she'd secured Chad's wound, she climbed back to her feet, turning to face wolf-Ruben. After crossing the space between them, she crouched down to put her face at eye level. Ignoring his bloody muzzle, she stroked him. "I need you to change back to man. Can you do that for me?"

Unbelievably, he felt a surge of calm radiating from her touch. Acquiescing, the wolf retreated, permitting Ruben to begin the change.

Though less rapid, the shift back to human felt nearly as painful as it had earlier, most likely due to the intensity of the first change.

Man once again, Ruben turned away from the now-moaning Chad and gathered up his torn trousers in an attempt to hide his nakedness.

"What have you done?" So much sorrow and disappointment rang in Willow's voice. Directed at him. He felt a twinge of pain before he realized that she didn't know the truth.

Slowly, Ruben turned. "He's the one who killed my servant. After he confessed, he was going to try to kill me. He cast some sort of spell that held me immobile." He pointed toward the knife. "He planned to use that to cut me into pieces."

To his relief, she nodded, accepting his statement as fact. She turned to eye Chad, who had passed out from the loss of blood.

"Can you heal him?" Ruben asked.

Willow shook her head. "I don't know. Mostly what I do is soothe troubled animals, calm them. It's more psychological than physical."

He held her gaze. "Are you willing to try?"

She looked torn. "But he's the killer."

"A killer who needs to be brought to justice. That means he gets a trial. Heal him. Please."

"For you," she said softly. "I'll try. But don't get your hopes up."

"I have faith in you." And he did. He truly believed she could perform miracles, if she had faith in herself.

Without another word, Willow crossed to the other man and laid her hands on him. Ruben turned away, exhaustion swamping him, unable to watch her. At least he now knew the truth. Not only about the killer, but about his war with his dual nature. He'd allowed himself hope, hope that had turned out to be false. He couldn't coexist with his wolf. The beast had wanted to blindly, savagely kill. His wolf hadn't cared about justice or trials. How could anything but madness await him now?

He sank to his knees, back still to Willow while she continued to try and heal the man he'd nearly killed. He wanted to weep, but didn't have the energy to do so. To think he'd actually let himself believe he had everything under control!

His eyes stung and he angrily rubbed them with his fist. He would not reveal—not even to Willow—the depths of his sorrow. Instead, he hung his head, shielding his face from her with her with his hands, trying to imagine what kind of future he had in store now. All he could see was blackness, which he fancied mirrored his soul.

"I did what I could. I think he's sleeping normally," she said, weariness making her voice tremble. "Perhaps you'd better secure him somehow so he doesn't escape."

Without a word, Ruben got up and used the bloody rope from Chad's belt, finding the discarded knife and using it to cut off the right length. Once he had Chad trussed up, he removed the sheath and attached it to his own belt, placing the knife safely inside it.

Staring down at the still-unconscious man, he reflected on how closely he'd come to being just like him. A murderer.

Defeated, he turned away, unable to stand looking at the bloody leaves any longer. He saw the earring, shimmering in the dim light. Legs shaky, he retrieved it, carrying it back to her. "Here's your mother's earring."

She accepted it solemnly, placing it in a small pouch she kept tied to her belt. "Thank you."

"I don't understand. He killed for that," Ruben mused.

"No. He killed because he takes pleasure in it." She sounded certain. "Which is why he was going to kill you."

Though Chad hadn't said as much, Ruben knew she was right. Stomach clenching, he turned away. He kept remembering how his wolf had attacked, fighting as if it was a battle for life and death. Hunching his shoulders, he studied the blood-stained leaves and dirt and considered how easily the outcome could have been different.

Maybe the wolf hadn't been wrong.

"You were fighting to save your life. What you did was self-defense," Willow said, placing her hand lightly on his shoulder. Once again she'd come up behind him without him noticing, proving his senses also had gone dull. Worthless.

"I was out of control." Slowly he sank to his knees, wishing he'd let Chad kill him. That would be infinitely better than succumbing to madness.

"You are not mad," Willow said firmly. "You defended yourself—and us." Kneeling next to him, she tried to wrap her arms around him, undeterred when he tried to shrug her off.

"Let me help you," she said softly. "Your psyche is wounded. I believe I can heal you, too."

"I'm beyond redemption," he said, bitterness coloring his voice. "Leave me alone."

"You don't mean that."

"Actually, I do."

To his disbelief, she succeeded in circling her arms around his chest and back, holding on to him tightly. "You did the right thing."

"How can you say that?" He let his mouth take on an unpleasant twist, fury almost choking him. "If you hadn't come along, I'd have ripped out his throat."

"Only to save your life." Her voice washed over him like a cooling balm. "You did what came naturally, what you had to do to defend yourself. Now do the right thing again and let me help you."

Glaring at her with burning eyes, he sneered. "Go away."

"I'm not going anywhere." Then, stunning him, she kissed him, her mouth soft as she moved her lips over his. "I promise I can help you, just like I helped him."

Swiveling his head, he eyed Chad, still crumpled in a heap on the forest floor. "You healed him? I thought you could only heal animals."

She shrugged, still keeping her arms locked around him. "Until now, I've never tried to help a person. I wasn't entirely sure it would work."

He tried being dispassionate and dragged his hands across his eyes. "What would you have done if it hadn't?"

"I don't know." She kissed him again, a whisper of her lips along the rigid line of his jaw. "I guess I'd have gone for help."

He shuddered; he couldn't help it. Though he didn't really understand how or why, her nearness calmed the storm inside him. His wolf leaned into her, drawing comfort from her presence. His human self…felt more confused than anything else.

"I think you should leave me alone." Trying for contempt, the most he could manage was a sort of tormented defeat. This too infuriated and enraged him.

"I'll never leave you," she promised. "Now let me help you."

"Do I have a choice?" Forcing himself to relax, which seemed counterproductive, he tried to harden his heart against whatever foolishness she would try to use to convince him he wasn't—

"Evil? A madman? A killer as bad as him?" She indicated Chad. "You're not, I promise you."

Glowering at her, he shook his head. "How did you do that?"

Again she lifted her slender shoulders in a shrug. "I don't know. I simply hear your thoughts inside my head."

Like a mate. Gut knotting, he closed his eyes. This couldn't be happening, couldn't be real. For all he knew, he was in the throes of a dream and would wake to find his madness had manifested itself once again while he slept.

"Whatever," she scoffed, softening her words with a quick kiss. "Magic is real, you know. And one thing I have learned is that magic takes individual forms with different Sidhe."

She caressed him, her touch sure and comforting. Even though he wasn't sure he wanted comfort, he held still, feeling a bit like she was trying to free him from invisible bonds, like he was a wild animal caught in a trap.

Which, he reflected grimly, he actually sort of was.

"All right," he finally managed. "Go ahead and try."

## Chapter 18

Warmth flowed from her fingers. More than that. Enchantment. Shimmering, beautiful, glorious.

Bright.

Stunned, he could feel it heating his skin, and deeper. His blood and his soul. Forgiveness, acceptance and hope. Hope was something he'd lost sight of a long, long time ago. Even as it washed over him, cleansing him, he tried to push it away, to resist. He wasn't certain he believed in such a thing any longer.

"Of course you do," she said, once again inside of his head.

As her fingers kneaded his skin, he closed his eyes, letting his head drop until his chin rested on his chest.

Inside, his wolf luxuriated in the sensation. No—*he* luxuriated. *All of him*.

"That's right," she murmured encouragingly. "You are no longer separate. You are one."

"Easy enough for you to say," he told her slowly. "But you

don't know how it's been for me. Becoming the wolf is like a drug for me. I love it so much—and when I'm wolf I don't want to ever change back to man."

"That's because you've been so busy suppressing the wolf inside you. When he finally got a taste of freedom, he didn't want to go back to his cage."

Reaching inward, he realized she was right. "How do you know this?" he asked, letting wonder fill his voice.

She smiled again, the beauty of it lighting up her face. "I told you I talk to animals. Your wolf part told me. You could have found this out yourself, if you'd only taken the time to ask."

Inside, his wolf rumbled his agreement.

Stunned, Ruben looked at her. This lovely woman who had come to mean so much to him. So much—he cut off the thought, afraid she would pluck it from his mind.

In truth, perhaps she already had. She beamed at him, contentment shining from her brown eyes. The same satisfaction filled him as well, making him realize until now, he'd never been fully alive.

Was this a new kind of magic? She was Sidhe after all.

"Yes." She gave him a tremulous smile. "All my life I've believed I was without magic. An outcast, bastard born, so different from everyone that even my own mother could hardly bear to look at me."

The sorrow in her voice touched him, breaking past the barriers his own inner agony had erected. "And now?" he asked.

"Now I've learned there is so much more to me than I ever could have imagined. My sister's taunts, my mother's contempt—none if it will touch me again."

"Easier said than done. We all want our parents to love us."

"True and while I'll always feel that lack, at least I now understand the reason behind it."

Wisely he considered her. "That will only lessen the sting."

She gave him a smile of such brilliance his chest grew tight. "Yes. But I can live with that." She considered him, her fingers tracing soft patterns on his skin. "Now, how about you? Do you understand what it is you have to do?"

"Only partly," he admitted, stretching as he realized he felt better than he had in years. "I've been treating my wolf as an enemy."

"When in fact he's only one aspect of you. You've got to accept yourself—all of yourself."

Grimacing, he nodded. "I was working my way through that when Chad attacked me."

They both glanced at the still unconscious man.

"We'll have to notify my father. I'm going to request a few guards accompany us back to SouthWard. His magic is pretty strong. I don't want to take a chance of him escaping."

Later, after King Drem had his guards temporarily quarantine Chad in a locked holding cell, Ruben and Willow found themselves alone in the castle.

Once his adrenaline had subsided, he was in a kind of hell. Even the merest brush of her fingers against his skin made him feel as if his heart was about to leap from his chest.

He wanted her, plain and simple. No, more than that. He needed her, the way his wolf part needed to break free and run.

When the king finally released them to get ready for their journey home, Willow came up to him and wrapped her arms around him. His reaction was swift and violent. It took every ounce of self-control he had to keep from shoving her against the wall and taking her right then and there.

She deserved so much more than that.

"Are you tired?" Her voice broke into his thoughts. Pink stained the creamy perfection of her cheeks.

"Tired?" he repeated, searching her face for signs of exhaustion. "Not particularly. You?"

Instead of answering, she flashed him a wicked grin. Glancing behind them and ahead at the deserted corridors, she turned toward him.

In one forward motion, she molded her curves against him. "Then kiss me," she ordered, softening it a second later with a "Please."

He needed no other urging. Desire swept over him as he crushed her to him, claiming her mouth with a kiss. She kissed him back, her mouth moving against his in the kind of kiss that told him she had craved him as badly as he did her.

Right then, with their mouths joined together and passion heating his blood, a vow was made and sealed, at least in his heart.

*His*, his blood sang. *Now and for all time.*

Somehow they managed to make it to his room, sharing each other's breath. She moved her hands, all over him, all trace of shyness gone. Her boldness enabled him to channel his darkness into passion, letting the other part of himself—his wolf—as close to the surface as he could without actually changing.

Pleasure, pure, explosive, arced between them. They were one and the same, skin to skin, heart to heart—two and then three—and, as he entered her, his mate, he almost gave her the words that would let her know she now owned his soul. *His mate.*

But something held him back, even after, when she curled her body into his and held him, smiling. He had made his choice. He had to allow her time to make hers.

Dawn was a short time away when Willow finally bid him good-night and made her way toward her room. Aching, he watched her go, ignoring the way he wanted to howl at her absence. He punched his pillow, closed his eyes and tried to rest. If he was lucky he could grab a few hours of sleep before they started out in the morning.

Now he would have to try and pretend that nothing had changed. In reality, he knew things would never be the same again.

Unfortunately, when Willow entered her sleeping chambers, it was to find a disheveled and grumpy Tatiana waiting for her.

"Where have you been?" her sister demanded shrilly. "I've been waiting here for hours."

Willow briefly closed her eyes, gathering her strength. Then she opened them and told Tatiana what had happened.

"I don't believe you," Tatiana said when Willow had finished. "Chad isn't a killer. You're just trying to frame him because you don't want to marry him."

Regarding her sister with total disbelief, Willow sighed. "That's ridiculous. He tried to kill Ruben tonight. And he admitted to everything."

"No." Tatiana crossed her arms. "You tricked him. I demand to see him."

Tiredly, Willow let herself sink down onto her bed. What she'd give to rest her head on the pillow and simply close her eyes. "Why do you care? I know a long time ago you wanted me to switch with you, but since I haven't seen any evidence of anything going on between the two of you, surely you're over that by now."

To her astonishment, Tatiana blushed a deep, fiery red. "Actually, we've been with each other. In the physical sense. I want to marry Chad, not Eric."

Oh for the… Now Willow did close her eyes. She opened them again when the room began swirling around her. "Tati, Chad's a vicious murderer. Not only that, but he tried to kill Ruben. We've taken him before King Drem. When we leave tomorrow, armed guards will be escorting us home. He'll be standing trial for his crime."

But Tatiana didn't want to hear. "I refuse to believe you. I need to rescue him. If you won't help me, then I'll find someone who will. I know." She snapped her fingers. "Eric won't let this happen to his brother."

"Go." Too drained to argue, Willow waved her away. "King Drem has already summoned Eric. I think you might find out that he wasn't surprised."

She didn't even react as Tatiana stormed out of the room, slamming the door behind her.

The next morning arrived much too quickly. Her entire body aching, Willow hurried through her preparations, aware that her sister would no doubt make this the journey from hell.

Once downstairs, she went to the banquet area. Ruben was already there, finishing his breakfast. She saw no sign of Eric or Tatiana, or anyone else from King Drem's Court.

Studying Ruben, she saw no sign of the bitter despair that had ravaged him the previous evening. In fact, as she returned his impersonal smile, it seemed like he'd put those momentous events temporarily behind him. At least, she hoped his blankness was only temporary. Sniffing, she searched the air to make sure he hadn't been placed under a spell. She found none of the lingering residue of magic, so she supposed he was trying to deal with things the best way he could at the moment. Time, like always, would finish healing his wounds.

After filling her own plate, she sat down across from him and filled him in with what her sister had said.

"Really?" Shaking his head, Ruben winced, then drained a large mug of coffee. "Did you see that coming?"

"Honestly, no. Though when the two princes first arrived in SouthWard, Tatiana did come to my room and declared she wanted Chad and would give me Eric. I chalked it up to her normal theatrics and let it go."

"Ah, well." He pushed his plate away. "Hopefully she'll let it go. I haven't seen Eric, so I don't know how he's reacting."

He'd barely finished speaking when Eric and Tatiana strolled into the room. Neither of them spoke or even glanced at Ruben and Willow. Instead, they filled their plates quickly and took a table in a corner as far away as they could get while remaining in the room.

Willow sighed. "So that's how it's going to be."

Ruben eyed them. "How much magic do the two of them have?"

Shocked, she forgot to chew. Swallowing hastily, she spoke. "Surely you don't think—"

"That they'll try to stage a rescue? Actually, that's exactly what I do think."

"Then ask King Drem to seal their powers." She resumed her meal. "Easy enough of a solution."

"You can do that?"

"Of course." Satisfied, she pushed her own plate away. "It's a simple spell for someone who's as powerful as him. He can even put a time limit on it. The only stipulation is to cast such a spell, the Sidhe must be more powerful than the ones he puts the spell on. And, since you don't get to be king unless you have a lot of power, I'm sure that's well within his capabilities."

"Thank you." Ruben pushed back his chair. "I'll find the king and ask him. I'll be back in a few minutes."

The instant Ruben left, the other two got up and carried their plates over to her table. Without asking, they plunked down in the chairs next to and across from her.

"We need your help," Tatiana said, her no-nonsense stare telling Willow she wouldn't take no for an answer. Which was too bad, since of course Willow couldn't help her with Chad.

"We've already been through this," Willow said, trying not to clench her teeth. "Come on, Tatiana. Please be reasonable."

Now Eric spoke. Leaning across the table, he took her hands in his and gave his best effort to hit her all at once with his masculine charm. Well aware of what he was doing, Willow hid her smile.

"Come on, Willow. Help us out. Chad is my baby brother," he said, his voice pitched low enough to sound both desperate and sexy. Not an appealing combination. "I can't let him suffer."

Willow decided to hear him out, if only so she'd have a better idea of what they were planning. "What do you want me to do?" she asked.

Eric's blinding smile would have been dazzling if she hadn't known what a complete narcissistic ass he was. He appeared to take her capitulation at face value, unlike Tatiana, who narrowed her eyes in suspicion.

"On the ride back, we need to free him."

"Really?" Crossing her arms, Willow leaned forward. "Exactly how do you propose to do that?"

Before Willow could answer, Ruben arrived back with King Drem. Immediately crossing the room to their table, the king regarded Eric and Tatiana with a thunderous frown.

"Both of you, stand," he ordered. "I've already taken care of Prince Chad. His magic is now rendered useless. The time has come to do the same to you."

"Why?" Tatiana asked, her tone wheedling. "Do you honestly think we would try to do something so foolish?"

Unsmiling, the king regarded her. "Yes," he answered. "Stand." Though he pitched his voice low, the power behind his words echoed off the walls.

Immediately Eric pushed to his feet, proving he at least, was no fool. Tatiana on the other hand, remained seated.

She continued to pick at her breakfast as though she hadn't heard a thing.

Smiling sadly, the king leaned down. "I'm talking to you also, Princess Tatiana."

Reluctantly, she stood. Raising her head, she glared at Willow before facing the king. With defiance shining from her face, she deliberately reached down and picked up her cup. After taking a long drink of juice—blatantly disrespecting the king—she swallowed and placed her cup back on the table.

"I have armed myself against you," she said softly. "So unless your magic is more powerful than mine, your spell of binding is worthless."

Eric snorted, rolling his eyes at her words. Willow exchanged a quick glance with Ruben, impressed that Eric hadn't completely swallowed Tatiana's nonsense. Evidently he was a bit more intelligent than Willow had given him credit for.

"Nice try." King Drem smiled, a hint of dark ruthlessness coming through. "I haven't held my kingship all these years with weak magic, I promise you."

She opened her mouth to respond then closed it. Staring at a spot beyond the king's head, she waited.

King Drem spoke a single word. Immediately, the air sizzled with his power. Impressed, Willow waited to see if he would do more.

He did not. Instead, he clasped Ruben on the shoulder before turning to Willow. "I'll miss you, daughter," he said, before enveloping her in a quick hug.

Releasing her, he walked away without saying anything else, though Willow thought she saw tears in his eyes.

Subdued now, Tatiana sank back down into her chair. Eric, who hadn't moved the entire time, pushed his chair back so hard it crashed to the floor. He stalked off without another word.

"This is going to be a long journey," Ruben said, glancing toward the departing EastWard prince.

"I know," Willow sighed. "You know they're going to try to hatch some other plan that doesn't involve magic."

"True." His smile felt as tender as a caress. "We'll be all right. King Drem is sending an armed escort, remember?"

Flushing even more, she nodded. "True, but you know his guards will not be able to travel into our kingdom. Once we reach Bright lands, they'll have to turn around."

"I'm sure we can manage. Now," he said, glancing at the huge clock near the unused fireplace. "Are you ready to ride?"

She nodded, taking his hand when he offered it. Again that feeling of warmth, of completeness, brought on by the simple act of skin touching skin. When he pulled her to him, she went willingly, burying her face in the hollow of his throat. He smelled of wood smoke and pine, a masculine scent that made her ache deep inside.

In silence they stood, holding on to each other as if neither ever wanted to let go. Refusing to allow herself to worry about the future and what would happen once they got back to SouthWard, Willow took pleasure in the moment. She drew strength from his quiet embrace and she fancied she lent him some of her own.

When he finally pulled away, his mouth curved into a warm smile which she felt all the way to her toes. "Let's head down to the courtyard. Our horses should be saddled and ready."

He held out his arm and she took it. Together, they left to begin the final part of their journey.

Though Ruben had known instinctively that King Drem had designed something to contain Chad, he wasn't prepared for the rolling prison that waited for them in the courtyard: a brightly painted wagon, so colorful it might have belonged to gypsies. Six huge draft horses were hitched to it, which might have been overkill had not the inside been entirely encased in iron, forming a cage. Inside, Chad sat quietly, head in his hands. Ruben almost felt sorry for the other man. Almost.

Eric and Tatiana, already mounted, alternated between glaring at Ruben and Willow and staring at Chad.

Astride a magnificent black horse, King Drem waited to lead them from his castle.

First Ruben helped Willow on her horse. Though she smiled bravely at him, sadness darkened her caramel-brown eyes to the color of chocolate as she gazed at King Drem. He knew she was going to miss him.

Though he definitely understood how she felt—he hadn't seen his parents in what seemed like forever—she'd be fine, he knew. Especially if she followed through on her promise to visit often.

King Drem blew Willow a kiss. Finally smiling, she blew one back. And then, at Ruben's signal, they turned their mounts to go.

They rode out without pomp or circumstance, the clip clop of the horses' hooves on the cobblestones the only sound. When they reached the path that led into the forest, King Drem reined in.

"I leave you here," he announced, his dark gaze settling on Willow. When she acknowledged his look with a smile, he turned to eye Ruben. "Take care of her," he ordered. "Or I'll find you."

Then, without giving Ruben a chance to answer, he signaled to his men and they rode away, leaving four behind plus the coachman who controlled the wagon. Throughout all of this, Chad never once looked up.

Riding alongside him, Eric and Tatiana exchanged a meaningful glance, as though they had something planned, but Ruben didn't worry. Their magical ability had been contained.

If they planned to try something else, something physical, they'd be easily overcome.

The guards, stern-faced men clad all in black, each with blank expressions, the magic pulsing off them palpable, even to Ruben. He was glad to feel it, well aware of how deadly it could be.

They rode hard that entire day, communication limited by the brutal pace they set. As dusk prepared to fall, Ruben began to scout a place where they could make camp.

Finally, he located a clearing large enough to accommodate them all. Signaling to the leader of the guard, they stopped. It didn't take long for the tents to go up. Unusually quiet, Tatiana immediately disappeared into hers. Instead of joining her, Eric went to attempt to speak with his brother.

Ruben watched them and noticed Chad kept his head lowered, apparently in an attempt to appear nonresponsive. The two brothers conversed, no doubt trying to come up with some last-ditch scheme before they reached SouthWard.

Looking up, he noticed one of the guards regarding them, as well. Good. Though he seriously doubted they'd be able to accomplish much, the fact that they were up to no good was disruptive enough.

"Ruben." Still standing next to her horse, Willow waved him over. "The animals are worried."

"About Eric and Tatiana?"

She nodded.

"With their magic bound, I don't think they'll be too big of a threat," he said.

She cast him a troubled glance. "They can still stir things up, even without magic."

Unable to resist touching her, even if only for a moment, he squeezed her shoulder. "I'll have a word with the guards."

With a ghost of a smile, she nodded. Then, standing up on tiptoe, she kissed his cheek, whisper soft. "I'm going to bunk down with the horses. There's no way I'm sharing a tent with my sister tonight."

"I don't blame you," he said.

Moistening her lips, she looked down. "Anyway, if you're not too tired, I wouldn't mind your company later."

The rush of heat her words brought made his pulse quicken, though he managed a casual nod. "I just might do that," he told her, before walking away to have a word with the captain of the guard.

Of course, over the next several hours, he could scarcely think of anything else.

Dusk had fallen, with darkness not too far behind. Almost everyone had retired to their tents, with the exception of the two men who were on guard duty and, of course, Chad.

As Ruben walked up to the jail-wagon, he gazed at the other man and waited for him to look up and acknowledge him. But Chad still sat cross-legged, his head down, as though lost in a deep meditation.

Finally, Ruben shrugged and moved away. Casually, he strolled to where the hobbled horses clustered. He went to his mount, scratching behind the animal's ears, smiling as the horse rubbed its massive head against him for more.

He stepped around the cluster of horses, and his heart stuttered when he saw her, fast asleep on a pallet she'd made of horse blankets and a saddle. A sense of completeness filled him as he gazed down at her. Shocked at the depth of his feelings, he realized he could no longer run from the truth. Willow was his mate. Whether or not she came from his world was immaterial.

Once he'd worked through the remainder of his problems, he wanted to claim her as his.

He turned away, his chest tight. While he had finally faced the truth, he had a long way to go before he'd be worthy of her. He couldn't exactly blame her if she wanted to take another path.

Returning to his tent, he debated going inside, but turned around, deciding to sleep by the fire instead. Though Eric and Tatiana's magic had been contained, he wouldn't put it past the other man to try something physical. If Ruben were in his tent, he'd have no way to see an attack coming.

And his intuition told him, Eric would try something soon. He just didn't know what.

In the morning as they broke camp, the leader of King Drem's guards came to Ruben. "Our border lies not more than a few paces south of here. We dare not ride onto Bright land. To do so could start a war. So at that point, we will return back to our own land."

"I understand." Turning to eye Chad who still slept inside his iron cage, he shook his head. "What about the coachman?"

"He can stay," the captain said. "He's human, so he'll be safe."

Human? Eyeing the man perched up on the odd wagon, he wondered why the man hadn't spoken to him. Still, he was glad for the coachman's assistance.

"He can't speak," the captain grimaced. "We found him as an infant, abandoned in the woods. Oftentimes he does work for us, traveling between our lands and into the human realm."

Interesting. Ruben inclined his head in a nod to acknowledge the coachman. A moment later the other man did the same.

Shaking the captain's hand, he thanked him for all his help.

As the man walked back to join his men, Tatiana emerged from her tent. Barely clothed, her lush figure on display for all to see, she sauntered over to Ruben, ignoring the lustful looks from the other men.

"I understand we have a few minutes before we ride," she purred, running her finger down his chest. "My back is stiff and sore from the long ride yesterday and I have need of a massage. Would you mind helping me out?"

Ruben couldn't help but laugh. "Get your fiancé to assist you. But you'd better be ready to leave when we ride out. And by that I mean fully dressed. Do you understand?"

Though she pouted at his harsh tone, he saw from her calculating expression that she really hadn't expected him to capitulate so easily. "Of course I do." Fluttering her eyelashes, she moved away.

She was up to something. But what?

Ruben watched as she strolled slowly past the guards on her way back to her tent. Being men, they all stared wistfully and when she crooked her little finger, he knew if they hadn't been on duty, they'd have trampled each other on the way to her tent.

Instead, they stood with their feet planted in place, as she disappeared.

A moment later Eric came out. When Ruben saw what the other man was wearing—or, to be more accurate, what he *wasn't* wearing—Ruben laughed out loud. This time, Eric approached Willow, who had her back to him as she checked her horse's cinch.

Ruben's jaw tightened. The half-naked man tapped Willow on the shoulder. She turned and as she realized he had on almost nothing, she blanched. Sidestepping him neatly, she moved to the other side of her horse, her face flaming.

"Enough," Ruben roared. "Eric, get dressed and then help take down the tent. We leave in ten minutes."

Eric waved, smiling broadly. As he strolled past the soldiers, one man eyed him in exactly the same way as his buddies had eyed Tatiana.

Scratching his head, Ruben went back to taking down his tent. Had the two of them really thought he and Willow were so foolish to fall for that? And even if they had, then what?

Had Tatiana planned to knock him out in the middle of love-making, with Eric doing the same to Willow?

His stomach churned as he realized he hated the idea of Willow with anyone but him. He felt possessive, like a wolf would toward his mate.

Hellhounds. There it was again, that disturbing truth. Yet while he couldn't deny the fact, what about her? Did she feel the same way? Did her people—the Sidhe—even believe in mating for life?

Her parents had sought a match with Chad. This brought another stomach-churning thought. Being royal, he knew how many intricacies were involved in a match. Of course, his own family was no obstacle. They'd be happy with any woman he chose.

Willow's parents were another matter entirely. King Puck didn't seem like a bad sort. He appeared relatively easygoing. Queen Millicent was not.

Ruben closed his eyes. Was he seriously considering asking for Willow's hand in marriage? Of course he would, provided she was willing. The attraction between them was powerful and she'd demonstrated numerous times her uncanny ability to read his thoughts. He ached for her constantly, and being with her briefly only made him want her more.

He hoped—no, he prayed—she felt the same way.

## Chapter 19

Pushing the thought from his mind for now, Ruben finished packing and mounted his horse. Already seated on hers, Willow waved, her dark hair looking almost blue in the morning sunlight.

Again, yearning swept through him. He supposed he should be glad she appeared to be trying to keep distance between them. He sighed. He couldn't exactly blame her. She probably thought he'd stood her up last night. In fact, he'd simply been a coward, unable to deal with all the emotions she aroused in him.

He'd tell her later that he hadn't stood her up, but he didn't need the distraction right now. Not with both Eric and Tatiana proving they were completely loose cannons.

Finally, with the camp disassembled, they rode again. At the designated place, King Drem's guards took their leave. As they rode off, their black-clad backs straight, Ruben didn't miss the way Tatiana and Eric exchanged covert glances. He nearly groaned out loud. They rode their horses alongside each other, speaking in voices too low to carry.

"Well, there's one good thing about all this," Willow said drily, riding up alongside him. "Maybe the two of them will finally get close enough to marry."

Ignoring the way his heart skipped a beat, he allowed himself a moment to drown in her smile.

"Maybe." He smiled and glanced back at the others. "But have you noticed the way your sister looks at Chad? I really think she fancies herself in love with him."

"She does," Willow sighed. "Even when they first arrived in SouthWard, she decided she wanted him instead of Eric. I'm not sure why. She and Eric are exactly alike."

"Maybe that's the reason. They're so similar, they'd despise each other in a matter of months."

"That's one possibility," she said. "But I'd like to think they'd learn from seeing their own flaws mirrored so clearly."

"Those kind of people rarely do." Shaking his head, he tightened his hands on the reins to keep from touching her. "You were asleep when I came last night," he murmured. "I didn't want to disturb your rest, so I left."

As she opened her mouth to speak, one of the horses whinnied, then screamed, a blood-curdling sound. Willow's mount reared up, as Tatiana's horse went down, pinning her under it. Blood pooled scarlet into the dirt.

Once Willow had her horse under control, she jumped down. Ruben also vaulted to the ground, handing her his reins. He rushed over, arriving at the same time as Eric.

One look at the Bright prince's face and Ruben knew this hadn't been staged. Appearing truly panicked, Eric tried frantically to free his fiancée from underneath the thrashing horse. An arrow protruded ominously from the animal's neck.

Unfortunately, his efforts only succeeded in terrifying

the wounded animal, which flayed about in a futile effort to climb to its feet.

"Stand back." Attempting to grab Eric's arm, Ruben slipped in the blood and staggered, just as the other man swung at him.

Eric glared at Ruben with murder in his eyes and resumed his efforts to free Tatiana. The horse's stomach heaved as he struggled. Still Eric tried to lift the beast, all the while attempting to dodge flailing hooves.

Meanwhile, Tatiana lay ominously still.

"Hold." The note of command rang unmistakable in Ruben's voice.

An instant later, Willow seconded his order. "Move away from the horse."

About to argue, Eric saw something in her face that had him jumping back. "You! How can you help? You have no magic," he spat the words. "Everyone knows that. And now you're going to let your sister die in the dirt just for spite."

She ignored him, running her hands down the horse's flank. Instantly, the animal went still. When she finally raised her head to look at Ruben, tears ran down her cheeks.

"My sister is grievously wounded and the horse has been shot," she said. "First, we need to move him off Tatiana. The arrow nicked his artery, so I can't help him. But I can ease his passage, very quickly, or at least try so he won't suffer, before I help you and Eric tend to my sister."

*Shot.* Glancing around them and realizing they were completely exposed, Ruben knew they'd have to find the shooter.

"Yes," Willow agreed, once again apparently reading his thoughts. "But first, we must free Tatiana. Then you can find the shooter."

Intuition clamoring a warning, nonetheless Ruben nodded. "What would you have me do?"

"You and Eric," she said, including the other man in her

gesture. "Each grab a pair of legs. Ruben, you take the front and Eric the back. I've sedated the horse so he will remain still, as long as you are gentle. Slide him this way, and we'll free Tatiana."

Though Ruben seriously doubted he could move even half of a one-ton horse, he was willing to give it a try.

"Ready?" Willow asked, crossing around to the other side to push while they pulled. She stood as near to Tatiana's prone form as she could. "One, two, three, pull!"

Ruben pulled. Next to him, Eric did the same, grunting loudly while Willow pushed. To his disbelief, they were able to slide the massive animal off Tatiana.

Willow went to assist her, to see if she could somehow use what little magic she had to help, but the instant her fingers touched her sister's skin, Tatiana began screaming.

When Willow took her hand away, her sister quieted.

"See?" Eric shot her a venomous look. "She doesn't want your help."

"Tend to her," Willow ordered, dropping to her knees next to the violently shaking horse. She began crooning low, nonsensical words that seemed to calm the beast. Ruben turned away, glancing from Tatiana to the woods.

"I don't think you should move her," he told Eric. Ignoring him, the other man slid one arm under her head and the other under her back, lifting her. He carried her over toward the wagon while Ruben followed behind.

"If I had my magic, I could heal her," Eric said bitterly.

"Look, I understand." Ruben clapped a hand on the other man's shoulder and tried to keep an eye on the trees. "I'm not sure how or why, but it would appear someone has a powerful bow and is trying to take us out. We need to find this person before anyone else gets hurt."

Without looking up from Tatiana, Eric nodded.

Inside his makeshift cell, Chad began to laugh. "Leave her, you fool. Do what I told you to do."

Eric swung his golden head to glare at his brother. "Hurting her wasn't part of the plan."

"Plan?" Ruben looked from one to the other. As he did, Chad brandished a wicked-looking crossbow.

Ruben dove behind the wagon just as Chad sent an arrow flying. "Take cover," he shouted to Willow, as she raised her head from her work on the horse. In plain view, with her back to Chad, she'd make an easy target.

"I'll kill her unless you free me," Chad said, the venom in his voice telling Ruben he meant it.

Seeing the danger, Willow froze.

"Take cover," Ruben shouted, his heart in his throat.

"I can't leave the horse right now," she shouted. "If I do, he'll die in great pain."

"If you don't, he'll kill you," Eric warned her, turning back to look at his brother. "And the horse will still die in pain. You promised no bloodshed, Chad."

"I lied," Chad told him smoothly, before shooting Eric in the leg. He laughed when his brother crumpled to the ground.

Willow took that opportunity to dive behind a large tree.

Chad grinned, bringing the massive crossbow to bear on Ruben. "Looks like you're next," he told Ruben.

"Kill us all and you'll be trapped in there forever," Ruben said. "There won't be anyone left alive to free you. You'll rot in your cage. A slow, painful death."

Chad cocked his head, considering.

A movement above Chad caught Ruben's eye. The coachman had climbed on top of the cage, unnoticed by the Bright prince. He held a long, deadly looking whip.

Quickly Ruben looked away. The coachman was their only chance.

Madness gleamed in Chad's eyes as he sighted the arrow on Ruben's heart.

"You don't want to kill me," Ruben said, knowing he had to distract the other man.

"Oh, but I think I do. But first, I want her to die." As Chad raised the crossbow again, aiming at Willow, the coachman snapped the whip, knocking the weapon out of Chad's hands with a loud crack. It discharged its arrow before bouncing into and through the bars onto the ground.

Ruben dove for it. Chad began cursing virulently.

Ignoring him, Ruben turned to check on Eric. The Bright prince had torn his shirt and made an efficient tourniquet over his wounded leg.

"I'm all right." Eric waved him away. "Please, check on Tatiana." The worry in his voice told Ruben the other man truly cared for his fiancée.

"Let me check her out." Pushing past Ruben and Eric, Willow knelt at her sister's side. She took Tatiana's pulse, then began feeling along her arms and legs and rib cage, searching for broken bones.

When she looked up again, her expression was tight with strain. "She has at least one broken rib, and I think her left arm is also broken. Beyond that—if she has any kind of other internal injuries—I have no way of knowing. She's unconscious."

Exhaustion was evident in the way she swayed, even from a crouched position. Though Ruben hated to ask it, he had to. "Can you try again?"

For a second she closed her eyes, appearing to muster up her last remnant of faded strength. "She's my sister," she said finally. "I'm not sure she'll let me, but of course I'll try."

Shaking with the effort, she began humming tunelessly as she let her hands hover over Tatiana's rib cage. Tears streamed down Willow's cheeks, but she held her position, until the tremors became all-engulfing shudders. As Ruben rushed to steady her, she collapsed in his arms.

"Is she…?" Eric asked tentatively.

Ruben cradled the woman he loved and glanced up at the other man, only to find him gazing at Tatiana with an eager, hopeful and completely besotted look.

"I don't know." Transferring his attention back to Willow, Ruben gathered her as close as he dared, wishing he could send some of his strength to replenish her limp body.

But whatever magic he possessed was limited to shape-shifting and he could do nothing but hold her.

Willow's chest rose and fell with shallow breathing, and she didn't appear hurt, just depleted.

Next to him, Eric gave a glad cry. "She's waking up."

Sure enough, Tatiana had begun to stir. Pink returned to her colorless skin as she regained her strength. Ruben wished he could say the same for Willow.

"Keep her still until she can focus," Ruben cautioned.

Eric nodded, reluctant to tear his gaze away from the woman he planned to marry. Tatiana moaned, trying to push up onto her elbows. She opened her violet eyes and blinked up at Eric. Realizing who held her, she tried to push him away, struggling to see beyond him. "Chad?" she cried out, her voice full of anguish. "Chad."

To his credit, Eric continued to hold her. "He's alive," he said drily. "As am I and your sister, I think."

But Tatiana did not hear him. She'd already slipped back into unconsciousness.

Ruben looked away, back at his mate. Her long lashes fluttered, and he saw a shimmer of awareness in her caramel-colored eyes. "Willow?"

A ghost of a smile touched her lips. "I think I healed her…"

"Shh." Placing a soft kiss on the smooth skin of her forehead, he held her close. "Conserve your strength."

"But Tatiana…"

"She woke up and then went back to sleep. I think she's going to be okay." He kissed her again, this time lingering. Inhaling the fresh lilac scent of her, he suppressed the urge to hold her tighter, afraid he might injure her.

"Great." Willow smiled sleepily up at him, then stretched. "Give me another minute to regain my energy and then I can help you two figure out how to get everyone home without injuring them more."

By the time Willow was able to stand—shakily, and while leaning heavily on Ruben—Tatiana had come around again. Despite Eric's protests, she had gotten to her feet and gone to crouch near the cage, where a furious Chad still sat, glaring at them all with murder in his gaze.

"Are you all right, my love?" Tatiana gushed, attempting to reach through the bars to caress Chad's face.

"Get away from me, you faithless whore," Chad snarled.

At his words, Tatiana drew herself up straight, her injury apparently completely healed. "What's wrong with you?" she demanded. "How can you speak to me like that, after we've made love? I know we're meant to be together."

Chad spat at her, contempt twisting his face. "I don't want you. I never did. You and my brother deserve each other. Two fools."

Shocked, Tatiana stumbled backward, nearly falling. Eric had come up behind her, and he caught her, though he moved now strictly from reflex, his jaw tight and his gaze hard.

"You slept with her?" Eric asked his brother, his voice completely without inflection. "The woman I planned to marry?"

Ruben couldn't help but notice how the other man used past tense now. He couldn't blame him. What kind of man would want a bride so faithless that she'd cuckold him with his own brother?

"What kind of man are you?" Revulsion plain in his every action, Eric set Tatiana apart, ignoring the way she desperately reached out to him, apparently realizing she'd lost it all.

When she touched his shoulder, he spun and turned on her. "For that matter, what kind of woman are you? We were supposed to wed. We'd even begun discussing wedding plans, for Bright's sake."

Most women would have hung their head in shame. Not Tatiana. She looked Eric straight in the face and smiled. "I will make it up to you," she promised. "If you'll let me."

Not an apology at all.

For a heartbeat, Ruben thought Eric might strike her. The thought apparently crossed Eric's mind, as he raised his hand before lowering it and clenching it in a fist.

This made Ruben actually like the pompous prince, who seemed to have a heart after all.

"The engagement is off," Eric declared, in a hard, flat voice. "Do not come near me again."

Disbelief flashed across Tatiana's face. "You can't do that. Our parents have already signed the marriage contracts."

"They will be voided," he said, and turned his back on her to mount his horse.

Since they were now one horse short, they helped Tatiana up on the front of the jail wagon, where she could ride with the coachman.

And then they set out as fast as they could for SouthWard. King Drem had explained that they would not be sent through the portal due to the prison coach and so would have a long ride ahead of them.

Ruben rode next to Willow, noting how she gripped the pommel of the saddle. More than once, she appeared to be nodding off.

"Are you going to make it?" he asked, aware he couldn't let her see how worried he was. Willow's earlier pale skin had now taken on a ghostly pallor. Even her lips, normally red, seemed bloodless. She barely showed enough strength to keep upright in the saddle.

Unsmiling, she nodded. "I think so."

"Let me know if you need my help," he said. "If you'd like to ride with me, I'm sure we can arrange something."

His words brought a faint smile, though she shook her head. They rode on, pushing as hard as they dared. Luckily, neither Tatiana nor Eric seemed inclined to talk. Chad had folded himself up into a close approximation of a ball. He must have been weak from loss of blood.

Several hawks circled overhead, keeping pace with them. Ruben also got a sense that other creatures watched them from the shadows. If they communicated to Willow, she didn't pass that information on. Perhaps they too were worried about her.

Finally, the landscape began to look familiar.

"We're nearly home," Willow said, confirming his thoughts.

The instant they reached the golden path that wound up the hill toward SouthWard keep, as though a message had been sent ahead, medics rushed out and tended to Tatiana and Eric. When they were deemed stable enough, they were transported to the hospital. Chad was also taken off, escorted by a regiment of guards, still trapped in his ensorcelled prison.

Though Willow needed to rest, she and Ruben were told that the king and queen wished to see them immediately.

They were taken into the castle, and without a chance to clean up or take refreshment, Willow and Ruben were ushered into a formal sitting area. The servant closed the door behind him, leaving them alone. Ruben helped her take a seat on a gilt-encrusted couch, then sat beside her.

"At least it's not the throne room," Willow joked, trying to sound lighthearted, though she betrayed herself by the way she kept twisting her hands anxiously. The slight sag of her shoulders and the persistent way she shivered revealed her exhaustion.

Aching to hold her, Ruben nodded, absently noting the dazzling gilt-covered chairs, gold-threaded upholstery and glittery wallpaper. *Bright* didn't even begin to describe the effects of it. "If I stayed in this room too long, I'd have a raging headache."

Though she laughed, her nerves were apparent in the sound. Her movements were shaky, but she got to her feet and began to roam the room. She picked up objects, studying them and setting them back down without ever seeing them.

Finally, she dropped back into her seat next to him. "They'd better make this quick, or I'm going to pass out," she whispered, leaning her head on his shoulder.

Stroking her hair, Ruben reached for her hand. Once her fingers were intertwined with his, he felt a little bit of calm peacefulness steal over him. No matter what happened, as long as Willow and he were together, everything would be all right. He had to believe that.

Finally, King Puck strode into the room, his narrow face pinched. There was no sign of Queen Millicent, Willow's mother, and Ruben didn't know whether to be relieved or worried.

Instead of greeting Willow, the king fixed his gaze on Ruben. "I see you've imprisoned the youngest EastWard prince. What evidence do you have against him?" he asked, crossing his arms.

"Against Chad?" Ruben sat up straight. "He tried to kill me. And then he admitted to murdering my servant. I request permission to bring him home so he can stand trial."

The king flinched. "He is the second son of a powerful king. I don't know that I can allow this."

Moving slowly, Willow pushed to her feet, bravely facing

down her father. "You don't have a choice. You must send word to EastWard. You know our laws. Chad will have to stand trial. Not only did he murder a human servant, but he attempted to kill Prince Ruben."

King Puck slowly nodded. "I'll have to speak with your mother."

Willow shrugged. "Go ahead. But no one is above the law. King Drem has put a binding spell on Chad to keep him from using his magic."

At the mention of the Shadow king, a look of sorrow mingled with pain flashed across King Puck's autocratic features. "You met your sire?"

Slowly, Willow nodded. "Why did you never tell me?"

"You mother did not wish me to." He reached out as if to touch her, but dropped his hand before making contact. "I abide by her wishes, as always."

"Where is my mother?" Willow asked, her voice steady. "I have much I want to discuss with her."

"She's with your sister. Until she's sure Tatiana is all right, I doubt she'll have time for you."

Though Ruben knew the king's words had to hurt, Willow's serene expression betrayed nothing. "Would you let her know that I need to speak with her?" she asked.

King Puck nodded. "Of course. Meanwhile, I'll go and prepare a message to be sent to the EastWard king."

As he turned to leave, Willow stepped in front of him, stopping him. "And after Chad is well enough, he must be sent through the veil to stand trial for his crimes among the humans," she declared, her tone daring him to disagree. "Prince Ruben has promised this to his father."

After a long moment, the king sighed. "I suppose you're right. Let me see what I can do."

As he reached for the door, Queen Millicent swept into

the room, her expression furious. "Arrest both of them," she ordered, motioning her guards to come in after her.

"On what charges?" Ruben asked. Willow stood like a statue, allowing the guards to place her in restraints.

"On what charges?" he repeated, when it seemed plain the queen had no intention of answering.

She waited until he was handcuffed before answering.

"On charges of conspiring against the royal family of East-Ward."

"What kind of nonsense is this?" Willow asked, facing her mother. "You know good and well—"

Queen Millicent's expression contorted, turning her beautiful face into one of ugly malice. "Tatiana has told me the truth. She said you and your human pet conspired against Chad in order to frame him for Eric's crimes."

"That's ridiculous," Ruben protested. "Ask King Drem's coachman. He can tell you the truth."

The queen looked down her aquiline nose at him. "He violated the treaty by trespassing on our lands. Like him, you and Willow are to be held until all of this is sorted out."

Exhaustion claiming her, Willow let herself be transported by the guards to her family's little-used jail in the ancient dungeons underneath the castle. She had no doubt that neither she nor Ruben would be kept here for long, despite Chad's apparent plan to deceive everyone. Even if Tatiana refused to tell the truth, there was Eric. As firstborn son and heir to the EastWard kingdom, his word would carry a lot more weight than Chad's.

"All very good reasoning," Ruben said from the cell next to hers. "Except for one major issue. Chad's trying to make it seem like Eric is the killer."

"Somehow, he must have persuaded Tatiana to go along with his story." That wouldn't have been too difficult. Now that Eric wanted nothing to do with her, her sister would have been quick to grasp at any straw Chad might have thrown out.

Though she tried to stay awake long enough to come up with a plan, Willow felt herself drift off to sleep. The last thing she saw before closing her eyes was Ruben's handsome face, peering worriedly at her through the bars.

When she woke, she felt sluggish, though she knew her strength had returned to her. Raising her head, she found Ruben in the exact same place, still watching her.

"How long was I out?"

He shrugged. "A few hours. I have no way to track time. But no one has come looking for us. If your sister doesn't recant her story…"

"She will. She has to. Tatiana is a lot of things, but she's not an idiot. She won't want to be with a killer, especially one who made it plain he was using her. Once she gets over her embarrassment, she'll tell my mother what really happened."

Ruben's expression was doubtful, but he nodded. "I just want to go home," he said.

Willow felt a pang at his words, though she was careful to hide it. "Of course you do. Why wouldn't you, now that you've completed your task?"

He searched her face. She couldn't decide if the tenderness she saw in his gaze was pity or something more.

"Now is not the time to talk about this," he finally said. "But once we get out of here…"

Chest tight, she turned away, not wanting him to see how much his words had hurt her.

Footsteps on the stone stairs had them both raising their heads. When Tatiana came into view, Willow smiled, glad she'd been right about her sister.

Ignoring Ruben, Tatiana crossed to stand in front of Willow's cell. "I'm sorry to have to put you through this," she said, her tone as conversationally pleasant as if they were discussing the weather.

Willow frowned. "Are you going to tell the truth so we can get out?"

"I haven't decided." Twirling a lock of her golden hair in her finger, Tatiana wrinkled her nose in a move she often practiced in front of a mirror, deeming it adorable. "I didn't want to marry Eric, but I refuse to let him humiliate me. At least now that everyone thinks he's a killer, they won't listen to anything he says."

"You can't do this. Not only will Chad—who actually *is* a killer—go free, but an innocent man will be tried for his crimes."

"So?" Tatiana's expression seemed carefully blank.

"Tati, Chad said he didn't want you. Remember?"

"He didn't mean that. He only said that to give him time to think of a better plan. Once he did, he told me the truth."

Willow let her disbelief show. "I have to believe you know better than that."

Her sister's face took on that mulish expression that Willow knew so well. "Say what you will. I have to do what makes me happy."

"This? This makes you happy? Not only are you helping a killer, someone who may just decide to slaughter you some day, but you're letting an innocent man suffer for his crimes." Willow took a deep breath, fervently hoping she could make Tatiana see reason. "Not to mention they've got us locked up for allegedly conspiring against him."

"Sorry. You're collateral damage." With a sigh, Tatiana swept her gaze over Willow. "You had no future here anyway. You should have stayed at NorthWard, with your own people."

Unable to believe what she was hearing, Willow regarded her older sister with a combination of pity and scorn. "Tati, you'll be queen someday. You have to do the right thing."

Then, not waiting for her sister to answer, Willow turned her back on her and went to sit on her cot.

Tatiana left without another word.

"Do you think she'll do it?" Ruben asked. "I knew she was awfully self-centered, but this is unbelievable."

"I can only hope." Willow let some of her glumness show in her voice.

When a few minutes later there were more footsteps on the stairs, she raised her head. Relief flooded her when she saw King Puck and Queen Millicent stride around the corner.

But neither one was smiling.

# Chapter 20

"I believe you have something of mine," her mother said grimly, holding out her hand.

The earring. Willow couldn't believe she'd completely forgotten about it. Slowly, she dug into her pouch and retrieved it. Dropping the bauble into her mother's hand, she sighed. "I'm sorry—" she began.

"Silence," the queen ordered, holding up the pearl. The earring began to glow as she closed her fingers over its luster. Closing her eyes, she listened to something only she could hear.

They all watched, Willow and Ruben confused, King Puck appearing wary.

Finally, Queen Millicent opened her eyes. Fixing her sharp violet glare on her husband, she made a sound of disgust. "The jewelry has told me everything. I now know Tatiana lied. These two are guilty of nothing."

The king flashed a look of surprise. "Then what do you want me to do with them?"

"Release them," the queen ordered, bitterness darkening her tone. She could hardly meet Willow's gaze. "Chad is the killer, as you said. Tatiana, for whatever foolish reason, seeks to help him." Making a dismissive gesture, she turned away, tossing her pardon over her shoulder. "You and your human are free to go."

"Wait," Willow called out. "We are not finished, Mother. I met my true father. King Drem has told me you forbid him to contact me."

The queen's expression, already cold, turned to ice. "So?"

"So? That's all you can say? Why did you hide this from me?"

"Because it doesn't matter. I never wanted you. You are nothing but a constant reminder of my sin."

Though in some small part of her soul, she'd known this, actually hearing her mother say these words had Willow reeling. "But you're my mother…"

"No longer." The queen lifted her chin, the gesture reminding Willow of herself. "From this day forward, you are the daughter of King Drem. You are no longer welcome here."

"Release them," the king ordered. As her guards unlocked the cells, Ruben stood. "What about Chad?" he asked.

From the doorway, King Puck answered. "Though we've not yet heard from his parents, I'm certain Eric will give approval for you to take him to Teslinko to be tried for his crime."

Ruben bowed. "Thank you."

"You're welcome," the king said, sounding anything but gracious. Then, without a word of apology or even a look at their youngest daughter, the King and Queen of SouthWard swept from the room.

Willow stared after the woman who'd birthed her and

briefly allowed herself to feel the old, familiar longing. Her entire life she'd ached for her mother's approval—no, more than that. She'd longed for her mother's love.

Apparently, as far as Queen Millicent was concerned, Willow would never be worthy. Maternal love was supposed to be unconditional, but not her mother's. Willow might as well have wished for wings to fly, or something equally unobtainable.

That's when Willow realized she could no longer stay here. No matter what happened, whether she went to Teslinko with Ruben or back to NorthWard to live among the Shadows, SouthWard was no longer her home.

Though she tried to tell herself it didn't matter, she felt like an enormous hole had been ripped in her soul.

Besotted. Glaring at Willow and Ruben while they made goo-goo eyes at each other, Chad silently sneered. He might have been defeated, at least for now—or however long King Drem's spell kept his magic contained. It wouldn't be forever, this he felt quite certain. The massive amount of energy it would take to cast a forever spell would have been more than King Drem and an entire army of Sidhe could have managed.

The question was, how long would it last? Patience wasn't something he had in abundance, yet Chad knew he'd have to wait. Because once his magic was released, no one—especially not one puny human Shape-shifter and a bastard Sidhe princess with no magic—would be able to stop him.

Then he would have his vengeance. And it would be bloody. Exactly how he liked it.

His brother Eric would also pay. The coward had simply turned him over to the SouthWard rulers, in effect washing his hands of his only brother. If Chad had been permitted to see his brother once before he was sent to Teslinko, he would

have spat on him. He suspected Eric knew this and that was
why he stayed away.

Curious as to what kind of punishment the humans would
try to impose on him, Chad settled in to wait for them to
come collect him. He'd already been told they'd be taking
him to Teslinko.

Coming through the portal with Willow, Ruben had never
felt so completely and utterly happy. Finally, he'd returned
home, along with the woman he loved. Though he hadn't yet
confessed his feelings to her, he planned to do so once he'd
delivered Chad to his father to stand trial.

Willow seemed unusually solemn, no doubt a direct result
of her parents' coldhearted actions. He planned to make that
up to her—once she became his wife, she would never want
for warmth and love.

Since metal wouldn't travel through the portal—or veil,
as Willow called it—new bindings had been fashioned for
Chad. Made out of some kind of heavy-duty rope, he'd been
bound with his hands behind his back and his ankles shack-
led, just loose enough to permit him to walk. King Puck had
assured them the bonds were magical, and that the magic
would transfer through the portal intact.

For safety's sake, Ruben kept Chad slightly ahead of him.
He didn't want to take a chance the other man would try to
escape the instant they crossed over.

They all went through at once. Ruben and Chad, with Willow right alongside them. Ruben landed on his feet on recog-
nizable ground, in his beloved, familiar forest and breathed
the pine-scented air. Taking Willow's hand, he swung it once,
laughing while Chad glowered at them.

Both surprised and relieved that Chad had put up no re-
sistance, Ruben ordered him to walk. He still held Willow's
hand and together they began to hurry toward home.

When they reached the first rise in the forest, he pulled her close and kissed her until they were both breathless. Smiling, he wrapped her in his arms and turned to face the first view of his family's castle.

Normally the ancient, crumbling tower where he'd often took refuge was the only part visible. But now…he saw nothing.

Ruben knew a moment of trepidation as he jerked the plastic rope that held Chad tethered. "Are you certain we've arrived back in Teslinko, in my world?"

The worry in his voice made Willow look up at him, frowning. "Yes, of course. The gateway is in the veil between my world and yours, not any others."

He took a deep breath, trying to slow his racing heartbeat. "We'd best hurry then. Something must have happened to my home."

Letting go of her hand, he ordered Chad to go as he started forward, slowing enough to reach out and steady Willow when the footing grew rough. As they reached flatter, more level land, he picked up the pace, urging Chad ahead of him the way he might have urged a packhorse.

The dark looks the EastWard prince kept shooting Ruben told him how little the other man appreciated this.

Willow kept pace with them easily. The sound of their running feet blended with the pounding of his heart. He could only hope his parents were all right. He'd never forgive himself if the extremists had succeeded in hurting his family while he'd been gone.

He hadn't remembered the landscape being so hilly, though to be fair he'd never tried to run it before, except as wolf. At the thought, his inner wolf stirred, though there was no struggle to try and change, just a deep feeling of contentment. This in itself was new, and slightly shocking. Maybe Willow had been right. Perhaps there was something to be said for this newfound acceptance of his dual nature.

Chad jerked his rope, probably deliberately, which made Ruben stumble. Like a chain reaction, Willow nearly lost her footing, too.

Instantly he grasped her elbow to steady her, even as he pulled back on Chad's tether.

"We're nearly there," he told her. She'd been to his home before, as had Chad, he remembered.

They continued at a slightly slower pace, though anxiety still churned inside him. He kept her elbow in his hand as he tried to brace himself for what he might find.

The path curved here; there was the stone bench surrounded by the rose bushes his mother had planted. There was the arbor of sturdy oak trees he'd helped his sister take care of when they'd been younger.

At the last bend in the path, he broke through the trees, tugging her along with him. Panting, he stopped, peering at the welcome sight in front of him. There sat the home, his castle, the slate-colored stones glowing warmly in the bright afternoon sun.

The building appeared exactly as he'd left it, except there had been quite a bit of repairs made already to the ballroom that had been destroyed in the explosion.

He swayed, his relief so great he couldn't speak. Slightly ahead of them, Chad looked back and sneered.

"See." Willow touched his arm and leaned into him. "It's all right. Nothing has changed."

But it had. Something was…different.

Not entirely sure what, he glanced past the renovated ballroom and up the small hill, searching in vain for his old hiding place. Where the tower had once cast a long shadow on that bit of lawn, he saw only sun. The old part of the keep was no more. This he couldn't fathom. The tower had stood for many centuries, withstanding storm and wind and the fallacies of man. What could possibly have brought it down now?

"Come on." Taking her hand once more, he pulled her around the huge gardens, toward the curved drive. He forced Chad to continue to move ahead of them. As they rounded the corner where repairs were still being made to the ballroom that had been destroyed by the bomb, he led her up weathered stone steps to a rise in the land.

"Here." Nothing left but several piles of stone. Grief filled him, sorrow for losing both the last piece of his family's past, and his only secret, special place. True, there were secret hallways and hidden rooms inside the newer part of the palace, which was actually a few hundred years old, but this had been *his*. Part of his family's history, part of his childhood, part of his life.

"What is it?" Willow turned, surveying the area. She lifted her head, sniffing the wind in a manner that reminded him so much of a wolf that he froze. "I sense something," she said. "Age and sorrow and history. Why?"

"An old part of the castle once stood here." He shook his head. "It was the only part that remained of the old keep. There was a massive stone tower here." He pointed. "With crumbling steps."

"Can we get a move on?" Chad said, his expression disparaging. Ruben ignored him, glad of the magical tether that kept the EastWard prince bound. King Puck had promised it would last until Chad had served his sentence, or been killed, whichever his punishment might be.

While Ruben was happy—so happy—that his home was unscathed, he'd lost something, too. This had been his refuge. And now it was no longer.

As he stood surveying the ruins, letting his sorrow show in the bend of his shoulders, she came up behind him and once again wrapped her arms around him. "I'm sorry. It obviously meant a lot to you."

"Yes. I'm not sure what happened to it. It looks like another explosion, though why the extremists would want to target this section..." But even as he spoke, he knew why.

"My father's father declared it off-limits, but of course I came here every chance I got. Even as an adult, this was where I came when I wanted to escape the rest of the world. They must have been targeting me."

"But how did they know?"

He shrugged. "All of my family knew I came here, as did most of the servants. No one spoke about it and I was never disturbed here. It's easy to see how, if word had leaked to the extremists, they could hurt me by destroying this."

"They didn't know you weren't here." Her caramel-colored eyes searched his face. "I'm very glad you weren't here."

"Me, too."

Standing on tiptoe, she touched her mouth to his. Gladly, he kissed her back, letting her touch erase the sorrow. He'd only lost a place. She—and his family—were what really mattered.

Chad grunted, grimacing. Ruben sent him a warning glare, then focused his attention back on Willow.

Chuckling, she broke apart. "It does have a beautiful view from here. Maybe you can put a bench here or something."

"Maybe. No more hiding away," he mused. "I'll miss it."

"I think perhaps its loss is fitting," she said, still holding his arm. "You no longer have a need to hide away from your life."

She was right. "And now it's time." Giving Chad's tether a shake, he linked arms with Willow as he forced his prisoner toward justice.

Recognizing him, the guards immediately sprang to attention and opened the door. Ruben kept Chad's tether a bit tighter and led him up the steps and into his home.

"My son!" Nothing but joy in his voice, King Leo rushed from around the corner, enveloping Ruben in a heartfelt hug. "Welcome home."

When he pulled back and caught sight of Willow, who hung back, he held out one arm and motioned her forward so he could include her in the embrace. "Princess Willow. Thank you for taking such good care of my son."

He glanced at Chad and his brows rose. "You caught him?"

"Yes. He's also Bright—from EastWard—and a prince. He's under a magical spell to prevent him from using his magic. The bonds are also ensorcelled, so that he cannot get away."

"Excellent." Giving Chad a hard glare, King Leo motioned to his men. "Take him below to the dungeon. He will stay there until he can be brought to trial."

"What of my bonds?" Chad spoke for the first time. "Surely you plan to remove these once I'm in my cell."

Ruben and his father shared a glance. Finally, Ruben shrugged. "King Puck didn't tell me how to remove them."

Willow didn't even try to hide her smile. "He told me. But I'm not sure you deserve to have them taken off. He said they'd remain until you received your sentence."

Narrowing his eyes, Chad glared at her. He said nothing as the guards marched him forward.

Once he was out of sight, Ruben looked at the woman he loved. "Are you going to remove them?"

"Maybe someday." Her smile widened, including King Leo. An expression of satisfaction shone in her eyes. "I can do it remotely. I don't have to be anywhere near him."

Linking arms with her, Ruben gazed down at her, matching his smile to hers. "I'm glad. I think we've both had enough of Chad to last us the rest of our lives."

King Leo cleared his throat, reminding them of his presence. "You've been gone about three months."

Again Ruben and Willow exchanged a glance. "I told you time passes differently in my world."

Though he wanted nothing more than to pull her close and kiss her, before asking her to stay with him forever, Ruben knew now wasn't the time. He turned to his father, letting some of his weariness show. "It was a difficult journey."

Face grave, the king nodded. "We had troubles here as well. The extremists stepped up their attacks."

"Is that what happened there?" Ruben asked, gesturing out the window in the direction of the ruins where his beloved tower had once stood.

"Yes." King Leo frowned. "The extremists apparently decided to capture you and must have learned that you often visited the old tower. So they set a trap." He grimaced. "Or tried to. There's a reason that place was condemned and deemed unsafe. Best as we can tell, there were six of them."

"Six to capture one man?" Willow sounded impressed.

King Leo gave Ruben a fond smile. "My son is known for his fighting ability."

Tilting her head, Willow considered him, the glow in her caramel-brown eyes making his face feel warm. To distract himself, he looked back at his father.

"Were they all inside when it collapsed?" Ruben asked.

"Yes. Four of them were killed instantly. The other two were badly injured. One died in the hospital. The other is still recuperating from his wounds."

"I'll talk to him later," Ruben said. "After I rest."

"Of course." His father clapped him on the shoulder, then held out his other arm for Willow. Grinning, she walked into his embrace.

When they broke apart, Ruben's throat was tight and Willow's eyes moist.

"Now why don't you two get some sleep? We can deal with all of this later."

"Agreed." Ruben held out his hand. He wanted nothing more than to be alone with Willow. She took it, exhaustion putting faint hollows under her eyes. "At least the hard part is behind us."

As they walked away, down the long corridors toward the staircase, heading for his bedroom where this incredible journey had first begun, she stopped and pulled her hand free.

"Ruben, I—"

A loud barking interrupted her. Cocking her head, she listened as the sound grew closer.

"York!" Ruben called. "My dog," he told her. "He must have learned I've returned home."

He'd barely finished speaking when a huge German shepherd dog came barreling around the corner, barking frantically and joyously. The canine leaped for Ruben, who dropped down and held out his arms, bracing himself for the one-hundred-pound animal.

With a powerful lunge, the ecstatic dog took him down, whining and licking as he welcomed his person home.

"There, there, boy," Ruben said, hugging his pet and burying his hands in York's short coat. Gradually, the dog calmed down, his delighted shudders disappearing. Finally, panting, York sat, leaning against Ruben's leg as if to warn him not to go anywhere else without him.

Eyes brimming, Willow made a sound low in her throat. "The purest sort of joy," she managed to say. "He loves you so much."

"As I do him." He motioned her to come closer. "Willow, may I introduce you to my beloved dog, York," he said, feeling only slightly foolish at the formal introduction. After all, this was a woman who could actually communicate with animals.

"York," Willow said, in that singsong voice of hers. "I'm pleased to meet you."

The German shepherd sniffed the air, tilted his head, studying Willow. Rather than approaching the big animal, she crouched down low, turning sideways so she didn't face the canine directly. The wolf in Ruben admired this tactic, well aware of the need to let the dog approach her of his own free will. *Especially since they were going to be a family, if he had his way.*

After a moment, York made a sound, low in his throat. A *woof,* which Ruben swore sounded as much like a question as anything else.

Willow nodded. "I do love him," she said, so softly that Ruben could barely make out the words. "More than I ever thought possible."

Then, rising and moving with great dignity, the huge dog went to her and raised his paw. Solemnly, Willow shook it. "I promise."

"You promise what?" Ruben asked.

Without lifting her gaze from York, Willow slowly shook her head. York whined and licked her, his large tongue sweeping her cheek. Willow laughed, delight making her eyes glow. And then she listened, her expressive face showing, at first seriousness, then wonder and finally a tentative sort of hopeful joy.

When she finally raised her gaze to Ruben, she looked shaken.

York got up and went back to Ruben, taking a watchful seat at his side.

Meanwhile, Willow appeared close to tears.

"What's wrong?" Ruben asked, helping her get to her feet. Though he still wanted to know what she'd promised his pet, he needed to make sure she was all right.

"He says that you love me," she whispered, a single fat tear rolling like silver down her cheek.

"I do." Ruben kissed her now, tasting salt and hope and more on her lips. "What did you promise him?"

When she raised her gaze to his, the emotion he saw shimmering there made him catch his breath.

"I promised that I would love you the rest of my life," she said, her voice husky.

"You know I'll hold you to that," he told her. "And I promise you the same. There will be no others."

Desire, electric and raw, hummed between them. Meeting her gaze, he willed her to read his thoughts.

A slow, sensual grin blossomed as she eyed him, the passion blazing to life in her whole face heating his blood.

"I want you," she breathed, standing up on tiptoe to kiss the pulsing hollow at the base of his throat, sending a rush of need through him.

"And I want you," he responded. "Forever and always."

"Starting right now," she said, laughing up at him, the sound full of life and joy and love.

"Wait." He took a step back, feeling as though a weight crushed his chest. "I can't ask you to give up your world and I can't leave mine." His voice broke. With great effort he steadied it. "Here, Teslinko—I'm the heir to the throne."

She cocked her head to gaze up at him, the sparkle in her rich brown eyes completely undimmed. "You can take vacations, can you not?"

"Of course," he answered, at first not completely sure where she was going with this. "You mean visits to South-Ward? You actually want to go to Tatiana and Eric's wedding?" The two had finally agreed to marry, which had made Eric ecstatic and Tatiana resigned.

A brief shadow crossed her expressive face. "No. Not there. I meant to visit my father, King Drem. And all my other relatives. I'm sure if I ask him, he'll arrange for a portal to take us there periodically."

"But after what happened to you there..."

She shook her head. "I spoke with him about that in private. He's promised to make sure no one else tries to put any spells on me. There's no reason we can't go. Especially once we have children. I want them to know their grandfather."

*Children?* The idea brought him such happiness, he could barely swallow past the lump in his throat.

Misreading his silence, she searched his face. "You do want to have children, don't you?"

Opening his mouth to speak, he realized he couldn't find the words. He nodded instead. Finally, hope bloomed in him, fierce and bright.

Which might have been a good thing. "Love will always win," she breathed, standing up again on tiptoe to press her mouth to his.

Then, grabbing his hand, she tugged him after her as they took off running for his room where they could consummate the lifelong pact they'd just made.

# *Epilogue*

The wedding was held in Teslinko, on a bright, cloudless day. Ruben's entire family was in attendance, including his sister Alisa and her husband, Dr. Braden Streib, who'd traveled from America.

And Willow's family, King Drem and his wife, myriad half siblings and cousins and family friends, filled up the chairs on one side of the outdoor tent.

At the last moment, Willow had asked Tatiana and Eric to come, telling Ruben she couldn't live with bitterness in her heart toward her sister. To Ruben's surprise, they both had agreed to attend, and sat in the front row next to King Drem's immediate family.

Queen Millicent and King Puck had declined, which had saddened Willow, though she refused to let this ruin her day.

King Leo and Queen Ionna had put on a lavish ball the night before, and all the Sidhes danced, appearing to enjoy themselves. Extra guards were posted to ensure that the extremists didn't cause trouble, but since a few arrests had been made while Ruben and Willow were gone, rumor had it that the group was on the verge of disbanding.

The ceremony was simple and lovely. Willow wore a dress of her own design, something ethereal and elegant rather than sparkly and bright.

Standing at the front of the gathering, watching his mate seem to float down the aisle toward him, his wolf at full attention, Ruben knew he'd been blessed. Not only with his own fairy princess to love and cherish the rest of his days, but with, at long last, coming to terms with his dual nature. Now able to enjoy being a man as well as wolf, he'd finally banished the deep darkness that had once haunted him.

He looked forward to joy and light—and children, lots of children, all resembling their beautiful mother, he hoped. And of course love. Love most of all.

As though she read his thoughts, Willow's mouth curved in a smile as she reached him. She took his hand, and her smile broadened into a wolfish grin, both a contrast and a compliment to the heartrending tenderness of her gaze.

As they spoke their vows, his heartbeat picked up, waiting for the kiss. Finally, they were man and wife. At long last, he swept her into his arms, she trembling and breathless, he exhilarated and strong and sure, and sealed the bargain they had just made.

Together. Forever and always, whether in his world or in hers.

\* \* \* \* \*

# NOCTURNE™

Available May 7, 2013

## #159 KEEPER OF THE SHADOWS
*The Keepers: L.A.* • by Alexandra Sokoloff

Rosalind Barrymore Gryffald is a news reporter and a
Keeper, one of an ancestral line of extraordinary mortals
charged with keeping the peace between humans and
shapeshifters. When she discovers an eerie parallel
between two murders and a fifteen-year-old Hollywood
tragedy, Barrie reluctantly teams with the gorgeous
and enigmatic Mick Townsend, a rival journalist on her
newspaper. As they dig into the cold case, more victims
surface, and Barrie can trust no one, least of all Mick, who
may well prove to be as inconstant as the shifters Barrie
is sworn to protect.

## #160 TAMING THE DEMON
by Doranna Durgin

Devin James wields a demon blade...and the demon
blade wields him, creating an irrevocable bond that
leeches into his soul, setting him on a path of loss and
destruction. Natalie James is a woman who knows how
to see through the darkness to Devin's heart. But neither
of them realize that her mentor will stop at nothing—not
betrayal, murder or selling his own soul—to acquire
Devin's blade.

# REQUEST YOUR FREE BOOKS!

## 2 FREE NOVELS FROM THE PARANORMAL ROMANCE COLLECTION PLUS 2 FREE GIFTS!

**YES!** Please send me 2 FREE novels from the Paranormal Romance Collection and my 2 FREE gifts (gifts are worth about $10). After receiving them, if I don't wish to receive any more books, I can return the shipping statement marked "cancel." If I don't cancel, I will receive 4 brand-new novels every month and be billed just $21.42 in the U.S. or $23.46 in Canada. That's a savings of at least 21% off the cover price of all 4 books. It's quite a bargain! Shipping and handling is just 50¢ per book in the U.S. and 75¢ per book in Canada.* I understand that accepting the 2 free books and gifts places me under no obligation to buy anything. I can always return a shipment and cancel at any time. Even if I never buy another book, the two free books and gifts are mine to keep forever.

237/337 HDN FVVV

| | | |
|---|---|---|
| Name | (PLEASE PRINT) | |
| Address | | Apt. # |
| City | State/Prov. | Zip/Postal Code |

Signature (if under 18, a parent or guardian must sign)

### Mail to the **Harlequin® Reader Service:**
**IN U.S.A.:** P.O. Box 1867, Buffalo, NY 14240-1867
**IN CANADA:** P.O. Box 609, Fort Erie, Ontario L2A 5X3

**Want to try two free books from another line?**
**Call 1-800-873-8635 or visit www.ReaderService.com.**

\* Terms and prices subject to change without notice. Prices do not include applicable taxes. Sales tax applicable in N.Y. Canadian residents will be charged applicable taxes. Offer not valid in Quebec. This offer is limited to one order per household. Not valid for current subscribers to Paranormal Romance Collection or Harlequin® Nocturne™ books. All orders subject to credit approval. Credit or debit balances in a customer's account(s) may be offset by any other outstanding balance owed by or to the customer. Please allow 4 to 6 weeks for delivery. Offer available while quantities last.

**Your Privacy**—The Harlequin® Reader Service is committed to protecting your privacy. Our Privacy Policy is available online at www.ReaderService.com or upon request from the Harlequin Reader Service.

We make a portion of our mailing list available to reputable third parties that offer products we believe may interest you. If you prefer that we not exchange your name with third parties, or if you wish to clarify or modify your communication preferences, please visit us at www.ReaderService.com/consumerschoice or write to us at Harlequin Reader Service Preference Service, P.O. Box 9062, Buffalo, NY 14269. Include your complete name and address.

When Shapeshifter Keeper Barrie Gryffald
investigates the death of a teenage shifter, she
is drawn into a fifteen-year-old mystery of a
"cursed" movie and its three iconic stars.

Enjoy a sneak peek from

# KEEPER OF THE SHADOWS

by Alxandra Sokoloff,
book 3 in THE KEEPERS: L.A. miniseries.

Barrie Gryffald was heading for the local crime editor's desk
when she saw the one person she didn't want to see coming
toward her.

Mick Townsend.

A newbie on the paper, and a thorn in her side from the
instant he'd show up. For one thing, jobs were scarce enough
without extra competition. But that wasn't even the start of it.

Townsend was *w-a-a-a-y* too good-looking to be a journalist.
In a city of surreally gorgeous people, he was truly heartstopping.

Only movie stars were supposed to look like that; there was
something almost preternaturally beautiful about him. Dark
gold hair and green eyes under perfectly arched eyebrows,
cheekbones you could cut glass with. The way he held himself,
that casually aristocratic elegance that was the territory of actors
and, well, aristocrats. He moved like a cat, strong as a panther
and just as lithe. He was tall, too, which made Barrie glad she

was wearing some serious heels tonight, Chanel pumps to go with the little Balenciaga number she'd found in her favorite thrift store.

Mick Townsend stopped right in her path, towering over her in an alarmingly commanding way. "Gryffald."

Barrie put up all her defenses as she coolly replied, "Townsend," and was proud that she didn't blush.

"You're looking very Audrey Hepburn tonight," he said lazily, and looked her over, a direct look that managed to be slow and sexy and aloof all at the same time, which didn't help her state of mind at all.

She sidestepped him and kept walking toward the crime editor's desk. Unfortunately, he turned and walked with her.

"A lady on the scent of a story, if I ever saw one."

"Looks like there's only one story tonight."

"Ah, yes. The Prince of Darkness. *Requiescat in pace.*" Rest in peace.

But there was a bitter quality to his voice that belied his words; it seemed more than mere journalistic cynicism, but some deeper feeling.

*Interesting,* she thought. *I wonder what that's about?*

**Find out in KEEPER OF THE SHADOWS by Alexandra Sokoloff, available May 7, 2013, wherever books are sold.**